MURDER ON PLATFORM FOUR

IRINA SHAPIRO

Storm

This is a work of fiction. Names, characters, businesses, places, events and incidents are either the products of the author's imagination or used in a fictitious manner. Any resemblance to actual persons, living or dead, or actual events is purely coincidental.

Copyright © Irina Shapiro, 2025

The moral right of the author has been asserted.

All rights reserved. No part of this book may be reproduced or used in any manner without the prior written permission of the copyright owner. This prohibition includes, but is not limited to, any reproduction or use for the purpose of training artificial intelligence technologies or systems.

To request permissions, contact the publisher at rights@stormpublishing.co

Ebook ISBN: 978-1-80508-665-9
Paperback ISBN: 978-1-80508-666-6

Cover design: Debbie Clement
Cover images: Trevillion, Shutterstock

Published by Storm Publishing.
For further information, visit:
www.stormpublishing.co

ALSO BY IRINA SHAPIRO

A Tate and Bell Mystery

The Highgate Cemetery Murder

Murder at Traitors' Gate

Murder at the Foundling Hospital

Murder at the Orpheus Theatre

Wonderland Series

The Passage

Wonderland

Sins of Omission

The Queen's Gambit

Comes the Dawn

The Hands of Time

The Hands of Time

A Leap of Faith

A World Apart

A Game of Shadows

Shattered Moments

The Ties that Bind

Echoes from the Past

The Lovers

PROLOGUE

Lord love a duck, but the trunk was heavy. It was one of those buckled traveling cases that could fit all of one's worldly possessions. Which raised the question—how could the owner not realize it was missing? Barnaby Lang mused on this as he hefted the accursed trunk onto a handcart. He lifted the worn card tag attached to the handle with one finger and peered at the address, but the only word he could make out was Birmingham. Barnaby gave up on the tag and pushed the cart with all his might until he finally reached the door to the unclaimed baggage storage room located at the far end of Platform 1.

One would expect the room to be stuffed full of cases, gloves, walking sticks, and other belongings that people tended to leave behind when getting off the train, but the items usually disappeared pretty quickly, and the storage area was nearly empty. Either the owners eventually returned to the terminus to claim their property, or the more likely scenario was that, if no one had come to inquire about a particular item within a day or two, the employees quietly helped themselves. Barnaby had yet to purloin anything. He'd started the job at the terminus only last month and was still on his best behavior, fearful that the station manager would sack him for some minor transgression.

Well, no one would be stealing this find, Barnaby concluded grimly. At least not without being seen. What on earth were these people transporting, cannon balls? He maneuvered the unwieldy cart through the door, deposited the trunk onto the flagstone floor, and pushed it into a corner. He breathed a sigh of relief and was about to tag the trunk with the date it had been discovered when he noticed something on the flagstones next to the outer right corner of the trunk. Was that...?

Barnaby bent down, pulled off his glove so as not to soil it, and touched the stain with his finger. He brought it to his nose and sniffed.

"Oh, Jesus," he cried when his worst suspicions were confirmed. No wonder no one had claimed this piece of luggage. It wasn't a trunk, it was a coffin.

ONE

THURSDAY, MAY 5, 1859

Sebastian Bell weaved through the throng of arriving and departing passengers, vehicles, and shouting vendors, and walked through the entrance that led to the Paddington terminus. He glanced around to get his bearings and headed down Platform 1, mostly to get out of the way of incoming travelers and their luggage.

Sebastian hadn't been to Paddington in some time, but not much had changed since the new terminus had opened nearly five years ago. Wrought-iron arches supported a glazed roof that soared above the platforms, where a thick mist diffused the sullen daylight and swirled above the train tracks that stretched into the distance. A large clock was mounted high above Platform 1, and several doors along the platform punctuated the wall, the areas beyond divided into various offices, dining rooms, and the royal waiting room that was off limits unless a royal party was expected. At least a dozen porters milled about, some wheeling loaded handcarts, others unencumbered and ready to offer assistance to anyone who needed help with their luggage. At a cab stand between the last two platforms, the line of hansoms constantly shifted as cabs at the front departed and new ones arrived to take their place at the back.

The terminus became more crowded after a hissing, smoke-belching train roared in and screeched to a stop at Platform 2, the doors of the compartments that ran the length of the cars slamming as passengers disembarked and called out to the porters. Many passengers carried their own cases and hurried toward the exit, where a boy of about ten was selling copies of a penny dreadful. A few people stopped to examine the front page, while others rushed past and through the doors that would take them outside into the overcast spring morning.

The locomotive was still puffing clouds of steam, and an odor of machine oil and smoke wafted from the cooling engine. The driver was hanging out the window, and a uniformed conductor stepped down onto the platform and walked briskly along the column of train cars, presumably to make certain that everyone had disembarked, and no one was in need of assistance. Satisfied, he returned to the front, exchanged a few words with the driver, then strode purposefully toward the station manager's office.

The clock showed 9:37. Sebastian had almost a half-hour to wait. He walked over to an unoccupied bench and sat down, looking at the glistening train tracks that disappeared into the tunnel beyond. He wasn't at all sure how he felt about the upcoming reunion. His brother Simian had finally responded to Sebastian's letter and had written to say that he would be arriving at Paddington on the 10:05 from Maidenhead and had suggested they meet. Sebastian had no idea what Simian had been doing in Maidenhead or why he preferred to meet at Paddington rather than invite Sebastian to visit the family home in Suffolk, but he wasn't going to question his brother's motives. This was a first step toward a long-overdue reconciliation, and Sebastian wasn't going to pass it up, even though he was nervous and unsure how to behave around the brother he hadn't seen or spoken to in years.

They had been close once, and had enjoyed a bond Sebastian had thought could withstand anything, but it had proved to be more fragile than he had imagined. His decision to move to London and join the police service had infuriated Simian, who had never dealt well with conflict, setbacks, or change in general. The brothers had kept in touch by post, with Sebastian writing to Simian monthly and receiving an annual reply that came around Christmas, but the brutal murder of Sebastian's wife and unborn child had driven a final wedge between the two men, since Simian had not seen fit to come to the funeral nor to ask after Sebastian during the three dark years that had followed. Adrift in a sea of despair, Sebastian had been left with nothing to cling to but a filthy cot in Mr. Wu's opium den that had become his survival raft. And now, after years of estrangement, the brothers were finally going to see each other in person and hopefully begin the process of rebuilding their relationship.

Sebastian glanced at the clock. 9:46. The minutes crawled by like the furry caterpillars he had liked to watch when he was a little boy, and he wished he had purchased a newspaper on his way to the terminus. He had the sort of mind that needed to be occupied at all times, and, when not working a case, he read voraciously. The stories kept him from overthinking and from worrying about a certain enchanting nurse he was always devising new ways to see. Sebastian was about to check the time again when an agitated youth hurried past him, his eyes bulging and his mouth hanging open in shock. His breathing was ragged, and his gangly limbs moved awkwardly as he sprinted down the platform.

"Slow your step this minute," a stern voice reprimanded the boy. "What do you think you're doing, carrying on like you're being chased by a pack of wild dogs?"

Sebastian turned to see a small, prissy man striding toward the boy, his cheeks mottled with anger.

"But Mr. Criss, sir," the boy cried. "There's a—"

"Nothing can be so urgent that it would require this sort of carry-on," the man hissed. "Now calm down and tell me what's wrong, Lang."

The boy stood still and gulped several shaky breaths in an effort to calm himself, but when he tried to speak his voice came out unnaturally high and quavered with anxiety. "There's a body, sir."

"A what?" Mr. Criss looked stunned, his dark eyes widening with sudden understanding as the boy's meaning seemed to sink in. "As in a dead body?" he asked, his voice low as he glanced around to see if anyone had overheard. He balked when he spotted Sebastian. Their eyes met for a brief moment before Mr. Criss looked away.

"In a trunk. In Unclaimed Baggage. Please come, sir."

Sebastian was on his feet before his mind had made a conscious decision to involve himself in the unfolding drama. He wasn't at Paddington in his professional capacity. Simian would be there in ten minutes—but, despite all logical objections, Sebastian found himself striding toward Mr. Criss, his hand already reaching into the pocket of his coat to pull out his warrant card. He held it up to the man's face.

"Inspector Bell. Scotland Yard. Show me the body," he said to the boy, who stared at him open-mouthed, as if Sebastian's words had summoned a demon.

"Cor, where'd you come from?" the boy muttered.

"Over there." Sebastian pointed to the bench less than two feet away. "It's all right, son. Just show me what you've discovered."

"Yes, sir," the boy said, louder now.

He seemed relieved to have someone assume control, since Mr. Criss had yet to take charge. The man appeared torn between irritation at this unexpected interruption and relief. On the one hand, he clearly preferred that someone else deal with whatever had happened, but on the other he had just lost control of the situation and would have to go along with whatever Sebastian decided to do, which could lead to all sorts of unpleasantness.

"What's your name?" Sebastian asked the boy.

"Barnaby. Barnaby Lang, sir. I'm a junior porter."

"Yes, I gathered as much. And you are?" Sebastian asked, turning to the older man.

"Frederick Criss, station manager. Inspector, I would ask for your discretion in this matter until we know what we're dealing with," he said in a pleading tone.

"You have it."

It wasn't Sebastian's intention to cause difficulties for the staff or alarm the passengers who swarmed past as they disembarked from a train that had just arrived at Platform 1. He also felt a twinge of sympathy for Barnaby, who looked terrified, his gaze sliding between the two men as if he were trying to figure out who was really in charge and who had the power to cause him the most bother.

"Please, follow me," Mr. Criss said, and the three of them strolled towards the unclaimed baggage area as if they were stretching their legs rather than going to look at a dead body.

Once they reached the door, which Barnaby had had the wits to shut behind him when he went for help, Sebastian stopped. There was no one at that end of the platform, so they could speak freely, and he thought he should be armed with the facts, no matter how scant, before going in and disturbing what might be a crime scene.

"Tell me everything, Barnaby. From the start," Sebastian invited.

Barnaby nodded almost violently. "After the train for Oxford departed, I noticed a lone trunk on Platform 4. It's my job to deliver unattended cases to Unclaimed Baggage, but I didn't get to it right away because I had to help several passengers with their luggage, and then I popped outside to get a sausage roll, on account of not having had time for breakfast." He stole a peek at Mr. Criss, who had compressed his lips into a thin line when he heard about Barnaby's transgression.

"Was the trunk meant to go on the train, or had it been offloaded?" Sebastian asked.

"I think it was meant to go on the train," Barnaby said. "If it had been offloaded, that would have been last night, and I would have seen it before I left."

"What time do you leave?" Sebastian asked.

"At ten. The last passenger train gets in at nine thirty."

"And I'm always the first to arrive in the morning, and there were no unattended cases on that platform," Mr. Criss said.

"What time did you get to the station?" Sebastian asked.

"Just before five, in time for the mail train. And I leave at half past six in the evening, sometimes seven."

That meant Mr. Criss and probably most of the porters worked a fourteen-hour shift, but that wasn't unheard of. Perhaps they were allowed to take both a lunch and a supper break during the day.

"What was the first train to leave from Platform 4?" Sebastian asked.

"Seven forty-two to Oxford."

"And was the trunk there then?"

"Impossible to tell," Mr. Criss said. "Some passengers arrive earlier than others, and their cases are taken directly to the platform while they visit the lavatory or purchase a newspaper or a cup of tea and something to eat from the dining room or the street vendors. If the trunk was already there, it wouldn't stand out."

"So, what made you think something was amiss?" Sebastian

asked Barnaby. "Surely you don't open every case that's left behind."

"The trunk seemed unusually heavy, and when I set it down I noticed something oozing from the corner. At first, I thought that maybe something inside had broken and begun to leak, but when I touched it, I knew it was blood," Barnaby explained, his voice shaking again at the memory of his gruesome discovery. "I undid the straps and opened the lid. I thought I should investigate before going for Mr. Criss."

"That was good thinking, lad," Mr. Criss said, and patted the boy on the shoulder.

Barnaby seemed glad of the praise, but then his face drooped with sadness. "It's a lady, Inspector. And she was murdered."

"How do you know that?" Mr. Criss demanded. "Are you a detective now, Lang?"

"Didn't take much detecting to see the knife sticking out of her chest," Barnaby replied, then hastened to add, "Begging your pardon, Mr. Criss."

Barnaby let out an exhalation of relief when Mr. Criss chose not to chastise him, then sucked in his breath when Sebastian pushed open the door.

"You two, wait outside," Sebastian said when Mr. Criss and Barnaby looked set to troop into the baggage area.

"I am the station manager, Inspector, and the responsibility for what happens in this terminus rests with me. I'm going in."

Sebastian didn't bother to argue, since Mr. Criss made a valid point. As he stepped inside, he heard the whistle of a train and thought that this was probably the 10:05 from Maidenhead.

"Barnaby," he called out.

"Yes, sir."

"Can you locate Mr. Bell, who's about to disembark at Platform 3, and bring him here?"

"Yes, sir, Inspector Bell, sir. Aren't you Mr. Bell?" he asked, looking a tad perplexed.

"Yes. I am here to meet my brother."

"On my way, sir," the boy cried, and took off.

Sebastian instructed Mr. Criss to shut the door behind him and walked over to the trunk in the corner. It was the only item large enough to hold a body and the only one that had a smear of dark liquid beneath the front right corner. Mr. Criss came up behind him, peering over Sebastian's shoulder as he carefully lifted the lid.

The woman lay on her left side, her knees bent to allow the body to fit inside the trunk. She wore a modest gown of black wool and black stockings that were visible because she wasn't wearing shoes. Her dark brown hair was pulled into a bun that had come partially loose, and several curls framed her pale face. Her eyes were shut, but her mouth was partially open, as if she had died in the middle of a scream. Even in her current position, it was obvious that the woman hadn't been very tall. She was plump, and, at first glance, Sebastian thought she might be in her early to mid-thirties.

An ivory-colored handle stuck out of the victim's chest, the fabric around the blade crusted with dried blood. The blood appeared to have flowed downward until it had puddled beneath the body and found its way out through what had to be an ill-fitting hinge. Sebastian leaned in and studied the weapon. Barnaby had said it was a knife, but the weapon didn't resemble any knife Sebastian had ever seen. A primitive design was etched into the handle, which appeared to be carved from bone. Sebastian was tempted to pull the weapon out and examine it more closely, but he knew Colin Ramsey would prefer that it was left as he had found it until he was ready to perform the postmortem.

"She must have been a maidservant," Mr. Criss observed.

He was visibly relieved that the woman didn't appear to be

a lady, since the death of a maidservant would be that much easier to downplay or dismiss altogether. Sebastian reached into the trunk and took hold of the woman's hand. It was the hand of someone who was accustomed to doing physical work, but that didn't necessarily mean she was a servant. Colin might be able to deduce more once he had her on the table.

"Here he is, Inspector," Barnaby announced proudly as he ushered Simian into the room.

Sebastian turned to find Simian standing by the door. He wore a black single-breasted frock coat and a black bowler that was pulled down low, casting a shadow over his eyes. A leather traveling case was gripped in his left hand, a simple black walking stick in his right. Sebastian smiled uncertainly, but Simian's mouth was pressed into a grim line, and his eyes narrowed in anger when he spotted the body in the trunk.

"Is this how we are to meet, Sebastian, over a dead body?"

"I apologize," Sebastian said stiffly, responding to his brother's curt tone. "I happened to be on the scene."

"Of course you did. That's you all over, isn't it? You could have sent this lad for a constable, but it would seem you had to get personally involved."

"Yes, I did," Sebastian snapped, angry himself now. "I am an inspector with the Metropolitan Police, Simian, and just because I'm off duty doesn't mean I can walk away from what is clearly a case of murder."

"Suit yourself," Simian barked, and turned on his heel.

"Wait," Sebastian called after him. "Simian, I'm sorry, and I'm glad you're here. Please, allow me a few minutes to deal with this, and then we can talk."

Simian paused. It was clear that he wanted to relent but also didn't want to lose face, so Sebastian added, "I'll take you to lunch. My treat."

Simian nodded and pointed to a nearby bench. "I'll wait over there."

He sat down with his back to the unclaimed baggage area, his shoulders rigid and his neck stiff as he stared at a train departing from Platform 2.

Returning his attention to Mr. Criss, Sebastian asked, "Mr. Criss, are you able to spare Barnaby for an hour?"

Mr. Criss looked annoyed, then sighed and nodded.

"Without garnishing his wages," Sebastian added.

"It's fine, lad," Mr. Criss said to Barnaby, who was looking worriedly from one man to the other. "Help Inspector Bell."

Barnaby stood straighter and adjusted his cap. "What can I do, sir?"

Sebastian pulled out a notebook and pencil from his pocket and jotted down Colin Ramsey's address in Blackfriars.

"Fetch a handcart, and let's get the trunk outside. I will find a wagon and pay the driver, but I need you to deliver the trunk to this address and help Mr. Ramsey get it down to the cellar."

"The cellar?" Barnaby repeated, clearly thinking something sinister was afoot.

"Mr. Ramsey is a surgeon who works with Scotland Yard," Sebastian explained.

"Oh. All right, then." Barnaby cast a sidelong glance at the trunk, and Sebastian realized the boy was probably afraid.

He followed Barnaby out and handed him a sixpence. "For your trouble."

It wasn't nearly enough, but that was all Sebastian could spare when he was about to pay for the body to be transported to Colin and then treat Simian to lunch.

"Thank you, sir," Barnaby said, and pushed the coin into his pocket. He was visibly worried and probably wished someone else had discovered the body, but it was too late. He was already involved.

Sebastian couldn't leave the terminus without speaking to the other porters. Someone must have delivered the trunk to the platform, since it was too heavy to move without a handcart or a trolley. The porters may have noticed something suspicious or might recall some detail about the owner of the trunk if they had seen him or her.

One man, John Derry, had seen a porter depositing what he thought was the same trunk on the platform that morning, which would support the theory that the trunk had been bound for Oxford, but there was no evidence to suggest that the owner of the trunk and the killer were one and the same. At least not yet.

"Which porter was it?" Sebastian asked.

Derry shook his head. "Sorry, I couldn't tell ye. I never saw his face. I just happened to notice that he were struggling with a heavy case."

"Didn't he have a handcart?"

"No, he had one of the hotel trolleys."

The Great Western Royal Hotel served as the main entrance to the station, and porters often helped the guests with their luggage. There was nothing odd about a porter wheeling one of the trolleys from the hotel. It probably happened all the time.

"When was this?" Sebastian asked.

"Around half past seven. I think the trunk were meant to go on the seven forty-two to Oxford, but by the time the porter made it to the platform the train was already on the move."

"What did the porter do then?" Sebastian asked.

Derry shrugged. "Left the trunk and pushed off."

"Thank you," Sebastian said. "Please contact me care of Scotland Yard if you remember anything else, Mr. Derry."

"I will be sure to do that, Inspector," Derry said, and walked away.

Sebastian nearly growled with frustration. There were six platforms and at least twice as many porters. The man could have been any one of them, and just because he had delivered the trunk to the platform didn't mean he knew anything about its owner. The fact that the trunk hadn't made it onto the train was either a stroke of bad luck or the plan all along. It was impossible to determine at this stage whether the killer had intended for the body to be discovered or had hoped to get it as far from London as possible in order to muddy the waters. The perpetrator might have boarded the train and watched the trunk disappear from view as the train chugged out of the station, or they could have sent the trunk on to Paddington and melted into the morning crowds, secure in the knowledge that the victim would never be connected to them once the body was discovered.

Sebastian would notify Superintendent Ransome that a murder had been committed, then attempt to identify the poor woman and see if he could manage to locate anyone who had known her in life. But just then, he couldn't afford to spend any more time on the investigation and jeopardize his fragile truce with Simian.

Sebastian strode back toward Platform 1 and made his way through a knot of disembarking passengers toward the bench where he had left Simian just over a half-hour ago, but when he got there he found the bench unoccupied. Simian had gone.

TWO

Gemma Tate gripped the wooden tray as she carefully made her way down the stairs. The tray was laden with soup plates, teacups and saucers, cutlery, and empty water glasses. As a nurse, it was her job to look after her patient, Anne Ramsey, whose cognitive decline had progressed rapidly and had left her with the sensibilities of a small child. However, for the past week, Gemma had been taking care of two patients, who had both come down with a lingering illness that had left them congested, feverish, and coughing until their sides hurt.

Anne spent most of her time dozing, but her son Colin was mostly awake, grumbling endlessly and refusing to submit to Gemma's ministrations. He had graciously allowed her to affix strips of mustard plaster to his chest that helped to loosen the phlegm in his lungs, and had grudgingly drunk the hot milk with honey and butter that helped to soothe his cough. But he had drawn the line at cupping, and wouldn't be persuaded to take the balsam of honey that Gemma had found so effective in treating the children at the Foundling Hospital when she had worked there.

Thankfully, Gemma and Mabel were still on their feet and

had been able to look after the Ramseys and take turns battling with them at mealtimes, since neither patient wanted beef tea or the thick porridge that would prevent them from becoming costive while lying in bed. They did acquiesce to endless cups of tea that soothed the inflammation in their sore throats, and Colin had begged Mabel to make a trifle to ease his suffering.

Gemma's gaze caught Mabel's as the two women met at the bottom of the stairs. Mabel held out her hands for the tray, and Gemma gratefully surrendered her burden.

"Please tell me they're on the mend," Mabel moaned and rolled her eyes in exasperation.

"Mrs. Ramsey is much improved, but Colin is still poorly," Gemma replied. "And very grumpy."

"Let me make you a cup of tea," Mabel offered. "You're looking a bit peaky yourself."

"I'm all right," Gemma replied with a heavy sigh. "It's just that Colin's coughing kept me up half the night."

"You should give him catarrh powder. I hear it does wonders for the sufferer."

Gemma chuckled tiredly. "Perhaps I should. He might not stop coughing, but the cocaine in the powder is sure to make him feel less aggrieved about his symptoms."

"Well, what about a thermal bath or a nasal douche?" Mabel tried again.

The two women snorted with shared amusement.

"You're right, Mr. Ramsey will never agree to either. No better than a child when he gets ill, and him a doctor," Mabel said with disdain.

"Physician, heal thyself," Gemma intoned.

"I doubt he can do that. That's your job," Mabel replied, and headed back to the kitchen.

Gemma was just about to return upstairs when there was a knock at the door. When she didn't answer quickly enough, the knocking became more frantic. A boy of about fourteen dressed in a slightly rumpled porter's uniform nearly fell on Gemma when she yanked open the door. He grabbed at the doorjamb to right himself, then let go, allowing his arms to dangle at his sides as he smiled awkwardly.

"Begging your pardon, madam, but I have a delivery for Mr. Ramsey. It's a body," the porter explained, lowering his voice to a whisper. "It's from Paddington. Inspector Bell sent me." He waited for Gemma to respond, then added, "I'm Barnaby. Barnaby Lang. Are you Mrs. Ramsey?"

"My name is Gemma Tate. I'm a nurse."

Barnaby scoffed. "No amount of nursing is going to help this 'un." He went quiet and stared at Gemma while he awaited instructions. He appeared to be vibrating with nervous energy and was clearly desperate to be relieved of his burden.

"Is this your first time transporting a dead body?" Gemma asked as she stalled for time.

Barnaby nodded. "I'm not afraid or nothing, but it did give me the creeps."

Gemma could see an innocuous-looking trunk sitting in the bed of the wagon that had stopped in front of the house. A burly middle-aged driver was on the bench. He wore a brown slouch hat and a sack coat that was patched at the elbows, and, although he was looking at Gemma with ill-disguised interest, she could tell that he too wanted to be rid of the grisly cargo and get on his way.

Gemma quickly ran through her options. She could tell Barnaby that Colin was ill and ask him to deliver the trunk to Scotland Yard, where Superintendent Ransome would no doubt pass the body to Mr. Fenwick. From what she had heard from Sebastian, the man was as indifferent as he was incompetent and more often than not settled on the cause of death without bothering with a postmortem. It was true that in some cases the cause of death was obvious, but sometimes there was more to learn from the body, and the biological factors could alter the course of an investigation. If Sebastian had sent the body to Colin, that meant he had questions he needed answered and trusted only Colin to furnish the information he sought.

How had Sebastian become embroiled in the case when he was meant to be meeting his brother? Given that the body had come from Paddington, Gemma supposed her question had been answered before it had even been asked. Sebastian would not walk away from a murder, nor would he entrust the investigation to someone else if there was any chance the killer could go free. Or maybe his involvement was the result of a catastrophic reunion with Simian, who, in Gemma's opinion, was a contemptible wretch. She would never say so to Sebastian, who was eager to mend bridges, but any man who could so thoroughly distance himself from his brother who had been shattered by grief and desperate for someone to hold him up when he was spiraling downwards had to be cruel and unfeeling.

Still, that was neither here nor there, and she had a decision to make, since both the porter and the driver were glaring at her with impatience. Gemma's motives were purely selfish since her brain was beginning to feel like the lumpy gray porridge she had just handed off to Mabel. She had to ensure that the poor victim who had been so unceremoniously stuffed into a trunk and left to trundle along in some baggage car until their remains were finally discovered got the justice they deserved, and she was eager to help Sebastian in his investigation. Detecting gave her a sense of purpose and made her feel useful and valued, sentiments she never took for granted, particularly when the praise came from Sebastian and made her glow with pride.

"Please take the trunk down to the cellar. I'll open the door that leads into the alleyway."

The driver shrugged and climbed off the bench, while Barnaby unlatched the back of the wagon bed and prepared to lower the trunk to the ground. Gemma shut the front door and hurried down to the cellar, where she unlocked the door and peered outside. The two men struggled to maneuver the trunk down the narrow stairs, but they finally got it through the door. Barnaby let out a strangled cry when he spotted a human brain that resembled pickled cauliflower and was floating in a jar of formaldehyde, and he nearly dropped his side of the trunk. He set it down with a thunk, and not a moment too soon, because, when he saw a five-month fetus with its nose pressed to the glass on the shelf below the brain, he gave a shrill cry of terror and fled, his boots pounding on the stone steps as he ran back to the wagon.

The driver, who seemed unperturbed, turned to leave, but Gemma called out to him before he disappeared through the door.

"Would you mind terribly setting the body on the table?" she asked.

The man looked annoyed, and with good reason. To deliver a trunk was one thing, but to touch the contents was something quite different. He probably thought she would pay him, but Gemma didn't have any money on her and in any case couldn't really afford to spend her wages on anything other than necessities.

"I would be most grateful," she added, hoping that would be enough.

The man nodded and went to open the trunk. He looked momentarily taken aback, then reached in, lifted the body with a grunt, and set the woman on her side on the dissecting table.

"Thank you kindly, sir," Gemma said.

"Good day to you, madam," the driver said, his voice firm in case Gemma was about to ask him to help with something else.

Gemma locked the door, rested her hands on her hips, and studied the victim. It was impossible to miss the object sticking out of her chest, and Gemma supposed a knife to the heart had to be the cause of death, but a postmortem would be able to tell Sebastian considerably more. Gemma knew more about the workings of the human body and had more practical experience than most of Colin's private students, but she wasn't equipped to perform a postmortem on her own. That would be not only presumptuous but also detrimental, since she could miss something vital and supply Sebastian with erroneous findings. What she could do, though, was examine the body and the trunk and see if there was anything she could learn that might be of use.

She wouldn't have dared to take such a decision in the past, but since the last case they'd worked on together her relationship with Sebastian had shifted. There was now a sense of inevitability between them and the certain knowledge that, whatever path life set them on, they would walk it together. Sebastian had accepted her as his partner, openly acknowledged her contributions, and given her the space to make her own choices. Despite an outcome that had very nearly ended in tragedy, Sebastian had seemed to realize that unless he gave up his position with the Metropolitan Police, any woman he loved, whether she was a partner who unapologetically meddled in his cases or a devoted wife who waited patiently at home, would always be at risk. The only way to protect the people he loved was to teach them to assess the situation and defend themselves should the circumstances call for it.

As proof of his capitulation, Sebastian had given Gemma an unexpected gift for her birthday—a beautiful American-made pistol that she now kept in a drawer by her bed. The pistol had been something of a surprise, and Gemma still wasn't sure how she felt about using it, but she understood that it was Sebastian's way of making sure she was safe and would be able to protect herself if he wasn't there to look after her. Gemma had yet to learn to fire the weapon, but just holding it in her hands had made her feel like a force to be reckoned with. She liked the power that had surged through her and the knowledge that she wasn't vulnerable as long as she could defend herself.

Sebastian had offered Gemma another gift as well, this one to safeguard her emotional well-being. He had arranged for her to say goodbye to Lucy, the little girl she had come to love while employed at the Foundling Hospital and had been forced to leave without a word of explanation. The promise of a meeting with Lucy had been an answer to a prayer, one that only Sebastian had heard and had taken upon himself to fulfill. He had never said so outright, but Gemma suspected he had realized that, once she'd had some time to consider the offer, she would change her mind. As much as she longed to see Lucy and tell her how much she cared for her, her desire was misguided and selfish and would only cause Lucy unnecessary pain.

To know that Lucy was well and settling into life at the Foundling Hospital would have to be enough, and, although it had hurt to say that final goodbye in her heart, Gemma knew it was time to let Lucy go. She had no claim on her, and Lucy was in the best possible place for a child who had been orphaned. Lucy would become part of the Foundling family and eventually have a chance at a safe and respectable future. Given Gemma's recent brushes with danger, she was no longer certain that her own path could be described in the same terms.

But respectable or not, for the first time since returning from Crimea Gemma felt a longing that was difficult to ignore. Some people called such feeling a vocation, and, although she could never become either a doctor or a detective due to the limitations placed on her sex, she could still carve out a place for herself in the male-dominated world she had been born into, and she would no longer apologize for either her intellect or her choices, because she had come to realize that she wasn't the least bit sorry.

Gemma rolled up her sleeves, carefully pushed the dead woman onto her back, and set to work.

THREE

Sebastian spent a quarter of an hour searching for Simian, but his brother wasn't at the terminus, and Sebastian had no way to contact him. Simian had never said how long he intended to remain in London or where he might stay—his letter had been brief and uninformative—but Sebastian knew that there was no direct way to get home from Paddington. Simian would have to make his way to the terminus at Bishopsgate in order to board an Eastern Counties Railway train that would take him to Colchester, where he would then switch to a train bound for Ipswich. It was a long and arduous journey, and, if Simian felt he had no reason to overnight in London, he was probably already on his way.

Although angry with himself for destroying any chance he had of talking things out with his brother, Sebastian was also deeply hurt. Simian might be ready to talk, but he clearly wasn't ready to forgive, and had chosen to punish Sebastian for a situation that was beyond his control. Would it have killed him to wait? Surely, after all this time, Sebastian deserved that much. But Simian had never been very flexible or capable of putting himself in other people's shoes. It was that rigid inability to compromise that was really at the heart of their estrangement. Well, if that was the way Simian wanted it, that was the way it would have to be. Sebastian had been on his own since he was eighteen and had managed to survive the worst life had to throw at him. He might no longer have a brother who loved him, but after years of self-inflicted exile he finally had people who cared about him, and he cherished them above all else.

Giving up on his search, Sebastian walked to the cab stand, climbed into the first hansom in the queue, and instructed the cabbie to take him to Blackfriars. The body would have been delivered by now, and, even though Colin would not have had much time to glean anything useful, Sebastian could remain on hand while he performed the postmortem, and spend some time with Gemma, which was sure to calm his troubled soul.

The streets were congested with the usual midday traffic, the hansom moving at a snail's pace as the cabbie guided the vehicle between lumbering dray wagons, sleek private carriages, and omnibuses that stopped every few minutes to load and unload passengers. In Oxford Street, the hansom got stuck behind a delivery wagon whose wheel had come off. The wagon completely blocked the road and made it impossible to either get around it or turn back, since the hansom was now surrounded by other vehicles. Street vendors took advantage of the congestion and swarmed the waiting vehicles, offering irritated travelers everything from newspapers to hot pies and boiled eels, and doing a brisk trade.

Exhaling deeply to combat his frustration, Sebastian decided to make the most of his time. He purchased a pork pie from a young girl who looked like she was about to buckle under the weight of the heavy tray slung around her neck, and leaned back against the seat as he consumed his pie, which was still warm and absolutely delicious. Once he had finished, he wiped his hands on his handkerchief, stuffed it back into his pocket, and considered what he had learned about the case, which regrettably wasn't very much.

Someone had either personally delivered or had sent the trunk containing the body of the woman to the station. She had been stabbed through the heart with a weapon that looked primitive and bore indecipherable carvings, and, although the heart would have stopped pumping blood once the woman was dead, enough must have seeped into the fabric of her gown to drip onto the bottom of the trunk and leak out through the hinge. The tag bearing the Birmingham address was almost illegible, and no one seemed to recall anything about the porter who had delivered the trunk to the platform.

The victim had been carefully positioned inside the trunk and wore no coat or bonnet, so chances were that she had been murdered at home and did not have anything on her that would point to who she was or where she lived. There didn't appear to be a reticule or even shoes, whose quality might tell Sebastian something of her circumstances. A person's footwear was always a good indicator of their financial situation since new shoes were dear, and old shoes were frequently reheeled and resoled to make them last longer. Sebastian's gaze slid to his own boots, which had seen him through the past three years. It was time he splurged on a new pair, and he had considered investing in a new suit and several new shirts as well since he was beginning to look a bit scruffy.

Sebastian pulled out his pocket watch, checked the time, and sighed in frustration, then returned to his deliberations. The victim had worn no jewelry that Sebastian could see, but it was possible that whoever had shoved her into that trunk had taken anything of value. They might have taken her shoes as well, if they were still in good condition, and her coat and bonnet, if she had been wearing them at the time. The items would fetch a few bob if sold to a thrift shop. It was unlikely that the woman had been stabbed through the heart in the middle of the street or while visiting some establishment, since the killer wasn't likely to have a traveling trunk on hand and would have needed to move the body and remove the items they wished to keep before putting the victim in the trunk and getting it to the station.

According to Mr. Derry, the trunk had been delivered to the platform early in the morning, so whoever had brought it hadn't been overly concerned with being seen. And why would they be? There was nothing unusual about someone arriving at the terminus with their luggage and instructing a porter to deliver the luggage to a particular train while they purchased tickets or visited the lavatory before starting on a long journey. There was nothing unique about the trunk or anything that revealed the identity of its owner.

When the hansom finally pulled up before Colin's house, Sebastian jumped down, paid the cabbie, and strode up the walkway to the front door. He had a dead body and not much else, and, unless Colin could extract new information from the corpse, whoever had killed the poor woman had committed the perfect crime.

FOUR

Mabel looked drained when she opened the door, and her relief at seeing Sebastian was palpable.

"Mabel, is everything all right?" Sebastian asked.

"Mr. and Mrs. Ramsey have been ill these past few days, and to be perfectly frank I'm a bit frazzled, Inspector."

"And Gemma? Is she ill as well?" Sebastian asked. He hadn't seen Gemma since her day off and now realized that she might have been unwell in the interim.

"She can't afford to get ill, can she?" Mabel replied peevishly. "Those two are worse than children when they're sick."

Sebastian was relieved to hear that Gemma hadn't succumbed to the illness, but the news put a damper on his plans. He knew he should probably leave, but he had come all that way, and he wanted to speak to her. Besides, he had to find out what had happened to the trunk and its contents.

"I won't stay long. I just need a word with Gemma."

"Oh, you'll be staying," Mabel replied cryptically, and held out her hand.

Sebastian shrugged off his coat and draped it over Mabel's

arm, then handed her his hat and turned towards the parlor, but what Mabel said next froze him in his tracks.

"Miss Tate is in the cellar. Working on your body."

"What?"

Mabel chuckled. "It was preferable to arguing with Mr. Ramsey about a nasal douche."

"Right," Sebastian muttered under his breath.

This day wasn't turning out as he'd expected, and he really wasn't in the mood for any more surprises, but he had to see for himself what Gemma was doing. Sebastian descended the steps and entered Colin's private sanctum to find Gemma, sleeves rolled up, a lock of hair falling into her face, bent over the corpse. The woman on the dissecting table was laid out flat, and her hair rippled over the sides of the table like a curtain of brown velvet.

"Gemma, what are you doing?" Sebastian exclaimed.

Gemma looked up, pushed the hair out of her face, and smiled a little guiltily. "Helping you."

"How do you imagine you handling the remains helps me?" Sebastian approached the table and was dismayed to discover that Gemma had pulled the murder weapon out of the woman's chest.

"Gemma," he began, but Gemma held up her hand.

"Before you say anything, hear me out."

Sebastian inhaled sharply, then nodded in acquiescence. What was done was done, and Gemma obviously had her reasons. To rebuke her would only lead to a row, which was the last thing he wanted after he had sabotaged his chances of working things out with Simian.

"All right. Tell me," Sebastian invited as he leaned against the wooden counter where Colin normally kept his instruments, and crossed his arms.

"Colin won't be in any condition to perform the postmortem for a few days yet," Gemma said matter-of-factly, "but the longer you wait, the greater the chance that the killer will escape. So I thought I would examine the remains and provide you with clues that would help you get started."

"That's very thoughtful of you."

Sebastian tried not to smile, but Gemma's eager expression had dispelled some of the frustration he had felt since he'd arrived at Paddington that morning and that had dogged him all morning, and he suddenly felt lighter, despite the corpse between them.

As a young constable, Sebastian had been dismayed by his mentors' ability to joke as they stood over a dead body or even eat next to a corpse while they waited for the police wagon that would cart the victim away, but over the years he had learned that carrying on as normal was the only way to deal with sudden and brutal death. The victim was gone, and no amount of somber reflection would bring them back, but an ability to set one's feelings aside and focus on the details without becoming emotionally unbalanced was what usually allowed one to solve the case in the end.

Sebastian felt pity for the woman on the table and was furious with whoever had taken her life, but at the same time he was also grateful that he could discuss the case with Gemma and relished the connection they had made over the past six months. He'd come to realize that, in the end, that was all there was—the people one loved and the joyful moments that elevated one's life from mere existence to glorious living. He had finally come to terms with his own grief and loss and acknowledged that he had Gemma to thank for holding out the hand that had finally pulled him out of the living grave he'd dug for himself after Louisa's death. It was time to move on, and he intended to go forward with Gemma by his side, if she'd have him.

"And were you able to discover any clues?" Sebastian asked, his attention returning to Gemma.

"Quite a few, actually," Gemma replied proudly. "For one, the woman was murdered more than eight hours ago, since rigor mortis has already passed, and I was able to straighten her limbs. Do you know what time the trunk was discovered?"

"It was delivered to the station around seven-thirty this morning, but the body was found not long before I arrived, which was shortly before ten o'clock. I thought the victim was probably murdered sometime during the night."

"Oh, so you already knew," Gemma said, her mouth drooping with disappointment.

"It's still important to establish the time of death," Sebastian hurried to reassure her. "Did you conclude anything else?"

"I did. The woman appears to be in her early thirties and comes from a working-class background. Her hands are rough and reddened around the fingertips, and I found fibers in her hair."

"And what does that tell you?" Sebastian asked, genuinely curious.

"I think she might have worked with yarn or in a textile mill, which would mean that she was probably not from London. This theory is further supported by her gown, which is made of thick wool. She would be comfortable up north but would be too warm in a woolen gown in London in May."

"The trunk was bound for Oxford, but the tag listed Birmingham as the final destination," Sebastian said.

Perhaps the Birmingham address was where the woman had lived, and the killer had tried to send her remains back to her family. There was a more direct way to get to the Midlands from London, but if Paddington had been the only option, the trunk could have been transferred at Oxford to an Oxford, Worcester and Wolverhampton Railway train bound for Birmingham.

Gemma nodded, clearly pleased to have her assumptions confirmed.

"Go on," Sebastian said, really listening now.

"The victim wore her wedding ring on a string around her neck, tucked under the bodice. If she worked around carding machinery, she would not be permitted to wear jewelry since it could get caught in the apparatus and possibly cripple her."

"Can I see the ring?"

Gemma reached inside the woman's bodice and pulled out the string. Sebastian leaned in closer to examine the ring, but, when his nose was practically in the victim's bosom, he straightened and reached for one of Colin's scalpels, which he used to sever the string.

"That's better," he said, and held the ring up to the light so he could study it more closely.

The narrow band of gold shone dully in the lamplight and appeared to be perfectly smooth.

"I don't think she ever wore the ring on her finger," he mused. "If she did, it would have minuscule nicks and scratches from coming in contact with various surfaces."

Louisa's ring had been scratched since she had never taken it off and had worn it while cooking, cleaning, and doing the laundry. Sebastian had considered keeping it, but had decided that Louisa would prefer to be buried with it, and it had remained on her finger. He peered at the underside of the band, then reached for the magnifying glass Colin kept on the counter. The inscription was difficult to make out since the letters were so tiny, but with the aid of the glass he was able to see it clearly. It read:

G♡H

"G loves H," Sebastian said. "Which one was she?"

"Definitely H," Gemma replied without hesitation. "The

wedding ring is given by a man to a woman as a token of his love and commitment, and when referring to a couple the man is always mentioned first, so G would have given the ring to H."

"Yes, you're probably right," Sebastian agreed, and smiled. "As you usually are. Did you notice anything else that might be important?"

Gemma nodded. "The gown is of reasonably good quality, and the stockings are in excellent condition. They have never been darned, not even on the big toe, where they tend to wear out first. And I think she was probably in mourning. I do wish I could examine her boots," she said wistfully, then continued, "The victim is well nourished, and her teeth are strong. She had a molar extracted, some time ago since the area is completely healed. Her hair is full and thick, and she probably used hot tongs or leather curlers quite recently."

"How can you tell?"

"The texture," Gemma replied, looking at Sebastian as if it was the most obvious thing. "See how her hair is woolly at the root but then becomes smoother? If she had set it in curlers or applied hot tongs, she wouldn't touch the root because she would burn her scalp. She wasn't the sort of woman men would call beautiful, but I think she took pains with her appearance. Perhaps she was preparing for a romantic assignation or a reunion."

Sebastian made a conscious effort to close his mouth, which had fallen open while Gemma was speaking. Now that she had mentioned these things, he could see that she was most probably right, but he would not have made the assumptions for himself, and he doubted Colin would either, being an unmarried man.

"There's also evidence of a physical altercation," Gemma added.

"Are you referring to rape?" Sebastian asked carefully.

The victim was still dressed, but Gemma might have

performed a physical examination if she had been so inclined. Gemma looked flustered, then shook her head.

"I didn't check to see if she had been assaulted, I was going to leave that to Colin, but there's bruising around her right wrist and also marks on her throat. Perhaps someone grabbed her by the neck with his right hand and then encircled her wrist with his left when she tried to push him off. That probably happened before she was murdered."

Sebastian's gaze shifted toward the murder weapon, which was covered in dried blood and quite oddly shaped.

"Is that an ice pick?" he asked.

Gemma shook her head. "It looks like an ice pick, but it's actually a bodkin. There's a hole near the end of the blade, but it's difficult to make out because it's clogged with blood."

"A bodkin? Like in *Hamlet*?" Sebastian asked.

He'd always assumed that when Hamlet had considered ending his life with a bodkin, he had been speaking of a dagger, but the tool Sebastian was looking at didn't have a steel blade and wasn't sharp like a knife.

"I suppose it can be used as a weapon, and it was in this instance," Gemma said when her gaze strayed to the wound in the woman's left breast. "But it's really a sewing tool. This one looks quite old. I think it's made of whalebone," she mused as she studied the ornate handle. "A bodkin is used for threading, but the sharp point is useful for making uniform holes in fabric or in leather."

"So not your usual weapon of choice," Sebastian remarked.

"Perhaps whoever the victim had been expecting came to see her, a violent argument broke out, during which he grabbed her violently and tried to choke her, and then he snatched a bodkin from her sewing basket and stabbed her in a fit of fury."

"That certainly sounds plausible," Sebastian agreed.

"And she didn't die quickly," Gemma said. "The heart stops pumping blood as soon as the person dies, but the bodice of her gown was soaked, and blood dripped onto the bottom of the trunk. Perhaps the killer missed the mark, and she died of internal bleeding. There's blood on her hands and beneath her fingernails, so she was probably conscious for a while and tried to stem the bleeding. There must have been quite a lot of blood at the scene."

"Yes, I agree, but we might never find out where she was murdered."

"How did she end up at Paddington?" Gemma mused.

"That's a good question," Sebastian replied, and went on to theorize out loud. If Gemma spotted a flaw in his reasoning, she would point it out, which would be extremely helpful. "Even if the trunk belonged to the victim or the killer conveniently had it to hand, how did he or she manage to get it to the terminus if they hadn't made prior arrangements?" Sebastian asked. "They would have needed a wagon to transport the body and help loading and unloading the trunk once they arrived at the terminus."

"And given the amount of blood, the killer would be taking a great risk since someone might notice the trunk was leaking," Gemma agreed.

"An unnecessary risk. Even if they didn't want to leave the body at the scene of the murder, they could have easily left it in some dark alley or thrown it off a bridge. Why take it to Paddington and leave it on the platform?"

"Perhaps the killer felt remorse and wanted to return the woman to her family so they could bury her," Gemma suggested, though Sebastian could hear her uncertainty about the idea.

"I suppose that's possible, but until we know more I'm not inclined to believe that the killer was motivated by sentiment," Sebastian said. "Not when they allowed her to die a slow and torturous death."

Gemma's eyes misted with tears as she looked at the

victim and laid a hand over the woman's bruised wrist. "She must have been in agony and absolutely terrified once the killer put her in the trunk. She would have known she was about to die."

"We can hope that she was unconscious by that point," Sebastian said. "I don't see any wounds on her hands, her nails are not broken, and there are no marks on the inside of the lid."

"I don't think she would have had the strength to try to open the lid," Gemma replied. "The hemorrhaging would have left her severely weakened."

"Is there anything that might help us to identify her?" Sebastian asked.

He could easily envision the victim's final moments and thought his anger would boil over if he allowed himself to dwell on her suffering. He also resolutely refused to draw a comparison between the way this woman had died and the manner of his wife Louisa's death, which would have been terrifyingly similar. All he could do for the deceased was find her killer and turn them over to the law, and, if the killer's own death happened to be drawn-out and horrific, then that would be poetic justice as far as Sebastian was concerned.

"I didn't find anything on the victim," Gemma said.

"So the ring is our only clue."

"Yes, but there must be countless couples whose initials are G and H. Without a surname, the ring is useless." Gemma sighed. "How do you intend to proceed?"

Sebastian's sigh was as heavy as Gemma's. "I honestly don't know. She could be anyone from anywhere, killed by someone she knew or someone she didn't. The trunk has no markings beyond a barely legible label, and the bodkin could have belonged to the victim or to the killer. Would you say this is the sort of thing many women would own?" he asked. He had never seen Louisa use such a tool.

Gemma nodded. "Yes, they would, particularly women who

sew their own clothes or work with leather. Mabel has one, only it's made of wood. This bodkin is actually rather distinctive."

"Is it?" Sebastian reached for the bodkin and lifted it by the handle, which wasn't as bloodied as the bone blade.

He brought the bodkin closer to the lamp and studied the symbols carved into the handle. They were difficult to make out since the handle had been rubbed smooth by constant use, but he could make out a flower at the top. It was a thistle.

"This is not the sort of flower someone would immortalize unless it meant something to them," he said.

"And what do you suppose it means?" Gemma asked.

"The thistle is a symbol of Scotland."

"Really? How do you know that?"

Sebastian hated to bring Louisa into the conversation, knowing that any mention of his late wife always made Gemma feel as if he were comparing the two women, but he could hardly lie or refuse to answer.

"Louisa had a Scottish nanny when she was a girl, who told her stories about the Highlands."

Nurse MacGillivray's grandfather had been killed during the Jacobite Uprising of 1745, and his brother had been transported to North Carolina and sold into indentured servitude. Her own father, who had been hardly more than a boy at the time, had spent years in prison but had eventually been released and allowed to return to the family's croft. Scottish independence was a subject that had been close to Nanny MacGillivray's heart, but Sebastian didn't think Scottish history had any bearing on the case and saw no reason to burden Gemma with the details of his wife's past.

"Perhaps our woman—H—came from somewhere near the Scottish border, or inherited this bodkin from a female relative who had Scottish roots," he said instead.

"Perhaps," Gemma agreed. "So, what's next?" she asked once Sebastian had replaced the bodkin in the kidney dish and wiped his hands on a towel. Her gaze kept straying to the still face of the unidentified woman, and Sebastian knew she felt a burning need to help her, even if that help was given posthumously.

"I have to give it some thought, but first I must inform Ransome. The case is not officially mine until his say-so."

FIVE

Gemma tore her gaze away from the victim and focused her attention on Sebastian. He was the most intelligent, resourceful man she'd ever met, but just now he looked completely worn out and, dare she say it, dejected. Gemma forced the plight of the nameless woman from her mind and came around the dissecting table to stand in front of Sebastian. She took his face in her hands and looked into the golden-brown depths of his eyes. What she saw was not a capable, confident man of thirty-two. She saw a wounded little boy who was desperate for the love and approval of his older brother.

Sebastian smiled sadly, then gently took Gemma by the wrists and lowered her hands, but didn't release them. He needed to talk about what had happened, but it was obvious he was torn between his need to confide in her and his desire to push his feelings aside.

"What happened with Simian?" Gemma asked softly.

"He left," Sebastian said after a slight pause. "He just left, Gemma."

"Why?"

"He was angry that I wasn't willing to walk away from this case."

"You could no more walk away from a murder victim than I could walk away from a person who's been injured. The things we do are not just our jobs. It's a calling, a vow to serve."

"Simian can't forgive me, and he can't understand. He's never been anything but a farmer."

Sebastian let go of Gemma's hands, and Gemma touched his face again, cupping his lean cheek.

"Sebastian, this rift with Simian is not your fault."

"It is," he replied. "I betrayed him."

"How did you betray him?"

Sebastian sighed heavily. "I knew Simian would try to stop me from leaving, he said as much when I tried to talk to him about my plans, so one day, when he was in the shed milking the cows, I took a few things and the money I had been saving for years and walked out. I left a note on the kitchen table, telling him that I would write once I was settled."

Sebastian shot Gemma an imploring look. "Don't you see, Gemma? I left him on his own at a time when he really needed me. I was thinking of myself and of what I wanted to do, but I never considered how Simian might feel. A few years before, it had been the four of us. A lively, loving family who lived and worked together. And then, after my father died, we suddenly became three. Then just two. And then Simian was left all alone in that house, with no means to hire help and with no one to talk to."

"You were eighteen," Gemma said softly.

Sebastian nodded. "Old enough to behave like a man, not a spoiled child. I didn't even give him the respect of telling him in person. I slunk off while his back was turned."

"And he's been punishing you ever since."

"I deserve it," Sebastian said quietly.

"You do not, and I don't want to hear such nonsense ever

again," Gemma said firmly. "Simian felt hurt and betrayed, I understand that, but you are his brother, his blood. I would have forgiven Victor for making a decision without consulting me. I would have forgiven him anything if it meant the difference between having him in my life and losing him forever. Simian is not alone. He has a family, and he got the farm. It's time he forgave you and stopped behaving like a petulant child."

Smiling wistfully, Sebastian said, "Simian was never the sort of person to make rash decisions. He liked to think things through, to let an idea sit with him until the outcome felt inevitable. He married Hannah a month after I left, as soon as the final banns were read. Which meant that he'd asked her three weeks before. He was so alone, he couldn't bear it for another moment."

"Sebastian, I was left alone when Victor died, but I didn't marry Mr. Gadd or join a vaudeville troupe just so I could have company. Simian was a grown man, and you cannot accept responsibility for the decisions he made. Besides, I thought he was happily married to a girl he had been sweet on before your mother passed."

Sebastian chuckled softly. "Simian was sweet on Hannah, but Hannah always preferred me."

"Were you in love with her?" Gemma asked carefully, and wondered if she wanted to hear his answer. Knowing that Sebastian had loved other women was surprisingly painful, even if those women were no longer in his life.

Sebastian smiled guiltily. "I don't know if I would call it love. We stepped out a few times, but I wasn't ready to take her on. That would have meant staying in Suffolk forever and working the farm with Simian for the rest of my days. I'm sure Hannah felt just as betrayed as Simian, but it was my only chance to change the direction of my life, so I took it."

"So you think they married to spite you?"

"I think they married because they needed to turn the pain I had caused them into something good."

"Did you make promises to Hannah?" Gemma asked, and wondered if she had any right to ask.

"No," Sebastian replied immediately. "I knew I would leave, and I didn't want Hannah to hold me back. But I think she might have pinned her hopes on me and was crushed when I left. I never meant to hurt her, Gemma."

"You don't owe me an explanation," Gemma replied, more gruffly than she had intended.

"But I do. I don't want you to think badly of me."

"I could never think badly of you," Gemma said gently.

Sebastian's eyes shone with relief, and Gemma smiled kindly at him. She had been so focused on the murdered woman that she hadn't immediately realized she should attend to the walking wounded first.

"Simian clearly does," Sebastian said with a sigh.

"Then I think you know what you have to do," Gemma said to the despondent man-child before her. "You must go home and make things right with Simian."

"How can I make it right? So much time has passed, and so much has happened."

"You can tell Simian what you just told me, that you're sorry for the way you behaved and that you should have given him the consideration and respect he deserved. And that you want to be his brother again, whatever it takes. You both need to set your pride aside and make an effort to move forward."

"He left," Sebastian reminded her testily. "Am I meant to beg for his forgiveness because I had to do my job?"

"Sebastian, if you are serious about mending your relationship with Simian, then you are going to have to take the high road."

"Yes, ma'am," Sebastian said, and smiled at last. "Thank you. I needed to hear that."

"Yes, you did. And now you need to hear this." She turned toward the woman on the dissecting table. "This poor woman has no one to speak for her. She was murdered and dumped at Paddington Station, her remains bound for some unconfirmed destination, where she would have most likely been tossed into a pauper's grave without so much as a prayer said for her soul. You must find her killer before you do anything else."

Sebastian's smile grew wider. "What would I do without you?"

"Exactly what you're doing right now."

"No," Sebastian said with a shake of his head. "I wouldn't be."

And Gemma knew he was probably right.

SIX

Chastened, Sebastian set aside his personal feelings and set off for Scotland Yard. There were still days when he walked into the duty room and expected to see Sergeant Woodward behind the desk, and was forcibly reminded that Sergeant Woodward had been transferred to another station—his punishment for betting on the wrong horse. No one ever mentioned Superintendent Lovell—who was now persona non grata—and every man at Scotland Yard stood in firm support of Superintendent Ransome, who had managed to endear himself to the men with his *I was once one of you and I understand what you need* approach. Sebastian had to admit that it was highly effective, and the men rallied around Ransome in a way they never had with Lovell.

Ransome had been in the job for only a month, but things had certainly changed, and, in Sebastian's opinion, for the better. Ransome was more willing to listen and didn't rely on threats of immediate dismissal as a form of professional motivation. He was quick to outline the stakes, but he also offered practical advice and whatever support was needed to get the job done. But Ransome's help wasn't entirely altruistic, since he stood to benefit from a positive result and hoped to impress his superiors. It would be his head on the chopping block if things went wrong, and he was acutely aware of that fact.

Sebastian greeted Sergeant Meadows, who had just finished taking down a complaint from a well-dressed gentleman who had been knocked down by a gang of street children and relieved of his purse, silver-tipped cane, and solid gold pocket watch. The knees of the victim's trousers were soiled, and there was a bruise on his ungloved hand in the shape of a hobnailed heel. Sergeant Meadows assured the man that all possible avenues of inquiry would be explored, then rolled his eyes, crumpled the report, and tossed it in the bin as soon as the complainant was through the door.

"Silly sod," Constable Bryant, who'd overheard the man's sad tale, exclaimed sympathetically. "His belongings have probably been split up and already changed hands at least once. He will never get them back. But it's nice to know that he believes in the reach and efficiency of the police service."

"Until he finds his hopes disappointed and tells anyone who's willing to listen that the service is a useless drain on already thinly stretched resources and the police service should be disbanded immediately in favor of privately funded law enforcers whose sole purpose would be to protect those who can afford to pay them," Sergeant Meadows replied sourly. "I've seen his type before, and their fury has no bounds once they have been humiliated and their pockets have been emptied."

Constable Bryant nodded. "Makes people feel helpless and small when they can't protect either themselves or their possessions, so they need someone to rage at."

Sergeant Meadows nodded in agreement, but his attention was on Sebastian. "Did you not have the day off, Inspector?"

"I did, but a murder victim was found at the Paddington terminus." Sebastian didn't bother to explain how he had come to be involved. "Did anyone report a missing woman either last night or this morning?"

"Yes," Sergeant Meadows replied. He seemed energized by his ability to offer assistance after the frustration of taking down the details of a street crime. "Let me see."

The sergeant took a neatly filled form out of a cardboard file and handed it to Sebastian, who looked over the details. The missing woman was forty-two, tall, and thin, and had red hair and green eyes. Sebastian handed the form back to Sergeant Meadows. "It's not her. Is the super in?"

"Yes, but you'd better hurry, Inspector. He's leaving in half an hour. Something about tea with the in-laws."

"I only need a few minutes of his time," Sebastian said, and headed down the corridor.

Ransome looked dapper in a black suit worn with a crisp white shirt, silver-gray puff tie, and matching waistcoat. His hair, which had been recently trimmed, was neatly brushed, his moustache was waxed into points, and his shoes shone with freshly applied polish.

"May I have a word, sir?" Sebastian asked once he'd been invited to enter and had approached Ransome's desk.

Ransome sighed. "Whatever it is, better make it quick. It's my in-laws' silver wedding anniversary. Mrs. Ransome and I have been invited to a *small* celebration for sixty," he said with a disgusted shake of his head.

"You look very smart, sir," Sebastian said, amused by Ransome's discomfort.

He wasn't privy to the circumstances of John and Laura Ransome's first meeting, the details of their courtship, or Sir David's feelings about his daughter marrying a commoner, but John Ransome, who was what Sebastian's mother would have called the salt of the earth, would have to learn to hold his own in a room full of influential men.

"I'd much rather be here, where I'm in my element,"

Ransome confessed. "I've never had to rub elbows with Sir David's cronies before. They kept their distance at the wedding, but tonight I'll be fair game."

It wasn't like Ransome to show vulnerability, but Sebastian supposed the superintendent thought Sebastian would understand and sympathize with his predicament. Ransome would have been treated with indulgence on the day of his wedding, but now he would have to try to fit in and not embarrass himself in front of a bunch of nobs.

"Think of it as a *silver* opportunity to make useful connections," Sebastian quipped.

"You mean, dazzle them with my roguish charm and quick wit?" Ransome grinned. He now seemed a little more relaxed.

"You wouldn't be where you are if Sir David didn't have faith in you, either personally or professionally," Sebastian said. "Remember that, and you'll be just fine."

"Thank you, Bell," Ransome said gruffly. "I appreciate that. And what brings you here on your day off?"

"A murder."

"Tell me," Ransome invited, and instantly adopted the calm, capable demeanor for which he was known.

Sebastian filled Ransome in on what he knew and shared some of Gemma's theories without revealing that she had examined the body without express permission from either Colin or Scotland Yard. He had learned to downplay her role in the investigations, but he wasn't about to dismiss her findings.

Ransome looked thoughtful. "To send a constable to check with the other stations if someone fitting the victim's description has been reported missing is a waste of time and resources," he said at last. "And if this woman arrived from Birmingham and was stashed in her own trunk, it's not likely that anyone in London has reported her missing."

"So, how do you suggest we identify her?"

Sebastian suddenly realized that Ransome might order him

to abandon the case. Much like the theft that had just been reported and wasn't going to be investigated due to the futility of such an undertaking, to expend resources on an inquiry that would likely lead to a dead end wasn't on Ransome's agenda. He believed in focusing on cases the Yard had a good chance of resolving and not wasting precious time or funds on ones that had no earthly chance of getting solved. Ransome was a political animal, and his leadership style was nothing more than a balance sheet in which losses and gains were measured not only in solves but also in positive publicity and renewed funding that would keep them all employed.

Having considered the situation, Ransome finally spoke. "If no one was aware of this woman's murder, I would recommend that you focus your energies on a case that can be brought to a satisfactory conclusion, but, given that you have already interviewed the station manager and the porters, there's a good chance the story will appear in the papers and make us look like incompetent clodhoppers if we don't find this woman's killer."

"What do you propose?" Sebastian asked again.

"I propose that we make a show of investigating this crime and see where it leads us," Ransome said.

Sebastian didn't like the sound of that.

"This woman deserves justice, sir, not a show," he said, no longer speaking to Ransome as a friend but as a superior who needed to be reminded why they were all there in the first place.

"And we will do our best to ensure that justice is served without throwing good money after bad," Ransome replied, his practical nature surging to the forefront. "I propose we have her photograph taken and issue a public appeal for information. If someone comes forward, then we proceed based on the facts they provide. If no one responds, then we have done our due diligence and can move on to another case without being accused of not investigating her death."

Ransome nodded, seemingly agreeing with his own proposal. "Yes, I believe that's a sound plan. Instruct Sergeant Meadows to allocate funds from petty cash," he said, then added, "The best person for the job is Zeke Robinson. He specializes in post-mortem photography and maintains a studio in Holywell Street. I've seen his work and was extremely impressed with the quality of the composition."

"Holywell Street?"

An address in Holywell Street spoke volumes since the area was best known for peddling pornography, the trade so rampant that it had resulted in the Obscene Publications Act a couple of years ago that threatened the shopkeepers with lengthy prison sentences if they were caught stocking illicit erotica. Despite the government crackdown, nearly all the shops that lined the narrow thoroughfare still sold graphic reproductions to both ladies and gentlemen who were in the market for forbidden and salacious images.

The shopkeepers hid their wares in books, almanacs, and sometimes boxes under the counter, and catered to every taste without judgment. Many photographs came from France, but there were studios in London that produced and distributed images of local talent. Since they were happy to pay a competitive rate to anyone who was willing to pose either by themselves or in compromising positions with members of either sex, there were always takers, especially when all they really had to do was drop their clothes. Young and beautiful prostitutes were eager to supplement their income, since an hour or two in the studio paid as much as servicing several punters.

Sebastian had seen a stack of illicit images on Lovell's desk after he had confiscated the contraband from two young constables, who had been daft enough to pore over the images in the duty room. The constables had been made an example of and sacked on the spot, and the images had been ceremoniously tossed into the potbellied stove in the breakroom. No one had dared to bring such filth into Lovell's station again, but that didn't stop the men from helping themselves to forbidden merchandise when they came across it in the course of their duties or from ogling the images over a late-night pint. Sergeant Woodward had kept a hidden stash at his home and had confided to Sebastian that he sometimes took the photographs out of their hiding place when his wife and children went to visit her parents. Some justified buying the photographs by suggesting that it was better than visiting prostitutes and reduced the possibility of catching the pox.

Having come face to face with his own failings, Sebastian no longer judged anyone too harshly. People would always succumb to their vices. Such was human nature, and there wasn't much that still had the power to shock him. Or so he had thought until Ransome went on to enlighten him.

"Zeke Robinson runs a respectable establishment and has a reputation for being sensitive to the feelings of the bereaved, but I have recently discovered that there's a niche market for certain types of images, and there are merchants in Holywell Street who cater to that sort of clientele," Ransome said with obvious disgust. "Necrophilia it's called, and I honestly can't think of anything more repugnant."

"What is it they're after?"

Ransome leaned forward and lowered his voice, even though there was no one in the corridor. "They will pay a premium for photographs of dead female bodies in various stages of undress, and even more for images of gentlemen making free with the corpses. The philistines find it arousing."

"Why would anyone...?" Sebastian spluttered. He couldn't finish the sentence, much less envision how someone could find a corpse sexually arousing, but, as he had learned in fifteen years on the job, there was no end to human depravity.

"The perfect women, they call them," Ransome went on. "Since they can no longer talk back or mount any sort of resistance." He consulted his watch, then, seeming relieved to find he still had time, asked, "Can you think of any leads we can pursue while we wait for a response to the appeal?"

"I was just thinking..." Sebastian began.

"Well, go on," Ransome demanded impatiently when Sebastian paused to organize his thoughts. "I don't have all day."

"To my mind, the bodkin speaks to a crime of passion. The killer grabbed whatever was to hand and stabbed the woman in the chest. Panicked, he or she then decided to dispose of the body before anyone found the victim. Unless they just happened to have a trunk and a wagon at the ready, they would have had to find both a large enough container and a mode of transport to get her to Paddington."

"So...?" Ransome drew out. "What are you saying, Bell?"

"The entrance to the Paddington terminus passes through the Great Western Royal Hotel in Praed Street, and the porters use handcarts and trolleys to deliver the guests' luggage to the platforms. The hotel would also have an abundance of trunks that could be appropriated if the situation called for it."

"Did your woman look like the sort who would stay in a hotel?" Ransome asked, clearly intrigued by the idea. "By herself?"

It wasn't common practice for women to stay in a hotel when traveling on their own. A lone female traveler would generally opt for a respectable boarding house. There she would be surrounded by other women and watched over by a landlady, who would keep the door locked for added security and provide meals so the lodgers wouldn't have to wander the streets in search of sustenance.

"We don't know that she was by herself," Sebastian replied. "She was in possession of a wedding band, so perhaps she was married. And I would assume that the hotel has budget accommodation for those who can't afford a suite of rooms or who are traveling alone. I don't imagine they would turn away female guests."

"It's certainly worth investigating," Ransome conceded. "But it's just as likely that the killer had meant to use the bodkin all along and had the trunk and a wagon at the ready. Somehow this doesn't feel like a random act of violence."

"No, it doesn't," Sebastian agreed. "The killing might have happened on the spur of the moment, but the disposal of the body was carefully managed."

"So, you think it was some hothead who cooled off quickly in order to save themselves from the noose?"

"Sounds that way."

"Well, it seems you have your work cut out for you," Ransome said as he pushed to his feet. "I must be on my way. Mrs. Ransome is already at her parents' house, helping with last-minute preparations, and I was warned repeatedly not to be late."

"Try to enjoy yourself," Sebastian said, and was rewarded with a sarcastic quirking of the lips.

"Enjoy is a strong word, but I will take your advice and try to make the most of the opportunity, or at the very least try not make an arse of myself."

Sebastian replied with a smile of his own and left Ransome to examine his reflection in the glass panel of the office door as he adjusted his tie before putting on his coat and topper. Stepping outside after Sergeant Meadows had handed him a few coins from petty cash, Sebastian considered his options. He could head to Holywell Street and arrange for a photograph of the victim, or he could go back to Paddington and question the staff at the Great Western Royal Hotel. The hotel would keep, but the corpse wouldn't, so Sebastian decided to start with Zeke Robinson and hoped that Ransome was right in his estimation of the man, and he could be trusted to do the job with integrity.

SEVEN

Holywell Street was lined with shops that sold old books, periodicals, and second-hand clothes. The windows displayed the shops' more innocent wares, and the tables set up outside competed for space on the narrow pavement. Sebastian held his breath as he passed Half Moon Passage, which was dim even on sunny days and reeked of urine and rot. The passage was located beneath the sign at number thirty-seven, which some said was the oldest sign in London, and which depicted a crescent moon. The face etched into the crescent wore an expression of disgust that seemed oddly appropriate given its location. The fetid passage offered a glimpse into the Strand, which was just on the other side but seemed a world away from the physical and moral shabbiness of Holywell Street.

Zeke Robinson's shopfront was at number forty-three and was so narrow, Sebastian nearly missed it. The door was unlocked but there was no one inside, only images covering the walls. There were photos of wives and mothers laid out in their coffins and surrounded by their grieving families, frightened children who propped up a deceased sibling between them, and elderly parents whose clawlike hands were gripped by their bereaved children.

Sebastian's chest constricted, and he suddenly couldn't draw a deep breath, his heart burning as he faced the unstoppable march of death and knew it was only a matter of time until he joined the ranks of the corpses that stared at him from the walls with unseeing eyes, their bodies already decomposing as the photographer posed them to create these gruesome mementoes of their passing. Sebastian was just thinking he'd step outside for a breath of air when a creaky voice addressed him from the back of the shop.

"Good afternoon, good sir. Zeke Robinson at your service."

The man was quite elderly, with a pointy beard and shrewd dark eyes that appraised Sebastian from beneath bushy gray brows. He was dressed like an undertaker, the black of his suit and tie contrasting sharply with his pallid skin and thinning white hair. Sebastian thought he detected a trace of a West Country accent, but it was so slight, the man must have lived in London for decades.

"I hope you like my work," Mr. Robinson said. "I take great pride in what I do."

"I can see that," Sebastian said, wishing only to get away from those dead-eyed stares.

Mr. Robinson cocked his head to the side and studied Sebastian. "Beloved wife? Child? Whom do you need me to photograph, young man?"

"I'm not here for me."

Mr. Robinson nodded, probably having realized that Sebastian was not dressed for mourning. "But you have lost someone. I can see it in your eyes," he observed.

"Haven't we all?"

"Yes, but some losses are more devastating than others. That's why I do this," Mr. Robinson said, spreading his arms to encompass his subjects. "I want to give those left behind something to remember their loved ones by. It's not death, it's eternal life."

The burning in Sebastian's chest eased, and his breathing felt almost normal once again. He studied Mr. Robinson more carefully, and, when he saw the lines of grief etched into the man's face and the pain reflected in his eyes, he understood.

"You didn't have anything to remember your loved ones by."

Mr. Robinson nodded sadly. "I come from a small fishing village in Devon. Every day, I went out hours before sunrise, hoping to return with my little boat full of the day's catch. One day when I woke, it was so cold inside, the water in the basin was frozen solid, so I made a fire before heading out. I wanted my family to be warm," the old man said miserably. "The hut burned to the ground, my wife and three children inside."

The photographer's eyes shone with tears. "More than anything, I wished I could turn back the clock and leave that morning without lighting the fire that killed them, but once I had finally accepted their passing I wished only to have something to remember them by. There was nothing left to photograph—their bodies were burned to cinders—but most people have an opportunity to capture their beloved's likeness before they are buried."

"How did you come to be here?" Sebastian asked, his gaze sweeping over the tiny shop.

"I couldn't remain in that village after my family died, so I worked as a navvy for a few years, and eventually I found my way to London. That was the first time I saw a postmortem photograph. And then I knew what I had to do."

Sebastian thought the man's calling was a noble one, but, unlike the grief-stricken families on the walls, he wanted to remember his loved ones as they had been in life, not in death. Louisa had been against wasting money they didn't have on a wedding portrait, but, once he had been finally able to look at it, Sebastian had been so glad he had insisted. Aside from the pain he carried in his heart, it was the only reminder of the girl he'd loved, and, although he kept the portrait safely locked in a drawer, he knew it was there, and he would treasure it for as long as he lived. And as he glanced at the macabre remains of dead children, he vowed then and there that if he was ever fortunate enough to be blessed with another child he would have a photograph taken every year, regardless of the cost.

"So, why are you here, then?" Mr. Robinson asked.

Sebastian pulled out his warrant card. "I'm Inspector Bell of Scotland Yard. I have an unidentified victim—"

"Say no more, Inspector. I quite understand," Mr. Robinson replied with a sage nod. "I've always thought the police service would benefit from keeping a photographer on staff. Imagine the possibilities."

Sebastian had never considered the idea, but Mr. Robinson made a valid point. To have a photograph of a crime scene or the victim would be immensely helpful to the investigator, who could refer to the details without having to rely on memory or other people's accounts.

"Where is the deceased?" Mr. Robinson asked.

"The victim is currently at a private mortuary in Blackfriars."

"And what was the method of murder?"

"Will the manner of death determine whether you're willing to accept the commission?" Sebastian asked, having suddenly realized that none of the subjects on the walls looked like they might have met with a violent end.

"No," Mr. Robinson replied with a shake of his head, "but I would like to know what to expect, and also to inquire whether you would like me to include the fatal wound in the frame or attempt to make the subject look as if they are still alive."

"The victim is a woman who was stabbed through the heart."

"A senseless death," Mr. Robinson remarked with a sigh.

"It obviously made sense to someone," Sebastian replied. "Her body was then hidden in a traveling trunk."

"Were her eyes open or closed when you found her?" the photographer asked.

"Closed."

"And her hands?"

"What about them?"

"Were they folded on her chest or left to fall where they would?"

"They were folded in front of her. What does that matter?"

"I think your killer felt some measure of affection for the victim and wanted to lay her out in the way of the dead."

Sebastian scoffed. "That's quite a lot to deduce from closed eyes and folded hands. She might have closed her eyes as she was dying. Or the killer could have folded her arms so she would fit in the trunk."

"Perhaps," Mr. Robinson said. "But sometimes people shut the eyes of the dead so that they don't feel judged."

Sebastian could understand the desire to avoid that sightless stare that was, nonetheless, filled with judgment. He had shut the eyes of countless victims, who, although they hadn't been able to see him, had still gazed into his soul and charged him with finding their killer.

"When was the woman murdered?" Mr. Robinson asked.

"Sometime last night. Maybe early this morning."

"So she's still fresh," Mr. Robinson said. "That's good news. How do you want her positioned? Eyes open or shut? Sitting or lying down?"

"Open. Sitting. I would like her to look as if the photograph was taken while she was still living."

"That's a tall order, but I'll see what I can do."

"I need the likeness as soon as possible."

Mr. Robinson pulled out his pocket watch and consulted the time. "Normally, I would leave the job for tomorrow, but, as it happens, Blackfriars is on my way home, so I will go now. I will have the portrait ready for you tomorrow morning, after ten o'clock."

"Thank you. I appreciate that, Mr. Robinson."

Sebastian took out his notebook and pencil and wrote down Colin's address, then tore out the page and handed it to the photographer. Mr. Robinson studied the address, then folded the paper and slid it into the pocket of his coat.

"Ask for Miss Tate, and tell her Inspector Bell sent you."

"Life goes on, eh, Inspector?" Mr. Robinson said, smiling knowingly at Sebastian.

Sebastian didn't bother to ask what the man had seen in his face. Just as Mr. Robinson identified grief, he surely recognized love, and longing. Sebastian wondered if the old man had ever remarried or had other children, but didn't think he had any right to ask. It was none of his affair.

"How much do I owe you?" he asked instead.

"That will be two shillings."

Sebastian paid the man and took his leave, exhaling in relief when he was finally out of sight of the staring dead. He decided to walk back to his lodgings. He needed time to clear his head.

EIGHT

When Sebastian arrived at home, he was greeted by a radiant Mrs. Poole, who appeared to be wearing a new gown of cobalt blue satin. A blue and white cameo brooch was pinned to the lace collar, and she had arranged her hair in a way that was more becoming than her usual bun. Wavy tendrils framed her flushed face, and her dark eyes sparkled maniacally. This was a new, romantically fulfilled, and recently betrothed Mathilda Poole, the source of whose joy was a porter by day and a writer by night, and was pontificating loudly in the parlor as he held forth on his latest literary triumph, *Murder at the Apollo*.

Bertram Quince's penny dreadful was based on the double homicide at the Orpheus Theatre that Sebastian had investigated only last month and had expressly warned Quince not to exploit. The author, who wrote under the nom de plume B.E. Ware, had renamed the victims, and the venue was called the Apollo Theatre, but it wasn't too difficult to draw the connections, since they were blatantly obvious. The only truly creative liberty Quince had taken was to alter the identity of the killer, since there were few people in London who didn't know who had committed the crime. Sebastian had to admit that he quite liked the new ending, since the killer wasn't someone the readers would expect to have done the deed.

"My dear Inspector," Mrs. Poole gushed, her bosom heaving with emotion. "Thank the good Lord you're finally home. I had quite despaired of seeing you tonight."

Sebastian took an involuntary step back, suddenly worried that he had been the one to propose to Mathilda while in the grip of an opium dream. He immediately reminded himself that such a thing could not have happened, since he hadn't set foot in Mr. Wu's den in six months and had only allowed himself the occasional drink that didn't result in a drunken stupor that took days to emerge from. There had to be another reason for Mrs. Poole's effusive greeting.

"I didn't realize you were anticipating my return so eagerly, Mrs. Poole," he replied. "Surely you haven't tired of Mr. Quince already."

"You foolish man." Mrs. Poole swatted Sebastian's arm playfully. "Of course not. I've never been happier or felt more valued. Well, at least not since Mr. Poole passed," she added, her voice quavering and a shadow passing over her eyes.

Sebastian had never met Mrs. Poole's husband, who had passed nearly six years ago, and had never heard his landlady speak of him. He had assumed that was because Mrs. Poole didn't miss him, but he now realized that perhaps she had genuinely grieved the man and couldn't bear to speak of him for fear of giving in to melancholy. She was clearly happy to have a new man in her life though, and looking to the future. Since announcing their engagement a fortnight ago, Mr. Quince had taken on the role of the man of the house, and carried on as if he were already the landlord. He would be soon enough if the marriage went through, and Sebastian was in no doubt that he would immediately raise the lodgers' rents and implement new rules.

Quince's first decision as Mrs. Poole's fiancé had been to

convince her to get rid of Hank, who'd helped her with whatever chores were too arduous for her to see to herself. Mr. Quince had announced that he would do the heavy lifting from then on and there was no need to waste money on a useless boy. Sebastian had been relieved to learn that Hank had found a position at a livery around the corner that included a place to sleep, since the boy had nowhere else to go and would rather starve on the streets than find himself at a workhouse.

The impending changes at Mrs. Poole's had prompted Sebastian to consider moving into a home of his own, but he had decided that the wisest course of action would be to wait, set aside a percentage of his wages, then start looking once things were settled with Gemma. He could bear the Quinces until then as long as they didn't interfere too much with his current arrangements.

"Mr. Quince and I have been waiting for you for hours," Mrs. Poole admonished Sebastian as she slid her arm through his and pulled him toward the parlor.

"Has someone died?" Sebastian asked.

The last time Mrs. Poole had urgently required his assistance had been when a past lodger, Herr Schweiger, had collapsed and died in his sitting room and his frantic cat had meowed pitifully for two days, clawing at the door in a desperate plea to be let out. Sebastian had been forced to break down the door and see to the body, and a grateful Gustav had moved into his rooms, adopting his savior as his new owner and granting Sebastian his miserly feline affections.

"No, silly." Mrs. Poole's laugh was so jarring, something inside Sebastian recoiled in dread, but the landlady went on, leaning in so close that he could smell the gin on her breath.

"Mr. Quince and I have a surprise for you."

The only surprise Sebastian would have enjoyed was if Mrs. Poole got out of his way and allowed him to sprint up the stairs toward his rooms and lock the door behind him, but she was bodily maneuvering him toward the parlor, her ample bosom nudging his arm.

"In you go," she said, and yanked him through the open door.

Mrs. Poole let go of Sebastian's arm and clapped her hands in delight. For the second time in as many hours, Sebastian found himself choked with emotion and wished he could have a moment to collect himself before three pairs of eyes bored into him in anticipation of his response. Simian sat on the settee, his expression tense as he waited for Sebastian to react to his unexpected presence. Mrs. Poole was still in the doorway, her hands clasped to her breast as if she were watching a heart-wrenching performance. And Mr. Quince looked on proudly, as if he had personally facilitated the reunion and expected to be thanked.

Simian stood but made no move toward Sebastian, his rigid posture speaking to his discomfort. "I hope it's all right that I'm here," he said.

"Of course," Sebastian replied woodenly. He was about to ask how Simian had known where to find him, then recalled that he had given his brother the address in his letter and had received a letter in return.

"You never told us you had a brother," Mrs. Poole exclaimed. "And he's so handsome," she gushed as if Simian weren't standing right there. "Why, I can hardly tell you two apart."

Mr. Quince appeared annoyed by his beloved's effusive admiration of the other two men in the room, but didn't censure her. Sebastian had a feeling that would come later, once they were married and Quince held the keys to the proverbial kingdom.

Once the initial shock of finding Simian at Mrs. Poole's wore off, Sebastian took a seat and, now that he wasn't distracted by the case, studied Simian discreetly. He could still see the young man his brother had been when Sebastian had left Suffolk, but the features that had been handsome in his youth were now softened by approaching middle age. Simian wasn't stout by any means, but his body looked bulkier and his face fuller, the extra flesh blunting the sharp cheekbones and angular jaw Sebastian remembered from his youth. But the familial resemblance was still there. Simian had the same dark blond hair and light brown eyes as Sebastian, and their tentative smiles were mirror images of each other, and so like their mother's, who'd smiled easily and often.

"You must join us for supper," Mrs. Poole exclaimed. "I have enough boiled beef and mashed turnips to go around. We'll just wait for Mr. Danvers and Mr. Rushton. They should be back from the hospital any minute now. The young gentlemen are surgeons."

Eugene Danvers and Giles Rushton were recent additions to Mrs. Poole's assortment of lodgers. Eugene was only twenty-one and one of Colin Ramsey's private students. He had been in search of new rooms, and Colin had helpfully mentioned that Mrs. Poole had a vacancy. Eugene had arrived along with his friend, whom he'd known for several years, and the two men resided on the top floor, renting the attic rooms to save money.

Eugene was a personable young man who made dinners at Mrs. Poole's table more bearable with his amusing anecdotes and witty remarks. Although not conventionally handsome, he had a certain charm, and a single-minded determination to become a renowned surgeon, which was why he had decided to spend his modest inheritance on private instruction. Giles Rushton was a few years older than Eugene and worked at St. Thomas's Hospital, where Eugene attended lectures and observed surgeries from the operating theater with other surgical students. Having completed his training, Giles was now a staff surgeon and a sort of mentor to Eugene, who treated him with obvious affection.

Giles didn't normally join them for dinner, since he rarely

made it home in time. His agreement with Mrs. Poole was that she bring him supper on a tray when he returned. Mrs. Poole wasn't overly pleased with this arrangement, but, given the recent exodus of lodgers, she clearly thought it best to secure Mr. Rushton's continued tenancy before he decided to find lodgings across the river, closer to the hospital. A savvy businesswoman, she hoped that Mr. Danvers and Mr. Rushton would sing her praises to their colleagues and ensure a steady stream of lodgers should anyone else decide to decamp in the coming days.

Mr. Homer, whose rooms were next to Sebastian's, had been unwell for several days and had not come downstairs. A mason, he'd hurt his back at work and could barely stand without moaning with pain. Mrs. Poole had been looking after him, but her irritation was beginning to show. Sebastian had heard her grumbling to Mr. Quince that Mr. Homer would likely be the next one to move, since he was getting on in years and would not be able to pay the rent if he could no longer work.

As if on cue, Eugene and Giles appeared in the doorway. Although no relation to each other, the two men could pass for distant cousins. They were both tall, lean, and fair, with Mr. Rushton sporting a waxed moustache, while Eugene Danvers wore a short beard. He said he thought it made him look more mature and helped him to fit in with the doctors and other students at the hospital, who were all older and at times quite patronizing.

Despite being the younger of the two, Eugene Danvers tended to speak for both men, with Giles Rushton interjecting only when he had a mind to add something he considered vital.

"Oh, I do beg your pardon," Eugene said as his gaze settled on Simian. "We didn't realize you had company. I wasn't aware you had a twin, Inspector Bell," he teased, "but then I wouldn't be overly surprised if a wife with six children in tow appeared on the doorstep. You certainly keep your cards close to your chest. Doesn't he, Giles?" He didn't appear to expect a reply, but Giles nodded and gave Sebastian a tight-lipped smile. "Are you moving in, sir?" Eugene asked Simian. "I didn't realize a vacancy had opened up, but I reckon you could always lodge with your brother until it does."

"I'm just visiting," Simian replied politely.

"Then I hope you enjoy your stay in our fair city. You have about a month until it really starts to stink."

"Mr. Danvers," Mrs. Poole exclaimed, feigning shock, but Eugene just shrugged, his expression saying, *You all know it's true.*

"Dinner in ten minutes, gentlemen," Mrs. Poole announced once she had recovered. "Will you be joining us, Mr. Rushton?"

"Not tonight," Giles Rushton replied in his usual economical way.

"My apologies, Mrs. Poole, but we only came home to change." Eugene Danvers smiled, clearly pleased. "Mr. and Mrs. Chandler are hosting a small supper party, and we are both invited." He tipped his hat. "Have a pleasant evening, everyone."

Mrs. Poole waited until the men's footsteps died away on the stairs, then hurried to explain for the benefit of Simian, who looked nonplussed. "Mr. Chandler is one of the directors at the hospital. From the way Mr. Danvers speaks of her, I'm quite certain he is courting Mr. Chandler's daughter, Charlotte. They met when she visited her father at the hospital." The landlady lowered her voice. "She was so shocked by the sight of a man who'd been gravely injured in a carriage accident that she fainted dead away, right there in the courtyard. Lucky our Mr. Danvers was there to look after her." Mrs. Poole sighed dramatically. "I expect Mr. Danvers won't be with us for long if his hopes come to fruition."

"But Mr. Rushton is here to stay," Mr. Quince replied soothingly. "He has no interest in marriage."

Mrs. Poole said, "Mr. Danvers shared with me that Mr. Rushton was married before he went to Edinburgh to study medicine. His poor wife died. Drowned. Mr. Rushton returned to England after he finished his studies, but he was on his own until he renewed his acquaintance with Mr. Danvers. It's a good thing he has such a devoted friend. I must admit, I will be sorry to see Mr. Danvers go. Such a charming young man, and the perfect lodger."

"What makes for a perfect lodger, Mrs. Poole?" Simian asked politely.

"Well, he's always respectful, cleans up after himself, and never asks for seconds." Mrs. Poole smiled. "And he compliments my cooking. You never compliment my cooking, Inspector," she said playfully.

"It's to die for, Mrs. Poole," Sebastian replied.

It literally was the closest thing to poison, but Mrs. Poole took his comment at face value, and her face broke into a joyful smile.

"Oh, really? You never said. Which dish in particular do you enjoy?"

"I couldn't possibly choose just one," Sebastian said. "They are all quite memorable."

"I will make boiled cod tomorrow," Mrs. Poole announced. "I know how you like it, Inspector, and I will set aside a nice piece for Gustav," she promised magnanimously.

Having recalled what had led to the discussion about food in the first place, she smiled beatifically at Simian. "Now it is even more important that you join us for supper, Mr. Bell. With Mr. Danvers and Mr. Rushton out for the evening, your presence would considerably enliven our dinner conversation." The smile slid off her face when her gaze shifted to Sebastian, who would never be accused of enlivening Mrs. Poole's gatherings and was tolerated only because he was a paying lodger and lent Mrs. Poole his cat.

"And if you would care to spend the night, we will offer you a very reasonable rate. Won't we, my dear?" Mr. Quince asked. "We happen to have a vacant guestroom."

"Of course," Mrs. Poole hurried to agree. "Very reasonable."

"Thank you, both, but I have booked into a hotel, and I was hoping to take my brother out for dinner," Simian replied politely. "I'm afraid we didn't get a chance to speak this morning since Sebastian got pulled into an investigation just as I arrived."

"Oh, please, do tell us," Mrs. Poole gushed. "I wager it was very exciting."

Sebastian preferred not to discuss his cases with either Mrs. Poole or the other lodgers, especially Mr. Quince. Whatever Quince gleaned from the newspapers was fair play, but Sebastian didn't think it ethical to give away any details that would find their way into his penny dreadfuls.

"I don't know what happened yet," he said evasively.

"But surely you can tell us something. Who was the victim? How did they die?" Mr. Quince asked. "Where were they found?"

Sebastian thought Quince probably wished he could take notes, and he would have liked to leave, but Simian wasn't one to ignore a direct question. Even as a boy, he hadn't had a duplicitous bone in his body and had taken everything at face value, especially other people's interest and attention.

"The body of woman was discovered in a traveling trunk," Simian said. "She was murdered, the trunk left at Paddington Station."

"Dear me, what a gruesome find!" Quince exclaimed. "Did you see it, Mr. Bell?"

"Just for a moment, but that was quite enough for me. I took myself off as soon as I realized what was happening."

"A body in a traveling trunk?" Mrs. Poole exclaimed, her gaze going to Mr. Quince. "That would make for an excellent story, don't you think, Mr. Quince?"

"Riveting," Quince said. "How did she die?"

"She was stabbed," Sebastian said before Simian decided to reveal any more details.

"How positively ghastly," Mr. Danvers said from the door. He was now dressed in evening clothes, and Giles Rushton loomed behind him like a shadow. "Forgive the interruption," Mr. Danvers apologized, and his cheeks turned pink with embarrassment. "We only stopped in to say we were leaving and to ask that you don't lock the front door."

"That's quite all right," Mrs. Poole replied graciously. "You both look very dashing."

"Why thank you, Mrs. Poole. Kind of you to say so," Eugene replied.

"Who was she, the victim?" Giles asked. His brows were knitted, and he appeared even more tense than usual.

"I'm afraid there was nothing on the body that would help us to identify her," Sebastian said.

"Oh, the poor dear," Mrs. Poole exclaimed, her hand flying to her bosom.

"Will Mr. Ramsey be charged with conducting the postmortem?" Eugene asked.

"The trunk was delivered to Mr. Ramsey this afternoon," Sebastian admitted with some reluctance.

"Splendid. I do hope he allows me to assist him. What was the cause of death?" Eugene asked. "Was the victim violated?"

"I don't believe this is a fitting subject for mixed company, Mr. Danvers," Sebastian replied sternly.

"Of course. How remiss of me. I do beg your pardon, Mrs. Poole. I spend so much time at the hospital, I tend to forget myself when speaking to individuals who are not committed to the medical profession."

"Your enthusiasm for your chosen profession is to be commended," Mr. Quince said. "A dedicated surgeon can save countless lives."

"That is my greatest hope," Eugene said. "If I can save even one person, I will feel that my life wasn't wasted."

"Why would you think your life was wasted?" Simian asked.

Eugene paused to consider the question, clearly searching for a way to explain his feelings to individuals who didn't share his passion for medicine.

"If I live to please only myself," he said at last, "then I contribute nothing to society or the welfare of my fellow man. I long to make a difference."

"You've made a difference already," Mr. Quince said. "Particularly to Miss Chandler."

The smile that spread across Eugene Danvers' face said it all. He was clearly besotted.

"She's an inspiring young woman," he said. "She hopes to attend Miss Nightingale's nursing school once it opens and then to go on to train other aspiring nurses, since her father won't hear of her working in a hospital."

"And a good thing it is too, since she can't abide the sight of blood," Giles muttered under his breath.

"Is the school ready to open, then?" Mr. Quince asked.

"Not just yet, but a substantial sum has been raised, and space has been allocated. The women will both train and reside at St. Thomas's Hospital until they are ready to take up full-time positions."

"These women will be expected to give up any hope of starting a family if they are to work full-time," Giles Rushton said disapprovingly. "Seems rather a big sacrifice for unmarried young ladies, but it is an excellent opportunity for nurses who were in Crimea and must now scratch out a living as best they can."

"Spinsters one and all," Mrs. Poole said. "It's too late for them to start a family, so they may as well have an opportunity to find respectable employment." She shot a look at Sebastian, then turned toward Mr. Quince, who was speaking.

"Surely you wouldn't wish Miss Chandler to work if you are to marry, Mr. Danvers."

"No talk of marriage has taken place, and I wholeheartedly support Miss Chandler's aspirations."

"Perhaps you should mention the school to Miss Tate, Inspector," Mrs. Poole suggested a tad snidely. "She would be the perfect candidate for such a position, wouldn't you say?"

Sebastian didn't reply. He wasn't going to discuss Gemma's circumstances with Mrs. Poole, but he did wonder if she knew about the school and if she had considered applying. Gemma cared deeply for Mrs. Ramsey and got on well with Colin, but he knew the position didn't offer her enough mental stimulation, and Gemma was the sort of woman who needed to use her mind. Perhaps if she found more fulfilling work, she wouldn't be so eager to assist Sebastian in his investigations. He didn't care to admit it, even to himself, but he would sorely miss Gemma's input, since he had come to rely on her astute observations and unique brand of sleuthing. There was something to be said for feminine intuition and a sympathetic approach.

He had read that the Pinkerton Detective Agency in America employed female agents, who often proved successful in situations where male agents had failed. Sebastian supposed it took a certain kind of woman to court danger for its own sake, and hoped that Gemma would never crave that kind of rush. People who were happy and fulfilled didn't seek that sort of stimulation, and he found that he thought about relocating to America less and less as the months passed, his focus on making a life here and now, and with a person he loved.

"Well, goodnight, all," Mr. Danvers said.

Mr. Rushton gave a stiff bow and followed Danvers out the door, right after shooting Sebastian a narrow-eyed look.

"I think we should be going too," Simian said, taking advantage of the opportunity to escape. "Shall we, Sebastian?"

"Oh, but you must stay," Mrs. Poole implored.

"Perhaps another time," Simian said politely, and moved toward the door.

"Thank you for your generous offer, Mrs. Poole," Sebastian said, then followed Simian into the night.

NINE

Simian looked relieved to have escaped from Mrs. Poole and Mr. Quince. "I'm famished, and I wouldn't say no to a pint," he said with feeling.

"There's a place just around the corner. I go there sometimes when I can't bear another evening at the boarding house."

"It does seem a lonely place," Simian agreed.

Sebastian couldn't keep quiet any longer. "You left! You bloody left and walked away, knowing I had no way to track you down. I thought you'd gone home."

Simian stopped walking and stared at Sebastian, clearly taken aback by the accusation. "What are you talking about?" he exclaimed. "I didn't just leave. You were busy, so I left a note with the station manager, telling you I'd call by the boarding house in the evening. Did you not receive it?"

"No."

Sebastian had not stopped in to see Mr. Criss after he'd interviewed the porters, so perhaps Simian's note was still sitting on the man's desk.

"You don't believe me?" Simian demanded, clearly wounded by the possibility.

"I do. That was considerate of you," Sebastian said in a placating tone, but despite Simian's explanation he was still upset, and Simian knew it.

"I didn't want you to feel rushed and neglect your responsibilities," Simian said.

"Is that a dig at what I do, Simian?" Sebastian bristled.

"Not at all. I was proud of you, Seb. I mean that."

That took the sting out of Simian's desertion and Sebastian permitted himself to relent.

"Thank you. That means a lot to me."

"Look, why don't we forget the pub and go to my hotel. There's a restaurant downstairs, or, if you prefer, we can order supper and a bottle of wine to be delivered to my room. We can talk."

The last thing Sebastian wanted was to hash out their differences in a hotel restaurant, but he did need to speak to Simian, and a conversation over supper seemed the best alternative. Food and drink always lent a veneer of civility, and the privacy would allow them to finally address the grievances that had been festering between them.

"All right. Where are you staying?"

"The Great Western Royal Hotel. I could have found somewhere cheaper, but I wanted to stay in a fine hotel just once in my life and to be the sort of man who could walk in and say, 'A room for the night,' and not inquire about the price," Simian said with a boyish grin.

"And how did it feel?"

"Not as gratifying as I had hoped. It would have been nicer if Hannah and the children had been there to share the experience with me."

"Perhaps one day they will," Sebastian said.

He raised his arm just as an empty hansom turned the corner. The driver pulled on the reins and brought the conveyance to a stop, probably relieved not to have to wait for his next fare at the cab stop, which was a few streets away and would already have a queue several cabs deep. The two men climbed inside and shut the folding doors, their faces immediately swallowed by the darkness within. It felt strange yet oddly familiar to be together after all these years and the brothers fell into silence, each lost in their own thoughts as they attempted to adjust to the transition and converse without awkwardness.

By the time the cab pulled up before the hotel the weather had turned. Rain was coming down in sheets, and the sky was as dark as if it were midnight, the cloud cover so thick it looked like a wool blanket had been thrown over the city. The building glowed like a multi-decked ocean liner on a stormy sea, the foyer and the windows bright against the gloom. The hotel was only five years old, and it was the most grandiose structure in the area, the design said to resemble a French chateau. It was a bold investment in a future in which everyone could afford train travel, had someplace to go, and could do so directly from the Paddington terminus, which was directly behind the hotel. The dome of the terminus reminded Sebastian of a turtle's shell, black and rounded as it melded into the sky above.

Several porters stood at the ready, smart in their uniforms and ready to assist the weary traveler with their luggage. Sebastian and Simian had no luggage, but the porters eyed them regardless, hoping for a tip should the men require help with something else, like a bottle of brandy or port delivered to their room if they preferred to avoid the crowded bar. Simian grinned at Sebastian, clearly proud to be able to afford such untold luxury, and asked one of the porters for a dinner menu. The man bowed from the neck and hurried toward the restaurant, returning a few moments later with a leatherbound folio that contained that evening's selections.

Two black-suited clerks were positioned behind the polished reception counter, occupied with guests who had either just arrived or had questions about their stay. There were vases filled with fresh flowers, comfortable seating areas grouped around plush carpets, and, off to the side, a discreet row of brass trolleys, used to transport the visitors' luggage to their rooms. Sebastian watched as a young porter loaded several cases onto the nearest trolley and pushed it toward an arch that led to a service corridor.

"Sim, can you give me a minute?" Sebastian asked his brother, who had just retrieved his key and was ready to go upstairs.

"Why? What's wrong?"

"I need to check something."

"I'm in room three-seventeen. Come up when you're ready. I'll wait for you to place the order."

Sebastian nodded, but he was already moving toward the corridor, his gaze fixed on the young man who was about to push the trolley into an opening in the wall.

"Oi," Sebastian called out to the porter. "How does that work?"

The young man looked startled, then smiled at Sebastian reassuringly. "Don't worry, sir, your luggage won't get lost or damaged. This is an ascending room that allows us to transport the heavier pieces upstairs without having to carry them up the stairs."

"So, once you send the luggage on its way, what happens?" Sebastian asked. "I've never seen one of these before."

"I wheel the luggage onto the platform, which will slowly rise up the shaft, then I take the stairs, just there," the porter explained, "and meet the luggage once it gets to the right floor. I then wheel the trolley to the room, deposit the luggage, and return downstairs."

The porter was about to close the door and send the contraption on its way when Sebastian said, "Wait."

"Wait for what?"

Sebastian pulled out the trolley, despite high-pitched protests from the young man, and got into the shaft.

"Hey, what are you doing?" the porter cried. "That's not safe for guests."

"Don't worry," Sebastian called back. "I'm not a guest, and I'm not going anywhere."

Sebastian had never seen an ascending room up close, but he had heard of mechanical lifts, which weren't deemed safe to transport the public. A snapped cable could result in death or grave injury, but such considerations didn't apply to mining or construction, which used the steam-powered lifts to move heavy materials up and down specially designated shafts. To utilize the system in a hotel was pure genius, and Sebastian would be remiss if he didn't examine the platform more closely.

He crouched at the center of the lift and peered at the floor. There was no light inside the shaft, but enough gaslight filtered in from the corridor that he could see a dark smear about the size of a half-crown that stained the wooden surface. Wetting his finger on his tongue, Sebastian rubbed at the stain until the substance was moist enough to come off on his skin. The finger came away red, and Sebastian was certain it was blood. This wasn't irrefutable proof that the murder had been committed at the hotel—the blood could belong to a porter who'd accidentally cut himself, or to a workman who'd been summoned to repair the lift—but, given the size and weight of the trunk and the proximity of the lift to the terminus, Sebastian couldn't dismiss the possibility of a connection without investigating further.

Climbing out of the shaft, he wiped his finger on his handkerchief and stuffed it into his pocket before heading to reception. He got in line and waited until one of the clerks was free to speak to him. Sebastian held up his warrant card and waited a few moments while the clerk studied it, his brow creasing with concern.

"Is there a problem, Inspector?" the man asked, lowering his voice so no one else could hear him.

"Has anyone reported any luggage missing in the past few days?"

The clerk made a show of thinking, then said, "Not that I know of. Why do you ask?"

Sebastian replied with a question of his own. "Has anyone checked out unexpectedly or skipped out on the bill?"

"No. Look, what's this about?" the clerk asked irritably, no longer bothering to moderate his voice.

"A body was discovered at the terminus this morning. The murdered woman was inside a trunk."

"Forgive the interruption, Mr. Henry," a uniformed porter said as he approached the desk. "I couldn't help but overhear."

The clerk looked annoyed but could hardly prevent the porter from having his say.

"Please, go on," Sebastian said to the man, who gave Mr. Henry a sidelong glance as if asking for permission.

The clerk nodded.

"Some porters work a double shift, Inspector, and they sometimes kip in the back room during their break. The room is used to store unclaimed luggage," the porter hurried to explain.

"Do many people forget to claim their luggage when checking out?" Sebastian inquired. To leave without one's things seemed a strange thing to do, even if someone could easily afford to replace the items.

"Sometimes there are extenuating circumstances," Mr. Henry explained.

"What sort of circumstances?"

"Such as when a guest dies or leaves in a hurry. There was an incident in December, where a guest was caught stealing silverware from the dining room. The manager had him detained and sent for the police. I believe he's serving time at Newgate. And last month a guest died in his sleep," Mr. Henry said. "We had a chambermaid pack up his belongings and moved the case to the storage room, in case a relation came forward to claim it."

"Did they?" Sebastian asked.

"No."

"Where was the guest from?"

"Leeds."

"And the thief? I expect he'd travel light."

The clerk shook his head. "He had a trunk, but it was half empty once packed. I expect he had intended to use the space for the items he'd pilfered."

"And where was he from?"

"I'm sorry, I can't recall."

Sebastian turned back to the porter. "You were saying."

"Peter Boyle found clothes, shoes, and toiletry items on the floor this afternoon. They were shoved into a corner. The trunk you just mentioned is missing, Mr. Henry."

"What did this trunk look like?" Sebastian asked the porter.

"It was about this big"—he spread his hands to illustrate the width of the trunk—"and had two straps with buckles."

"Did it have a tag?"

Mr. Henry nodded. "It did. Attached to the handle. Does that sound like the trunk you found?"

"It does," Sebastian said.

The porter looked like he was about to ask more questions or offer a theory, but Mr. Henry cut across him just as he began to speak.

"Thank you. You can return to your duties."

"Yes, sir. Good luck with your case, Inspector," the porter said before he walked off.

TEN

Sebastian felt a spark of excitement. He had yet to identify the victim, but it seemed the trunk had been stolen from the hotel and the ascending room had been used to transport the body downstairs, which meant that the woman must have occupied a room on an upper floor.

"Mr. Henry, was anyone expected to leave today but didn't?" Sebastian asked. He could tell by the clerk's face that this time he had asked the right question.

"A guest in room four thirty-seven was due to check out, but she had hung the Do Not Disturb sign on her door, so the chambermaid left her in peace."

"And did no one check on her?"

"We don't normally barge in on our guests, Inspector. People have all sorts of reasons for staying an extra night, and as long as they pay their bill we don't question their decision."

"What is the guest's name?" Sebastian asked. "Was she staying at the hotel by herself?"

"Since you have no proof that the guest in four thirty-seven was the victim, I'm afraid that information is confidential," Mr. Henry announced haughtily.

"Is the manager still here?" Sebastian asked, his gaze sliding to the clock mounted on the back wall.

It was a quarter past eight, and Simian would be wondering what had happened to him, but he could hardly walk away now. Sebastian hoped his brother would understand and forgive him, but he desperately wished that just this once he could hand over the case to someone else and spend the evening with Simian. But even if he sent word to Scotland Yard, there would be no one about at this hour, and nothing would happen until tomorrow, by which time the trail could grow cold. Or colder, Sebastian amended. He had to verify the facts before he was able to declare them relevant.

"No, Mr. Sykes left at six, but there's a night manager if you'd like a word, sir."

Mr. Henry made it sound as if Sebastian was a difficult guest who wanted to lodge a complaint, probably on account of the well-dressed couple who had just come up behind him and were clearly waiting to speak to Mr. Henry. The last thing the clerk wished to do was to alarm the guests and allow them to suspect that something was wrong. Murder was bad for the hotel business.

"I would," Sebastian said. He wasn't going to make trouble for Mr. Henry, who was just doing his job, or intentionally frighten anyone, but he wasn't about to abandon the investigation either.

Mr. Henry beckoned to an adolescent porter, who hurried toward the desk. "Escort this gentleman to Mr. Holden's office," the clerk said.

"Yes, sir," the boy replied, and beckoned to Sebastian to follow.

The manager's office was located in a corridor that ran behind the reception area and was a utilitarian room devoid of any personal touches. Mr. Holden appeared to be in his early forties. His dark hair was parted in the middle and thickly pomaded, his moustache was waxed into sharp points, the collar of his shirt was stiff with starch, and his dark gaze was solicitous behind wire-rimmed spectacles that reflected the light from the wall sconce.

"I'm Mr. Holden. How can I help you, sir?" the manager asked, smiling warmly as he gestured to Sebastian to make himself comfortable in the guest chair. The porter left them to it and shut the door behind him.

Sebastian showed Mr. Holden his warrant card and watched the man's demeanor undergo a transformation. The helpful smile slid off his face, and his expression became closed as he sat up straighter and clasped the armrests of his chair.

"Mr. Holden, this morning, I was made aware that an unattended traveling trunk was left at the terminus. The trunk contained the remains of a woman who'd been stabbed in the chest."

"And what makes you think your discovery has anything at all to do with the Great Western Royal Hotel?"

"A trunk is missing from the storage room, I found dried blood on the floor of the ascending room, and one of your guests failed to check out this morning. No one bothered to check on her well-being despite the fact that she evidently never emerged from her room."

Mr. Holden's mouth fell open, and he looked like he would have dearly liked to refute Sebastian's findings, but he quickly realized he had no choice but to cooperate. If Sebastian decided to descend on the hotel with reinforcements, the manager would probably lose his job and the wages he was still owed, and have no hope of finding work in a respectable hotel without a glowing character reference from his previous employer. His purpose was to keep things running smoothly and to avoid any incidents that might tarnish the reputation of the hotel and alarm its patrons.

"You are right, Inspector. We should have made certain

the guest in question was not in need of assistance, but I'm afraid I cannot permit you to invade their privacy on a hunch."

"Mr. Holden, it is very possible that the guest whose privacy you're so concerned with is, in fact, dead."

"Or they could be unwell and would prefer not to be disturbed."

"Allow me to point out that if a guest felt unwell, they would still require service, such as food, drink, and someone to empty their chamber pot if they were unable to make it to the communal lavatory, if there's one on their floor. When was the last time anyone has seen or been in communication with the guest in room four thirty-seven?"

"I... er, don't know. I would have to ask the chambermaids who are tasked with cleaning the rooms in that corridor."

"I would be most grateful. In the meantime, I must request that you check the room." When Mr. Holden opened his mouth to protest, Sebastian forestalled him. "At best, there's nothing wrong and the guest will feel gratified to know that their welfare is of the utmost importance to the staff. At worst, the poor woman will no longer mind about her privacy and will need me to determine what exactly happened to her and who's responsible."

Mr. Holden appeared to appreciate the wisdom of Sebastian's argument, and nodded. "All right. Come with me, please."

The manager strolled towards an ornate staircase that led to the upper floors. He talked as he walked, carrying on as if he were giving Sebastian a tour rather than going to a guest's room to obtain proof of life. "The hotel is one of the grandest in all of Europe," he gushed. "We have one hundred and sixty-five rooms, some of which are two-story apartments. There are more than a dozen sitting rooms, and our restaurant is not only highly rated but also affordable, which makes it accessible to all our guests."

"Does everyone who stays here have to reserve a room in advance?" Sebastian asked as they walked up the stairs.

"Individuals of quality, who want only the best rooms, generally reserve a suite in advance and in writing, but we also have a number of single and double rooms that are available for immediate occupancy. This is a railway hotel, Inspector, so we cater to all travelers, who sometimes need to find reputable accommodation upon arriving."

"What do you know about the woman in room four thirty-seven?"

They were now on the third floor, and Mr. Holden's breath was coming in short gasps. Sebastian suspected he didn't visit the rooms on the upper floors too often, since they were reserved for guests who were on a budget and didn't expect any special treatment from hotel staff.

"Absolutely nothing," Mr. Holden said. "You can't expect us to remember everyone's details."

"But you were aware that the guest had failed to check out."

"I was informed that the guest didn't check out by Mr. Henry when I arrived, but it's really not such an unusual occurrence. Sometimes, guests decide to stay for an extra day or two. They might want to extend their holiday, or perhaps their business isn't complete. We're happy to let them stay, since we have a number of vacant rooms at any given time."

"How often are the rooms cleaned?" Sebastian inquired.

"Every day."

"That's a lot of rooms to clean. You must have dozens of chambermaids."

"Several chambermaids are assigned to every floor. They're very efficient."

"Meaning they do a cursory check of the room?"

"Meaning they do whatever is required to keep the room tidy."

They had finally reached the fourth floor, and Mr. Holden

led Sebastian down the corridor, which was illuminated by two-armed brass sconces with frosted glass shades. Room four thirty-seven was on the left, towards the far end of the corridor, and a narrow plaque with the words *Do Not Disturb* hung off the door handle.

"Is every room equipped with one of these signs?" Sebastian asked.

Mr. Holden stopped, an expression of consternation passing over his face. "Now that you mention it, no. The signs are generally reserved for the more—how should I put it—comfortable rooms."

"You mean the more expensive ones," Sebastian translated.

"Well, yes. I'm not sure how the lady procured one for this room."

Sebastian stood back while Mr. Holden crept toward the door as if he expected to be shot at through the wooden panel. The manager rapped three times, then stood back, in case the door should open. No movement could be heard inside the room, so Mr. Holden knocked again. Nothing happened.

"Please unlock the door," Sebastian said, but Mr. Holden stood stock-still, frozen with indecision.

ELEVEN

A few moments had elapsed, but Mr. Holden had yet to open the door, seemingly torn between his duty to the hotel and his civic responsibility. He'd lifted his arm several times to insert the key into the lock, then yanked his hand away, reluctant to follow through. Sebastian was quickly losing his patience, but he couldn't force the man to comply, not without a warrant signed by a judge that would convince the hotel manager he had no choice in the matter and wouldn't be held accountable by his employers.

"Mr. Holden, kindly open the door," Sebastian said, more forcefully this time. "Or I will have no choice but to obtain a warrant."

It was an empty threat since Sebastian could hardly apply for a warrant at such a late hour and would have to wait until morning. He'd have to make his case to Ransome, who might have to involve the commissioner before approaching a well-disposed judge. By the time a warrant was issued, Mr. Holden could clear out the room and dispose of any evidence that would tie the hotel to the investigation.

"Mr. Holden."

"Perhaps the guest is asleep."

"I highly doubt that."

With great reluctance, Mr. Holden fitted the master key into the lock. He opened the door with excruciating slowness, calling, "Hello. Is anyone there? It's Mr. Holden, the night manager. I do beg your pardon if I'm disturbing you."

As expected, there was no answer, and, having finally lost what was left of his patience, Sebastian approached the door. "Step aside," he said to Mr. Holden, who was bodily blocking the entrance.

"Inspector—"

"I need you to step aside," Sebastian repeated.

Having done everything he reasonably could to justify his actions, Mr. Holden moved away from the door. Sebastian pushed it open and surveyed the empty room by the light of the nearest sconce. It didn't give off enough light to illuminate the room, so, walking carefully across the uncarpeted floor, Sebastian approached the nightstand, lifted the glass chimney of the oil lamp, and lit the wick with a lucifer match he'd found in a wooden box that had been left near the base of the lamp. Mr. Holden was about to enter the room, but Sebastian held up his hand to forestall him.

"Please remain where you are," he told the manager, who was peering into the room with apprehension.

Sebastian didn't move from his spot by the bed as he looked around, which took no more than two seconds. This had to be one of the cheapest rooms in the hotel since it was hardly bigger than a train compartment. There was a narrow bed with a tall wooden headboard and low footboard, a nightstand, a narrow wardrobe, and a washstand. The latter was equipped with a pewter ewer and basin, which were probably more economical than earthenware, since they wouldn't break if they were dropped and need to be replaced. A small, frameless rectangular mirror hung on the wall above the washstand, and the wardrobe was across from the bed. The bed was neatly made, and the wardrobe had just enough space to hang two garments from hooks fitted into the back panel and three drawers on the side. There was a space next to the drawers where the occupant had placed her traveling valise.

The wardrobe still held clothes and undergarments, and ladies' lace-up boots stood near the door. A black bonnet and a velvet cape hung from the hooks, and kid gloves were tucked into the bonnet, which hung upside down by the ribbons. The outer garments and the boots were proof that the woman had not left the room of her own accord. Sebastian pulled out the valise, the size of which was in keeping with the number of possessions in the room, and opened it. The case was empty, since the guest had unpacked when she'd arrived. He looked through the drawers, but there was nothing there save a high-necked nightdress, a pair of stockings, and folded squares of fustian that were hidden beneath a pair of cotton bloomers. Had Sebastian not been married, he might not have known what the fustian was for, but he thought that the woman had used the thick, absorbent fabric to line a sanitary belt.

When Sebastian raised his eyes as he shut the top drawer, he noticed a slip of folded paper inside one glove. He pulled it out and unfolded the note. The page was dogeared, the paper worn thin with frequent handling, and the penmanship barely legible, but he was sure it was an address. The letters were smudged, the blotches the result of either raindrops or tears that had fallen onto the page. One of the water stains had almost completely dissolved the second digit of the house number, but Sebastian thought it was either a three or an eight, making the number thirteen or eighteen. He couldn't quite make out the name of the street. Moving closer to the lamp, he held the paper to the light and experienced a jolt of recognition when he finally deciphered the address.

1 _ Albion Street, Clerkenwell, London

Mrs. Poole's boarding house was number eighteen Albion Street, and there was a boarding house at number thirteen. Sebastian didn't know the lodgers by name, but he had seen them come and go and was certain that at least two of the four men worked at King's Cross and had probably chosen the boarding house because of its proximity to the terminus, much as Mr. Quince had done. If the address was of any significance, and it must be if the woman had kept it in her glove where she could pull it out at any time and refer to it, then she had come to London to see someone who lived on Sebastian's street, possibly even in the same house. But if that were the case, why had she decided to take a room at the Great Western Royal Hotel? Was it because she had intended to depart from Paddington and had thought it easier to stay near the station? Sebastian folded the paper and slipped it into his pocket. He would consider the implications of this unexpected find later, but now he had to search the room for any other clues.

Sebastian peered into the basin and the ewer, which were both empty. Someone had used up all the water, but he didn't see either fresh or used towels. The drawer in the nightstand held a compact sewing case that contained several skeins of thread, a thimble, a brass needle case, and a bit of lace that would have been a collar once it was finished. The stitches were even and neat, and so tiny he could barely see the seam. There was enough space for a bodkin, but there was no way to verify that the case had contained such an implement. There was also a small linen bag that held a dozen leather strips, presumably for curling hair. Sebastian had to admit that what he had discovered so far did not conclusively prove that the occupant was either missing or dead. Perhaps the woman owned more than one pair of boots and had another bonnet and cape. It wasn't uncommon.

The victim could be someone else entirely and might or might not have been staying at the hotel. The description of the case and the Birmingham address of the owner coincided with the details of the trunk the victim had been found in, but by itself the case going missing proved nothing. But as Sebastian's gaze swept across the room, now from a different angle, he suddenly got his answer.

TWELVE

"There's no one here, Inspector," Mr. Holden announced, now visibly less concerned and eager to be rid of Sebastian. "The lady is clearly out, so let's leave before she realizes her privacy has been grossly violated."

"The lady is not here because she's dead," Sebastian replied.

"And how do you know that?" Mr. Holden demanded. He remained by the door, hesitant to enter the room he still believed to be occupied.

"There are traces of blood on the footboard and bloodstains beneath the bed, and the towels are missing."

"Maybe she pricked her finger or cut herself with sewing scissors," Mr. Holden suggested.

"And bled so much that the blood soaked through the mattress?"

Sebastian pulled back the coverlet to reveal a large brown stain just beneath the pillow and closer to the outer edge of the bed. The substance was without doubt blood, and it had saturated the bedding and the mattress beneath. Mr. Holden gasped, his face turning a greenish gray, while Sebastian permitted himself a small nod of satisfaction. This was indisputable evidence that the victim had been stabbed inside this room. When Sebastian had attended his first postmortem in Colin's cellar, Colin had said that the human body contained approximately ten pints of blood. Sebastian envisioned a pint of ale and tried to estimate how many pints it would take to create such a large stain. He decided that the victim had lost at least two pints of blood, possibly more since a lot of blood had also soaked into her clothes and there had been a stain at the bottom of the trunk.

He was sure a man's strength would have been required to transfer the body from the bed to the trunk and then deliver the trunk to the station, but to completely exclude a female suspect was premature. The victim could have been murdered by a woman who'd had a male accomplice. But whoever had done the deed, man or woman, would have had blood on their hands. They had probably brushed their hand against the footboard, then used the water and the towels to clean up before disposing of them. Sebastian thought they might have tossed the bloodied towels out the window, but didn't see anything on the ground when he looked out. Perhaps they'd stuffed them somewhere they wouldn't be easily discovered or had dropped them into the laundry cart on their way out.

And they had to have entered and left using the door. The window was too high off the ground for the killer to have climbed up, even if they had come over the roof, and too narrow to climb inside unless they had suspended a very small child. It was much more likely that the victim had opened the door to whoever had come knocking and had either been pushed back inside the room or had known her assailant and admitted them voluntarily.

"So, what do you suppose happened?" Mr. Holden asked as he looked around in panic. He would have to explain this to his superiors and possibly defend his actions if it was proven that the woman had been attacked on his watch.

Before answering, Sebastian examined the door and the jamb as Mr. Holden silently looked on.

"I think the victim let the killer in, since there is no evidence of forced entry," Sebastian said at last. "It's difficult to say if she knew her attacker or happened to open the door to someone who knocked. Likewise, it's impossible to tell if a physical altercation took place since the killer obviously cleaned up after themselves and put the room to rights. I would venture to guess that the victim was pushed onto the bed and stabbed, or maybe stabbed and then was either pushed or fell onto the bed. Perhaps she rolled onto her side, which would account for the amount of blood on the bed and the location of the stain. The killer likely fetched the trunk afterwards, once they realized they needed something large enough to move the body. And if they were familiar with the hotel, they'd know just where to look. Then they transferred the dead or dying woman to the trunk and used the ascending room to lower the trunk to the ground floor."

"And then they delivered the trunk to the station?" Mr. Holden asked.

"That's where it becomes a little murky," Sebastian replied, speaking more to himself than the manager. "I believe the murder took place sometime last night, but the trunk was most likely delivered to the station this morning. So the killer either took the trunk away and returned to the terminus, or they hid the trunk somewhere overnight, returning in the morning to take it to the platform."

"Why did they want to load the body on a train?" the manager asked.

"I don't know. If it were me, I would have left the body here and let the hotel deal with the woman's remains." Sebastian fixed Mr. Holden with a hard stare. "Would you have reported it to the police or disposed of the body before anyone got wind of what happened?"

Mr. Holden looked deeply uncomfortable, and Sebastian could tell he wasn't sure. It would be much easier to deliver the corpse to the nearest dead house and be done with it rather than alert the authorities and thrust the hotel into the unwelcome spotlight of a police inquiry.

"We would inform the police," he finally said, but the lengthy pause had spoken for itself. The killer couldn't have known what the manager would do if they had been seen and had decided to dispose of the body themselves.

"Where's the door to the ascending room on this floor?" Sebastian asked once he was ready to leave.

"It's at the other end of the corridor," Mr. Holden said as he locked the room behind them.

Sebastian walked very slowly, studying the floor beneath his feet, but didn't spot any bloodstains. That could be because the trunk had been placed on a trolley that had kept the blood from dripping onto the floor, or maybe the blood hadn't pooled at the bottom of the trunk until it had already been in the lift.

"I will need to see the back room and the trolleys, and I would like the details for the occupant of this room. I will also need to speak to the chambermaids assigned to this corridor."

"Of course," Mr. Holden replied woodenly. "I will ask them to come to my office."

"I will be down in a moment," Sebastian said.

He waited until Mr. Holden had gone, then made his way down to the third floor and walked down the corridor until he located Simian's room. Simian answered the door right away, his expression both irritated and eager.

"What took you so long?" he demanded. He was already in his shirtsleeves, and a menu was open on the small table by the window. "Beef Wellington looks good."

"Sim, I'm sorry, but I won't be able to join you. The victim was staying at the hotel, and it looks like she was murdered in her room. I must speak to the chambermaids while their recollection of events is relatively fresh, and examine the storage room, where I think the body was kept overnight."

Simian looked disappointed, his shoulders drooping and his mouth turning down at the corners, but, as much as Sebastian wanted to appease his brother, he simply couldn't take time out and resume the investigation in the morning.

"Do you think the maids saw something?" Simian asked, but he didn't seem genuinely interested.

"They may have. I will need to speak to all the porters as well," Sebastian mused out loud. "They might have noticed someone moving a heavy trunk."

"I'm going home tomorrow," Simian said, unspoken words of reproach hanging in the air. *I don't know when we'll see each other again. I made time for you, but you chose your job over me. You let me down again.*

"I'm very sorry," Sebastian said again. Then on the spur of the moment, he offered, "Is there any way you can stay one more night? I'll pay for the hotel."

Simian looked uncertain, then seemed to come to a decision. "I can stay at Mrs. Poole's. I don't feel right asking you to pay for the room. It's too dear, and, if I'm honest, it's a bit lonely anyway. I'm not much used to being on my own. It'll be nice to know you're there."

"We can have dinner tomorrow," Sebastian promised, the tension he'd felt earlier dissipating at Simian's suggestion. "I'll try to get back by seven o'clock."

"We really do need to talk, but all that can wait," Simian replied resignedly. "Go get your man, Seb."

"I will," Sebastian replied, and then he was striding down the corridor, his mind instantly returning to the details of the investigation.

THIRTEEN

The night had grown cold and a murky, rain-sodden darkness had settled on the city long before the sun had set. The house was chilly and damp, but it made little sense to waste coal when no one was downstairs to enjoy its warmth. The rooms were empty, and the parlor was silent and dark, the only sound the ticking of the carriage clock on the mantel. Once Gemma's patients were comfortably settled for the night and Mabel had retired to her own room in the attic, Gemma made her way downstairs.

Any other woman might have devoted the time to making domestic plans for the following day, or given in to private thoughts of the man she loved, but Gemma was not like other women, and, even though she did think about Sebastian, her mind soon leapt to his latest case. She was an experienced nurse and an amateur detective whose contributions had helped Sebastian unravel four complex cases. There had to be a way for her to help him solve this case as well.

The woman from Paddington was still in the cellar, laid out on the dissecting table and covered with a linen sheet. Gemma had been hard-pressed earlier to find something for the woman to wear, since her dress was soiled and stiff with dried blood, and the photographer Sebastian had sent had needed her to look presentable. In the end, Gemma had borrowed one of Anne's old shawls and draped it over the woman's shoulders, after Mr. Robinson had positioned her in a chair he had brought down from the parlor and set against the wall.

Mr. Robinson had taken a small wooden case out of his valise and unlatched it to reveal a color palette and brushes, like those of a painter. Once the woman's eyes were open and she stared blindly at the two people before her, he'd gone to work, dusting rice powder over her graying skin, rouging the cheeks and nearly colorless lips, and adding a bit of moistened soot to her lashes and brows. Gemma had twisted the woman's hair into a knot and even considered pushing a book into her stiff hands, to give the impression of someone who had been interrupted while reading, but quickly realized that she shouldn't wash the woman's hands in case there was something to be learned from the matter beneath her fingernails.

Gentle candlelight had gilded the woman's features, and one could almost believe that she was still alive, sitting still for a portrait. Mr. Robinson had set up his camera and taken a photo, but once he had checked the exposed plate had decided that there wasn't enough light to see the woman's features clearly. With a sigh of irritation, he had blown out the candle and moved an oil lamp closer to his subject before trying again. Satisfied at last, he had helped Gemma to return the body to the dissecting table, packed up his camera, and taken his leave. Having covered the body, Gemma had returned upstairs, but something niggled at her and, now that everyone had retired, it was time to test her theory.

The smell of putrefaction that had long seeped into the walls assaulted Gemma's senses as soon as she pushed open the door to the cellar and descended the stairs. even in the light of her lamp the space seemed eerie and watchful. Colin's specimens floated inside their jars and, although Gemma had seen them many times before, she was struck anew by how grotesque they truly were.

Setting the lamp on the counter, Gemma approached the table. She knew she should feel frightened, but she no longer feared the dead. They meant her no harm. It was the living one had to look out for. Their seamy secrets and innate sense of self-preservation made them a threat, and, as Gemma had recently discovered, almost everyone had something to hide. She pulled back the sheet and gazed down at the dead woman, whose made-up features were jarring in the shimmering light.

Gemma hated what she was about to do and knew it to be a violation, even if the poor creature was dead, but she had to confirm her suspicions before she brought her theory to Sebastian. She laid a hand over the woman's wrist and murmured a quiet apology before setting to work.

The bodice and the buttons that ran down the front were covered with dried blood and rough to the touch. Gemma undid the buttons and pushed the fabric aside to reveal a blood-soaked chemise. She had felt something unexpected when she had tried to arrange the shawl around the woman's shoulders to cover the wound on her breast, and had examined the woman's silhouette more closely. The victim was slightly overweight and thick around the middle, but her bosom seemed strangely disproportionate to the rest of her body. Her breasts were too small and flat. The unflattering shape could be the result of an ill-fitting corset, but Gemma had realized there could be another reason, one she couldn't verify in the presence of Mr. Robinson. She pulled down the neckline of the chemise to reveal a thick band of fabric that tightly bound the woman's breasts.

Apologizing one more time, Gemma opened the rest of the buttons, then undid the hooks of the corset until the restrictive garment parted, leaving the woman clad in nothing but the thin chemise. Gemma pulled the chemise free of the waistband of the skirt and lifted the fabric to expose the flesh beneath. Where the area wasn't bloodied, the skin was milky white and dissected by blue veins that resembled rivers on a map. The belly was soft and jiggly, and livid stretch marks extended from firm sides toward the puckered navel like spindly twigs. Bracing for the final test, Gemma lifted the skirt and the petticoats underneath to reveal the woman's pantalettes. The sanitary belt clearly visible through the thin fabric was enough to confirm her hunch.

Gemma had never examined a pregnant woman or someone who'd recently given birth, but as a nurse she was in possession of the basic facts, and she was certain that the deceased woman had delivered a child within the past few months. The fact that she had bound her breasts to suppress lactation could mean one of two things. Either she had left her baby in someone else's care, or the child had died. Given the woman's plain appearance and her serviceable gown and stockings, Gemma didn't think she was the sort to employ a wet nurse. That prerogative was exercised by women of quality, who didn't mind the expense and preferred not to nurse their children. Severing the physical bond to their newborn allowed them to re-enter society and join their husbands in social engagements that were denied a nursing mother. It was possible, however, that the victim couldn't afford not to work and had left her baby at one of the many baby farms that had sprung up to help working mothers.

The farms were usually a last resort, since they were nothing more than money-making schemes designed to keep the children alive for only as long as the mother continued to pay. The care was woefully inadequate, and the children were often dosed with opium to keep them from getting hungry or crying for attention. Gemma might never have known about the horrors the babies endured if one of the nurses she'd met in Scutari had not worked at several such establishments before answering Florence Nightingale's call. The stories of abuse had brought Gemma to tears, and she had raged against a society where so many children were born only to die soon after, their short lives made unbearable with suffering and neglect.

And if the victim's child had died and the woman had traveled to London, what had compelled her to leave her home at a time when she should be healing, or grieving, or both? What had she hoped to find? Had she come in search of her husband? It was possible, but Gemma had nothing to go on to flesh out this theory except the ring. She adjusted the woman's skirts and did up the corset, which proved unexpectedly difficult with the woman lying down and her unyielding flesh sliding sideways. Gemma's forehead was beaded with sweat by the time she closed the last hook and rebuttoned the bodice. She was about to cover the body with the sheet when something crinkled next to her hand.

Gemma patted the woolen skirt and discovered a discreet slit that gave the wearer access to a deep pocket worn underneath. She pushed her hand in and extracted two folded sheets. Both pages had been torn from a penny dreadful, the sort one could buy on the street or at any railway station in the city. Although the title page was missing, Gemma had no difficulty identifying either the publication or the author, since she immediately spotted the words *Apollo Theatre* and *Shakespeare* and knew the pamphlet to be written by B.E. Ware, who happened to be Sebastian's neighbor, Bertram Quince.

The date at the top revealed the pamphlet to be the most recent edition, which wasn't surprising. The woman could have purchased the penny dreadful for entertainment and once she'd read it might have kept the paper in her pocket to be used for her more personal needs. Few people threw away newspapers, and squares of print eventually found their way to privies, where they served a less intellectual but equally important purpose.

Gemma set the penny dreadful aside, pulled the sheet over the body, picked up the oil lamp, and trudged wearily up the cellar steps, her mind teeming with questions. She would jot down her findings as soon as she returned to her room, mostly so she wouldn't forget anything before she had a chance to share her conclusions with Sebastian, but also for her own benefit. Just as Colin wrote up a detailed report on every autopsy he performed, perhaps she could start keeping notes on every case.

Each body had something to teach her, and Gemma needed to make certain she took full advantage of the opportunity to learn. She was certain the knowledge would come in handy, even if she could never become a doctor in her own right, but for the first time in her life she realized that she could be more, do more, and no one had the power to stop her.

FOURTEEN

After making certain that Mabel had locked up for the night, Gemma continued upstairs, grateful for the sanctuary of her bedroom. She settled at the small writing desk, took out a fresh sheet of paper, and itemized everything she considered noteworthy, before folding the paper and sliding it between the pages of her book. It really wouldn't do for Colin to learn what she'd been up to, and Mabel could unwittingly say something if she saw Gemma's report on her desk.

It was too early for bed, but Gemma was tired and not really in the mood to read, as she normally did before she turned out the light. She washed her hands thoroughly, then undressed, pulled the pins out of her hair, and ran her hands through the heavy tresses before brushing her hair and braiding it into a loose plait. She turned out the lamp and climbed under the covers, but, despite the pleasant warmth that ensconced her, she couldn't stop shivering. When she shut her eyes, the dead woman's face hovered just inside her eyelids, her made-up face contorted into a grimace of suffering.

Try as she might, Gemma couldn't keep from picturing the woman's final moments. What had the victim done to bring about such a brutal end? Had she been such a grave threat that she'd had to die to make the killer feel safe? Was there someone waiting for her to come home, her loved ones frantic with worry and keeping vigil by the window, or had no one realized she was gone? Perhaps she had been all alone in the world, except for the man whose ring she had worn on a string around her neck. Was he the one she had been in mourning for? Had she been planning to come to London, or had it been a decision made in a moment of desperation that she'd possibly regretted once she was on her way? She had to have known someone and alerted them to her presence. Why else would they murder her and stuff her body into a trunk?

And why go to such lengths? Surely there were easier ways to dispose of a body, especially in London, where the killer could simply leave the victim where she fell and lose themselves among the multitudes. By the time the corpse was discovered, there'd be no trace of the killer and nothing for the police to go on. Every question led to another question, but Gemma didn't have any answers, and her exasperation mounted, her frustration compounded by the impenetrable darkness that pressed on her eyes and weighed on her chest as she imagined what it would feel like to be trapped in a trunk.

She needed to lighten her spirit, or she'd never get to sleep, and if she did her dreams would be plagued by nightmares. There was one way to do that, and she had relied on this method in Crimea when she had been desperate to erect a barrier between the horrific reality of her days and the cherished memories of a life forever changed. She had even taught Lucy to do the same in the hope that it would help the child keep bad dreams away.

Gemma straightened her limbs, shut her eyes, and tried to summon an image of a beach. After several failed attempts, the memory finally came to her, and she lost herself in the poignancy of the moment, reliving every detail as if it had been only yesterday and not twenty-one years before. The sun shone in a cloudless summer sky, and frothy waves rolled lazily onto the shore, the blue-green water sparkling in the sunlight as if its surface were strewn with thousands of diamonds. Two small figures came into view, a boy and girl, laughing and running down the rocky beach, their fingers interlaced as they held on to each other, the ribbons of the girl's bonnet whipping in the breeze. The hem of her dress was damp, and the boy's shins were as pale as milk beneath the short pants he wore. He let go and ran into the surf, laughing uproariously as a wave rolled over his bare feet, and the girl hitched up her skirts and ran after him, her mouth opening in shock as the cold water swirled around her ankles.

Gemma smiled shakily into the darkness as silent tears slid down her temples and into her hair. The memory was bittersweet, but she treasured it and reached for it whenever she needed to remember that life could be beautiful. That day, when she and Victor had seen the sea for the first time, had been perfect. They had played on the beach for hours until their parents had shepherded them to the seafront hotel where they were to stay for the remainder of their week-long holiday. Every day had been sunny and bright and filled with warmth and laughter, and the memory of it still made Gemma smile, even if the pain of loss squeezed at her heart. They were all gone now, except for her, a stubborn little weed that had managed to grow between the stones that marked the resting places of the people she loved.

FIFTEEN

Mr. Holden was in his office. He looked tired and resigned, but good manners prevailed and he asked Sebastian if he would care for a cup of tea or coffee before they got started.

"Coffee, please," Sebastian replied, and waited while Mr. Holden stepped out and asked a passing porter to fetch a pot of coffee from the restaurant.

That done, the manager returned, assumed his seat behind the desk, opened a leatherbound ledger, and flipped the pages until he reached the current week. He turned the ledger toward Sebastian and pointed to a line midway down the page.

"The guest in room four thirty-seven checked in on Monday and specified that she would be staying with us for three nights. The room was paid for in cash rather than with a bank draft."

"And the name?" Sebastian asked.

Mr. Holden's smile was apologetic. "I can't make it out. The signature is barely legible."

The handwriting in the ledger matched the one on the note in the victim's glove, but that was all Sebastian could deduce. He wondered if the woman had owned a reticule. She would have needed a place to keep her money when traveling to

London, so why had she hidden the address inside her glove? Perhaps she had been afraid of losing it in case her reticule was stolen, as it must have been since Sebastian had not found it inside the room, and it had not been in the trunk.

"Do the reception clerks not take down the person's name?" Sebastian asked.

"They do when the booking is made by post or when the guest pays with a draft, but when it's cash up front they get rather lax and allow the guest to sign the ledger."

"Surely someone must know her name."

Sebastian turned the ledger toward the gas sconce and leaned over it, staring at the page until his eyes watered. Mr. Holden leaned in as well, staring fixedly at the name.

"I think her Christian name was Helen," Sebastian said. Helen would fit with the engraving inside the wedding ring, but he needed a surname.

"I think you might be right," Mr. Holden replied. "But I can't make out the surname. It looks like it begins with O."

"Yes," Sebastian agreed. "Looks like Owens, but the handwriting is so cramped, I can't be sure."

"It's still something, I suppose," Mr. Holden said, clearly pleased to have been of assistance. "Helen Owens."

Their speculation was interrupted by a waiter, who delivered the coffee along with a plate of fairy cakes. He set the tray on the sideboard, inquired if there was anything else Mr. Holden might need, then departed.

"Can I get you a cup of coffee?" Mr. Holden asked as he got up to make one for himself.

"Milk and two sugars," Sebastian replied, his attention still on the register.

Mr. Holden handed him a cup of coffee and had thoughtfully set three bite-size cakes on the saucer. Sebastian popped a cake into his mouth and took a sip of coffee. It had been a long day, and it was nowhere near finished. He hoped the coffee would revive him and sharpen his faculties, since he still had several people to interview and the storage room and baggage trolleys to inspect before he could go home.

"I would like to help, if you would allow it, Inspector," Mr. Holden said. "I can speak to the porters, take a look at the trolleys, and search the storage room."

Sebastian considered the manager's proposal. It would certainly help, and he thought the man could be trusted. At this point, he had no reason to sabotage the investigation, since it would reflect badly on both him and the hotel and might put off potential guests if news of the hotel's culpability got out.

"All right," Sebastian agreed. "Please let me know right away if you discover anything."

"You can count on me," Mr. Holden said.

He gave up his chair and invited Sebastian to take a seat behind the desk, and, as soon as one of the chambermaids he'd sent for arrived, he introduced her to Sebastian and left.

SIXTEEN

The girl was about sixteen. She was short and thin and had bright red hair that she nervously tucked beneath her cap as she entered the office. She looked positively terrified, and seemed even more taken aback when she realized that Mr. Holden would not be present for the interview and she would be alone with a strange man. Sebastian didn't think he was particularly unapproachable, but had been told often enough that he could be quite intense, and took the comments into account when speaking to individuals who were easily intimidated. He made a conscious effort to relax his features and smiled at the girl in what he hoped was a reassuring manner.

"Please, sit down," he said as the maid stood before the desk.

She seemed unsure what to do with her hands, and clasped them before her before changing her mind and allowing her arms to fall to her sides. She balled her hands into fists, then seemed to realize how that might look and instantly straightened them. The poor girl looked exhausted, so Sebastian pointed to the guest chair.

"Go on. Sit."

She perched on the edge of the chair and folded her hands in her lap.

"What's your name?"

"Martha Drum, sir."

There were two fairy cakes left, so Sebastian reached for the plate and pushed it toward Martha, who looked utterly scandalized and shook her head.

"They'll only go to waste," Sebastian said. "You may as well have them."

She was salivating, and Sebastian hoped she would overcome her reservations and enjoy the cakes. She probably never got anything more enjoyable than porridge or a cup of broth.

"Thank you, sir," she whispered, and reached for the cake nearest to her. She took a tiny bite and closed her eyes momentarily, unable to contain her bliss.

Sebastian waited until Martha finished chewing, then asked, "How is it that you're still here so late in the evening?"

"I don't go home until ten o'clock."

"And what time do you start?"

"Ten."

"That's a long day."

"I can take a shorter shift, but then I will be paid less. The morning chambermaid, Betty, works from six to two, so we overlap during the busiest time. And then Polly comes in from two till ten."

"Why is that interval the busiest time?"

"Some guests wake early and ask for hot water, a fresh towel, or breakfast to be brought to their rooms. Most sleep in, then go downstairs to the dining room. That's the best time to clean their rooms, since we can finish by the time they return."

"Did you see the woman who was staying in four thirty-seven, Martha?"

Martha nodded vigorously. "I saw her several times." She

didn't inquire why Sebastian was asking, so he assumed that Mr. Holden had explained the situation.

"Can you tell me about her?"

Martha cast her gaze to the ceiling as she tried to recall the details. "The first time I saw her was when she first arrived. She nodded when I wished her a good afternoon and then went inside."

"What was her demeanor like?" Sebastian asked.

"Demeanor?"

"How did she seem?"

Martha pondered for a moment before replying. "She seemed nervous. Frightened almost."

"Was she alone?"

"Yes."

"Why do you think she was so nervous?"

It was an unfair question, since Martha had no way of knowing how Helen had felt, but she seemed an observant girl and probably noticed more than she let on and came to her own conclusions.

Martha shrugged her narrow shoulders. "Maybe it was her first time staying in a hotel. We don't get many single women travelers, and there were two gentlemen in the corridor."

"Did they do anything that would make her feel intimidated?" Sebastian asked.

"Not at all, sir. They tipped their hats and wished her a good afternoon. They were just being polite," Martha explained.

"When was the next time you saw the woman?"

"I saw her on Wednesday, around five o'clock. I was sweeping the corridor. She looked like she had been crying, and her hand shook when she tried to fit the key in the lock. I asked if she needed help, but she waved me away."

"Did the woman look as if she had been accosted in any way?" Sebastian asked.

"No," Martha replied right away.

"Martha, did you happen to notice if the lady carried a reticule?"

"She did. It was pretty."

"Was Wednesday the last time you saw the woman?"

Martha nodded. "I was due to clean her room today, after she checked out, but she had the Do Not Disturb sign on, so I didn't go in."

"Where would she get the sign?" Sebastian asked. "Mr. Holden said the rooms on the fourth floor don't normally have them."

Martha shrugged again. "I don't know. Maybe she asked at the reception desk."

"Do the reception clerks normally hand out signs?"

"Some guests want to have a lie-in and don't wish to be disturbed. They can ask for a sign at the desk, and whoever is on duty will give them one."

Sebastian made a mental note to inquire if anyone recalled the victim asking for a sign. Maybe she had said something or had given her name.

"Did you hear anything when you approached the door this morning?" he asked.

"No, sir. All was quiet."

"And did you happen to see anyone going inside or leaving? Perhaps the guest had a visitor?"

"If she did, I never saw them. Mr. Sykes says we are to keep the room doors shut while we clean. If we leave the doors wide open, someone might come inside and try to help themselves to the guests' personal possessions. I don't spend that much time in the corridor. Only when I sweep and polish the sconces and such."

"Do you and Polly work together, or do you split up the rooms along the corridor?"

"We prefer to work together," Martha said, "but sometimes Polly leaves me on my own."

"Where does she go?"

"She takes long breaks," Martha said resentfully. "But I can hardly report her, can I? She'll just say I'm lying, and Mr. Holden will believe her because she's been here longer. I can't afford to lose my position. I'm supporting my mother and two younger sisters."

"And where's Polly now?"

"I don't know."

"Martha, is there anyone staying in the rooms adjacent to four thirty-seven?"

"There's an older gentleman staying in room four thirty-nine, but four thirty-five is empty at present."

"How long has the room been vacant?"

"Since Monday."

"And was the guest in four thirty-nine in last night?"

"He came back around half past seven. I saw him go inside."

"I see. Thank you, Martha."

"You're welcome," Martha replied shyly. "Thank you for the cake. I've never had anything so delicious before."

"Take the last one," Sebastian urged her.

Martha looked conflicted, then reached for the cake and fled.

SEVENTEEN

Sebastian found Mr. Holden in the storage room. The manager was bent low as he examined a spot by the back wall, but he straightened and turned around when Sebastian called out to him.

"I've found a bloodstain," Mr. Holden said.

Sebastian crossed the room, which wasn't difficult since there were only a few traveling cases, several wooden crates, and a stack of soiled mattresses draped with a sheet by the side wall. A pile of clothes occupied the narrow space between the edge of the mattresses and the wall. The clothes must have come from the stolen trunk. Sebastian joined Mr. Holden and peered at the spot the manager pointed at. The smudged streak looked like the blood had been smeared when the case had been moved away from the wall and possibly loaded onto a trolley.

"I didn't find any bloodied trolleys though," Mr. Holden said.

"Are there any trolleys missing?"

"No, they're all accounted for. Perhaps the killer cleaned it before returning it."

"Which would ensure that no one connected the victim to the hotel," Sebastian said.

"I checked with the men, and no one saw anything," Mr. Holden said. "But the porters who were here this morning went off shift hours ago."

"How is it that the maids are still here but most of the porters have left?" Sebastian asked.

"Few people arrive or check out after eight o'clock, so there's no need for additional porters," Mr. Holden explained. "And since there are more people at the hotel in the evening, the maids have to remain until the dinner service is finished and the guests retire to their rooms."

"Is there anyone here after ten o'clock?" Sebastian asked, having recalled that Martha finished work at ten.

"Only me," Mr. Holden said. "I check in any late-arriving guests and help them with their luggage."

"And when does your shift end?"

"I'm here until eight in the morning, and then Mr. Sykes takes over."

"And do you remain in your office the entire time?" Sebastian inquired.

Mr. Holden nodded guiltily. "I usually go to sleep after I lock up. If anyone needs anything, there's a bell at reception."

"And are you often woken during the night?"

"Hardly ever."

"When does your day begin?" Sebastian asked.

"At six, when the kitchen staff and the porters begin to arrive."

"So, what you are telling me, Mr. Holden, is that if the killer waited long enough he'd have the run of the hotel?"

"Yes, I suppose he would," Mr. Holden admitted. He looked at Sebastian imploringly. "Do you think you might see your way to not informing Mr. Sykes?"

"That largely depends on what I discover. It's not my job to protect your reputation, Mr. Holden."

"No," Mr. Holden agreed, but Sebastian could see fear in the man's eyes. His oversight could cost him dearly.

"I need to speak to Polly."

"I'll find her for you," Mr. Holden said as they left the storage room and headed towards the stairs.

"In the meantime, I will have a word with the guest in room four thirty-nine."

"Do you suspect him?" Mr. Holden exclaimed. He appeared both alarmed and hopeful. It would make his life easier if the crime could be blamed on a deranged guest.

"No, but I would like to ask if he saw or heard anything from next door."

"Do you think the killer might still be on the premises?" Mr. Holden asked.

"I doubt it," Sebastian replied, more to reassure the manager than because he was sure.

Sebastian didn't think the culprit worked at the hotel, mostly because the man seen delivering the trunk had been wearing a railway porter's uniform, but the uniform could be an intentional misdirection. He had to keep an open mind and remain vigilant. Given the killer's actions thus far, he or she just might be brazen enough to remain close on hand to follow the investigation.

"Come to my office once you have finished," Mr. Holden said when they reached the fourth floor and parted ways.

EIGHTEEN

The guest in room four thirty-nine appeared to be in his late forties, possibly early fifties. He was heavyset, with wide shoulders, a thick neck, and a ruddy, lantern-shaped face that must have been clean-shaven that morning but was now covered with black stubble. He was in his shirtsleeves, his hair was mussed, and the bed behind him had rumpled bedding.

"Good evening, Mr....?"

"Garfield. Bruce Garfield. What can I do for you, good sir?" Mr. Garfield asked genially. He didn't seem the least bit annoyed to find a stranger on his doorstep after he'd clearly retired for the night.

"I'm Inspector Bell of Scotland Yard," Sebastian said, and showed Mr. Garfield his identification. "I'd like a moment of your time."

Mr. Garfield's surprise was evident, but he stepped aside and invited Sebastian in. The room was identical to its neighbor in both size and décor. Mr. Garfield sat on the bed, while Sebastian remained standing, since there was no chair.

"Mr. Garfield, a woman was murdered in the room next

door sometime last night. Did you see or hear anything unusual?"

The man's mouth fell open in shock, and he shook his head slowly as if still unsure of Sebastian's meaning. "Murdered? How?"

"She was stabbed through the heart with a sewing implement."

"A sewing implement?" Mr. Garfield stared at Sebastian as if he had taken leave of his senses. "Why would anyone do that?"

"That's what I'm trying to find out. Did you see anything or hear anything?" Sebastian asked again.

"No. All was quiet after I came upstairs after dinner, and once I fell asleep I wasn't likely to hear anything at all. I'm a heavy sleeper."

"What time did you come up?"

"Just after nine o'clock. My dinner booking was for eight."

"When did you arrive at the hotel?"

"Monday morning."

"From?"

"Swindon. I'm here on business. I sell leather goods. Belts, purses, small frames, and the like."

Sebastian had noticed a large black case next to the wardrobe that probably held samples.

"Do you ever make adjustments to the samples?"

Gemma had mentioned that the bodkin could be used to make holes, but it seemed to be a feminine implement, and Sebastian didn't think a salesman would be traveling with a carved stake. But he couldn't be sure.

"How do you mean?"

"Perhaps punch an extra hole in a belt," Sebastian improvised.

Mr. Garfield appeared genuinely surprised by the idea. "No, never."

"And if you needed to make a hole, what would you use?"

"An awl."

"May I look inside your case?"

"If you must."

Sebastian laid the case on the floor and opened it. There were about two dozen items, all fairly innocuous, and there were no tools inside the case.

"I know you're only doing your job, Inspector, and I take no offense, but believe me when I tell you I did not murder anyone."

"Mr. Garfield, did you see the woman in four thirty-seven yesterday?"

"No, I didn't. I didn't hear her either. She was very quiet. In fact, I thought the room was unoccupied." Mr. Garfield made a show of thinking, then said, "I don't know if this is important, but when I went to the lavatory just before going down to the dining room I saw a man walking towards the room in question."

"How do you know he was walking towards that room?" Sebastian asked.

"Well, my room is the last room on this side of the corridor, and I know he wasn't coming to see me. And there's a supply cupboard and the lavatory just across the hall. Since he kept walking, he had to be going towards one of the two rooms just before mine."

"So, he must have come quite close to you if he was going to four thirty-seven and you were headed to the lavatory."

"He did."

"What can you tell me about him?" Sebastian asked, hoping Mr. Garfield had been as observant of the man's features as he was of the floorplan.

"I didn't see his face. He was wearing a porter's cap and lowered his head when he spotted me. The visor cast a shadow over his features."

"Was he one of the hotel porters or maybe the doorman?" Sebastian asked.

"No, he was a railway porter. His uniform was dark blue, and the coat was short, not like the long coat the doorman wears."

"So, what did this man do?"

Mr. Garfield gave an apologetic shrug. "I stepped inside the lavatory and shut the door. He wasn't there when I came out. I thought I heard a door opening and closing though."

"Are you certain he entered room four thirty-seven?"

Mr. Garfield nodded. "I believe so, but I did not see him go inside with my own eyes."

"Is there anything at all you can tell me about this man? Height? Weight? Gait? Did he wear a beard or a moustache?"

"He was tall and slender. And his gait was brisk, purposeful. I'm not sure about a beard. I think he might have been cleanly shaven."

"Was he carrying anything?"

Mr. Garfield smiled at that. "Yes, he was. I remember now. He carried a single red rose."

"Did you hear him say anything to the person who opened the door?"

"I wasn't really listening, you understand, but I think he might have called her sweetheart."

"Thank you, Mr. Garfield. Kindly inform the hotel manager if you recall any other details."

"I'm leaving tomorrow," Mr. Garfield said. "My business in London is done, and I'm eager to return home, more so now that I know some poor woman was murdered right next door. Best of luck with your inquiry, Inspector."

"Thank you. Good evening to you, Mr. Garfield."

Sebastian left the man in peace and returned downstairs, where an anxious Polly waited for him in Mr. Holden's office.

Where Martha had looked young and innocent, Polly had the air of a woman who had something to hide, and Sebastian fervently hoped his instinct would prove correct.

NINETEEN

"What's your full name, miss?" Sebastian asked sternly as he studied the young woman across from him. He knew his inquiry would alarm her, which was his intention.

Polly was very pretty, with wide blue eyes, fair tendrils that escaped her cap and curled gently around her face, and an hourglass figure accentuated by the apron tied around her tiny waist. Sebastian put her at around twenty, but she might have been a few years older.

"Polly Crosby," Polly said quietly. Gripping the seat with both hands, she stared at him as if she half-expected to be charged with a crime.

"I hear you like to take unauthorized breaks, Polly," Sebastian said, and watched the young woman shrink into herself and hunch over like an old woman.

"Where do you go during your breaks?"

"I just need a breath of air sometimes," Polly hurried to explain. "I have a weak chest, and all that dust settles in my lungs and makes me cough and sneeze."

Sebastian was no physician, but Polly appeared to be in robust health and didn't have the watery eyes or runny nose of someone afflicted with frequent bouts of coughing and sneezing. She also looked like someone who would think fast on her feet and come up with a reasonable excuse.

Leaning back in his chair, he studied her until she had the grace to blush. "In my experience, when a woman sneaks off without telling anyone it's because she's meeting a man."

Polly's flaming cheeks and furtive gaze said it all. Sebastian had hit the mark.

"Does your young man work here at the hotel?"

Polly stared at her folded hands and shook her head.

"Where, then?" When the young woman refused to answer, Sebastian said, "Polly, I have no interest in making difficulties for you. I simply need you to answer a few questions."

"What about?" Polly asked sullenly.

"The guest in room four thirty-seven was murdered last night."

Polly gaped at him, her flushed face turning very pale. "Murdered?" she whispered. "Last night?"

"She was stabbed."

Polly was trembling now, her eyes huge.

"What time did you leave the hotel?"

"Ten o'clock, like always." Polly's voice quivered with fear, and Sebastian thought she was finally ready to be truthful with him.

"And where did you disappear to before that? Martha said she didn't see you for quite a while."

"I was called to another floor, to help out."

"Who called you, and to which floor?"

Polly squirmed in her seat, and Sebastian was positive she was lying, so he pushed harder.

"I will have to confirm your story with Mr. Holden. He would know if you were asked to assist on another floor, would he not?"

"Please, don't tell him. I need this job," Polly said, her eyes pleading.

"So why do you jeopardize your position by sneaking off?"

"Because I'm twenty-one, and I'm desperate for a bit of joy," the young woman cried. "There has to be more to life than waking at dawn, washing and feeding my da, who's too ill to look after himself, cleaning and cooking, then going to work and slaving away until I'm ready to drop."

"I'm sorry. That must be hard," Sebastian said.

"It is," Polly said miserably. "My father is bedbound, so I must see to him as soon as I get home, or he'll soil himself. I have no time for myself, Inspector, not even on Sundays."

"So, where do you go with your beau?" Sebastian asked.

He didn't think Polly was making up an invalid father to court his sympathy. Her desperation was right there in her eyes, and he understood her plight now that he'd seen the dedication that was required when looking after Mrs. Ramsey. Anne wasn't bedbound, not yet, but she could no longer see to her most basic personal needs and needed round-the-clock assistance and supervision. No doubt Polly felt awful knowing that her father had to wait for her to get home so he could use the pot and have something to eat.

"He works at Paddington, as a porter. We can hardly meet at the station, in full view of everyone, so we see each other at the hotel, after he gets off work."

"Where exactly do you meet?"

"In whatever room is empty on the fourth floor."

"What's your beau's name?"

"Jory Dixon. He's a good man, Inspector. He wants to marry me," Polly exclaimed, and her face lit up with hope. "He loves me."

"What time did you and Jory meet last night?"

"Around eight."

"Which room?"

"Four thirty-five."

"Did you hear anything from next door?"

Polly's cheeks blazed and she lowered her eyes in embarrassment, and Sebastian thought that, even if there had been cries for help coming from next door, Polly wouldn't have paid them any mind. She was clearly in love with her Jory and eager to enjoy his affections. Sebastian hoped her plan worked, since there were plenty of men who'd lie to a girl to get her into bed and then leave her when they either grew bored or discovered their lover was with child and didn't care to take on the responsibility.

"Did Jory bring you anything?" Sebastian asked.

Polly nodded eagerly. "He brought me a red rose. He bought it from a flower seller," she clarified, in case Sebastian assumed that he'd stolen the rose from one of the vases in the foyer.

"Will Jory confirm your story?" Sebastian asked wearily.

Polly's account had served to eliminate his only suspect since Mr. Garfield had seen Jory Dixon and not the killer last night.

"He will," Polly hurried to reassure him. "We had nothing to do with that woman getting killed, Inspector. Please, don't tell Mr. Holden I was in that room," she begged. "I swear, I'll never bunk off again. I'll tell Jory we can't meet at the hotel anymore."

Sebastian nodded, but his mind wasn't on Polly's romantic assignations. "What time does Jory finish his shift?"

"At eight, but he waits for me and walks me home."

"Good man," Sebastian said, and nodded approvingly. It wasn't safe for a young woman to walk home by herself so late at night.

He checked the time. It was nearly ten o'clock.

"Where does he wait for you?"

"By the side door that leads to London Street. May I go now?"

"Go on," Sebastian said.

He followed Polly outside and went to speak to Mr. Holden, who was waiting for him in the foyer.

"Anything?" Mr. Holden asked eagerly.

"Not as such. Polly didn't see anything."

Mr. Holden shook his head. "How is it that no one saw or heard anything? Surely the killer didn't just walk into the room, stab the woman to death, then walk out. An altercation must have taken place, and she would have cried out in fear and pain."

"Mr. Garfield went down to dinner, the room next door was empty, and the two maids were about their work. And the entire episode might have lasted no more than a minute."

"What about the disposal?"

"That would have taken longer, but, as you yourself admitted, the corridors and the foyer are virtually empty after hours."

"What will you do?" Mr. Holden asked.

"I will return in the morning and question the clerks and porters on the morning shift. Perhaps they saw something."

"Perhaps," the manager said, but he didn't sound convinced.

"I might have a word with Betty as well."

"Betty has the day off tomorrow. I can give you her address if you like, but I doubt she saw anything since she normally cleans the other side of the corridor."

"I will let you know if I should need it. Thank you for your assistance, Mr. Holden," Sebastian said, and headed toward the door. As he stepped outside, he wondered why he had covered for Polly, then realized that perhaps he had developed a soft spot for star-crossed lovers.

TWENTY

Jory Dixon wasn't difficult to find. He was the only young man standing near the side door on London Street. He was about twenty-five, and Sebastian could immediately see why Polly was smitten. Despite the uniform that was meant to make all porters look the same, and the neatly trimmed hair, there was something untamed about the lad, an intensity in his dark eyes, and a suppressed energy in his movements. He wasn't waiting patiently by the exit. Jory vibrated with impatience, his gaze frequently straying to the door as he waited for his girl. When hailed, he smiled and raised a hand in greeting.

"Good evening, Inspector. I saw you at the terminus this morning," he said in response to Sebastian's obvious surprise at being recognized. "What a hullabaloo. Everyone was talking about it. What are you doing here?" he added, having probably realized that Sebastian had come looking for him.

"I have it on good authority that you were canoodling with Polly Crosby last night in room four thirty-five."

Jory gaped at Sebastian. "Polly told you that?"

"She didn't have much choice, seeing as I could tell

Mr. Holden about her unauthorized breaks and have her dismissed."

"It wasn't her fault," Jory cried. "It was me. I begged her to see me in private. I put pressure on her."

"Mr. Dixon, I don't care what you get up to in your private life, but if the two of you hope to retain your positions I suggest you think twice about breaking the rules."

"I know. It's just that I miss her so much," Jory exclaimed. "There's nowhere for us to meet, not privately. Polly has her father to look after, and I have a mother and two sisters who rely on my wages. You have no idea what it's like to long for someone so much and not be able to spend time with them."

"As a matter of fact, I do. Perhaps combining your resources might solve your problem."

Jory nodded. "I thought the same, and I was going to ask Polly to marry me last night. I even brought a red rose, but then I changed my mind."

"Why was that?"

"It wasn't the right moment. I thought I should take her somewhere special, not ask her to marry me in that mean little room with a couple quarreling next door and Polly worrying about getting back to work."

"You heard an argument coming from next door?"

"Yes. Why?"

"The victim was staying in room four thirty-seven, and she was murdered sometime last night."

"Blimey!" Jory exclaimed. "You think she got snuffed while Polly and I..." Even in the feeble light of the streetlamp, Sebastian could see the young man's cheeks go pink. "While we were talking," he finished lamely.

"What did you hear, Jory?" Sebastian asked.

"Just raised voices. I couldn't hear what they were saying."

"And you heard a man's voice?"

Jory nodded. "But the woman's voice was louder. She sounded really upset."

"What time did you leave?"

"Around half past eight."

"And did you see anyone come out of room four thirty-seven?"

"No."

"Did you see anyone with a hotel trolley at the terminus this morning?"

"Yeah, I did. At least four different blokes. It's not unusual for hotel porters to wheel a guest's luggage directly to the platform. Sometimes a railway porter will help out and then bring the trolley back."

"Did anyone look shifty or nervous?"

"Not that I noticed. Everyone just went about their business."

Jory's eyes suddenly widened, as if he'd remembered something important. "You know, now you mention it, Inspector, I did notice a bloke whose cap said GNR. Everyone at Paddington works for the Great Western Railway—GWR. That cap was for the wrong railway line."

"Where does the Great Northern Railway come into London?"

"King's Cross."

"Thank you," Sebastian said just as the door opened and Polly stepped outside, looking demure in a coat that was clearly a hand-me-down and a drab bonnet. "Goodnight to you both."

"Goodnight," Polly murmured. Her look of alarm was replaced by one of relief when Jory smiled down at her and held out his arm.

Sebastian strode down the street, his mind buzzing like a hive. If Jory's observation was accurate, a porter from King's Cross had been at Paddington around the time the trunk had been delivered to Platform 4. Coupled with the address Sebastian had discovered in the dead woman's glove, that tidbit could prove to be monumentally important.

TWENTY-ONE

By the time Sebastian finally returned to the boarding house, it was well after eleven. Mrs. Poole normally locked up at ten, just before she retired, but Sebastian found the front door unlocked, and the light was on in the parlor. Mr. Quince was reading by the fire, but when Sebastian walked past the door he called out and gestured to Sebastian to join him.

"I was waiting for you," Quince admitted shyly.

"Is something wrong?"

"No, not at all." Mr. Quince suddenly looked less sure of himself than he normally did, and smiled awkwardly. "Please, join me for a drink, Inspector. There's something I'd like to discuss with you."

Sebastian wanted only to go upstairs. It had been a long and emotional day, and he still felt guilty about choosing his professional responsibilities over his duty to Simian. Sebastian would have loved to refuse, but the address in his pocket, coupled with the fact that Mr. Quince worked at King's Cross, reminded him that walking away wasn't really an option. Perhaps Quince wished to speak to him about the case and had waited until he could do so in private. Sebastian didn't think the man was about to confess to murder, but he looked nervous, possibly even a little scared, and Sebastian might not get another chance to hear what he had to say.

"All right. But just one," Sebastian said, mindful as ever of his hard-won sobriety. He would have joined Simian in a glass of wine, but he would have preferred not to drink with Quince.

He removed his hat, shrugged off his coat, and left the items on a chair by the door. Settling in a wingchair, he accepted a drink from Mr. Quince, who poured himself a rather large brandy and sat across from Sebastian.

"What did you want to speak to me about?" Sebastian asked once both men had sampled their drinks.

"I know this is a bit sudden, and I'm well aware that you have reservations about me, but I really do care for Mathilda, and I would be honored if you would act as my best man at the wedding."

These days, few things took Sebastian by surprise, but Quince's request took him completely unawares. They weren't friends. In fact, Sebastian found the man intensely irritating and tried to avoid him whenever possible. And given the direction his investigation was taking, he would have preferred to keep his distance, but Bertram Quince was looking at him with such trepidation, Sebastian couldn't find it in his heart to just say no.

"Surely you must have family or friends who should have the honor," he demurred.

Quince shook his head. "I have a brother, but we were never close and don't see each other very often. Gerald is based in Birmingham."

"Is he, indeed? Are you originally from Birmingham, Mr. Quince?" Sebastian asked. Quince did not have an accent that would mark him as a newcomer to London, but some people were able to lose an accent faster than others.

Quince shook his head. "I was born right here, in Clerkenwell, but we moved to Birmingham after my father died. My mother couldn't manage on her own, and her brother, who lived up there, offered to help."

"What does your brother do, Mr. Quince?"

"Gerald is a railway conductor. He works for the Great Northern Railway, but once his father-in-law passes he will inherit a textile mill."

"Why does he work for the railways when he could be learning the family business?" Sebastian asked.

It seemed an incongruous thing to do, especially since the life of a conductor was a nomadic one. Gerald Quince would surely hold a senior position at the mill until he became the owner, so why leave?

"Gerald and his father-in-law don't get on," Bertram said with a sigh. "The mill is struggling, has been for some time, but the old man refuses to make improvements or take any advice from Gerald."

"And is your brother qualified to offer managerial advice?"

"Before taking the job with the railway, Gerald worked for Robert Speers—that's his father-in-law," Quince explained. "Gerald visited other mills in the area in his spare time and consulted with the owners. He presented Speers with well-thought-out, practical ideas on how to increase output and lower operating costs, but rather than hear him out Speers dismissed him and forbade him to set foot inside the mill."

"Surely his wife had something to say on the matter," Sebastian said, wondering how Mrs. Quince felt about her husband leaving the family home for weeks at a time.

"Hettie took her father's side, and it's caused a bit of a rift between her and Gerald. He even took a room in Peterborough, which is on the Great Northern Railway line and more convenient to his work, and left Hettie the house."

"Hettie?" Sebastian asked, his ears instantly pricking.

"Harriet. But Gerald always called her Hettie."

"And is Gerald certain he will inherit the mill once his father-in-law passes?" Sebastian inquired.

Bertram looked uncertain. "There is another daughter, Cordelia, but she's unmarried. I can't imagine Mr. Speers would leave the mill to her, but you never know. He's a spiteful old bugger, so I wouldn't put anything past him."

"When was the last time you saw your brother, Mr. Quince? Surely he comes into London sometimes."

Given that the Great Northern Railway operated out of King's Cross and Bertram Quince worked at the terminus, the Quinces' paths were bound to cross on occasion.

Quince smiled sadly. "Gerald and I see each other from time to time, but he is never in London for long, and I don't care to delay the wedding until he's able to attend."

"What about friends?" Sebastian asked.

He still hoped to extricate himself, but didn't think Quince would let him off the hook. He wouldn't have asked if he hadn't considered all the other options and arrived at the conclusion that Sebastian was his last resort.

Bertram Quince smiled ruefully. "I'm embarrassed to admit it, Inspector, but I don't have many friends. My literary success has set me apart from my coworkers, and they give me a wide berth. Some openly mock me, while others accuse me of turning them into characters in my publications."

"And do you ever use your coworkers for inspiration?" Sebastian asked.

Quince had drawn on Sebastian for his latest penny dreadful and had named his detective Samuel Knell, which had annoyed Sebastian no end, but he could hardly demand that Quince not publish his story since he'd lifted the account directly from the papers and didn't need Sebastian's permission. Thankfully, Gemma's role in the investigation had not been mentioned, and she had been spared a less-than-thinly-veiled reference and a new name.

"To be frank, none of my coworkers are interesting enough to deserve the literary treatment," Quince replied. "Someone has to leave quite an impression on me to make it into a story."

"I must admit, it's a dubious honor."

"I assure you, Inspector, when I created Inspector Knell I meant only to commend rather than disparage. I would have gladly used your real name, had you permitted it," Quince said with obvious regret. "For whom the Bell tolls?" he intoned morbidly. "For the unsuspecting victim. I can still immortalize you, Inspector, if you let me. All of London reads my penny dreadfuls. Imagine the notoriety you could achieve."

"I'm not looking for notoriety, Mr. Quince."

"And that's what I so admire." Quince cleared his throat. "So, will you do it, Inspector? Will you stand up with me? It would mean the world, especially since Mathilda holds you in such high regard."

"Of course," Sebastian choked out. "I would be delighted."

Quince sprang to his feet and pumped Sebastian's right hand. "Thank you. That's very kind. Very kind indeed. Mathilda and I were thinking Saturday of next week, but we weren't going to finalize our plans until I'd spoken to you."

"Next week?"

"Why wait?" Quince exclaimed excitedly. "I want our life as man and wife to begin as soon as possible."

Sebastian couldn't fault Quince's thinking, and found that he envied the man. He would have liked his own life to start as soon as possible as well, but he had to wait until Gemma was out of mourning and ready to entertain his proposal.

"I'm going to take Mathilda away for a few days. A wedding trip to Edinburgh. She's never been away from London."

"What about your job?" Sebastian asked. "Will they be able to spare you?"

Quince smiled conspiratorially. "I haven't told anyone

except Mathilda, but I resigned my position at King's Cross last week."

"Really? Why?" Despite his resolve not to get involved with his neighbors, Sebastian was curious, and Quince's decision might have a bearing on the case.

"I will help Mathilda run the boarding house and write in my spare time." Mr. Quince smiled self-deprecatingly. "I have always dreamed of writing a novel. I think I have one in me, but the creative process is considerably more time-consuming than people realize, and one has to be in the right frame of mind to embark on such a complex undertaking."

"What will your book be about?" Sebastian asked.

"Why, Inspector Knell, of course. Solving an unsolvable crime. Such a book has never been written," Quince gushed. "Penny dreadfuls and broadsheets, yes, but not a full-length novel. I believe there's a market for such a thing."

Sebastian wasn't sure if he was impressed or annoyed by Bertram Quince's idea. A complicated case could make for an absorbing narrative, but it would also thrust Inspector Knell even more into the spotlight, not an outcome Sebastian hoped for.

"Would you be writing this novel as B.E. Ware or Bertram Quince?"

"I haven't decided yet. On the one hand, I have a devoted following as B.E. Ware, and I stand to capitalize on that, especially since I have already introduced Inspector Knell. On the other hand, I want to be taken seriously and not treated like some hack, so perhaps I will try to publish under my own name. What do you think?"

"I don't know anything about the publishing business, Mr. Quince, but I do know that I don't care to be made into a caricature."

"I would never," Quince cried. "Inspector Knell will be the

sort of protagonist the readers can respect, Sebastian. May I call you Sebastian now that you're to be my best man?"

"It would be best if certain boundaries were to be observed," Sebastian replied.

"Of course. I do apologize for the breach of etiquette. It won't happen again. But I would like to thank you, if I may," Quince said.

"There's really no need."

"There's every need. You're doing me a great favor, and it would be remiss of me not to acknowledge that in some small way." Quince smiled proudly. "I am prepared not to raise your rent once your lease agreement is up."

"Thank you. That's very generous," Sebastian replied. "Have you discussed this with Mrs. Poole?"

"Not yet." Quince chuckled. "In fact, she told me not to bother asking you since you were sure to refuse. I'm happy to have proved her wrong."

"Then perhaps you had better clear it with her before making a firm promise. Until you're married, this establishment still belongs to Mrs. Poole," Sebastian reminded Quince, who seemed to be making himself at home a bit too soon for his liking and negotiating on Mrs. Poole's behalf.

Sebastian renewed his rental agreement every year, and, although he had lived at the boarding house for three years, Mrs. Poole had yet to raise his rent. He supposed things were about to change drastically, but with any luck he would be gone before that happened.

"If I might ask you a question, Mr. Quince," Sebastian said once he'd finished his drink and set the glass on the low table between them.

"Of course. Ask anything you like."

"Is this to be your first marriage?"

"It is," Quince admitted. "Until I met Mathilda, I had never considered marriage and was quite content to remain a bachelor."

"What changed?" Sebastian asked.

"I fell in love," Bertram Quince replied, smiling beatifically.

Sebastian's expression must have conveyed his skepticism because, after a long moment, Quince's smile slid off his face. "I turned forty," he confessed. "Reaching such a significant milestone makes a man think."

"What about?"

"Life, death, old age, one's legacy. One starts to grow fearful."

"And Mathilda Poole has the power to dispel those fears?"

Quince sighed dramatically. "Mathilda is a good woman, Inspector. I might not be the man of her dreams, but I will look after her to the best of my ability, and I know she will look after me. It will be me and Matty against the world. My only regret is that we're too old to have children. I would have liked to be a father, and I know Mathilda longed for motherhood in her younger days."

"London is full of children, Mr. Quince, and some child would find themselves lucky if they were taken in by you and Mrs. Poole."

Quince shook his head. "I don't want to raise an orphan, Inspector. I want a child of my own. I think every man wants to leave something of himself, proof that he walked this earth and made his mark. Did you never long for a family of your own?"

When Sebastian didn't answer, Quince pushed to his feet. "It seems I've imposed on you long enough, Inspector. I'll say goodnight."

"Goodnight to you, Mr. Quince. Incidentally, do you happen to know anyone named Helen?" Sebastian asked as he picked up his coat and draped it over his arm.

Quince looked taken aback. "My mother's name was Helen. Why do you ask?"

"No reason. I must have heard you mention her."

Quince looked like he was about to question him, but Sebastian didn't give him the chance. He grabbed his hat and hastened up the stairs, then shut the door as soon as he entered his tiny sitting room. Gustav was happy to see him, until he realized that Sebastian had not come bearing gifts and retreated to his favorite corner, from which he fixed Sebastian with a sour look.

"I'm sorry, old son. I'll bring you a treat tomorrow," Sebastian promised.

For a moment he thought Gustav would remain where he was, but the cat eventually relented and followed Sebastian to the bedroom, where he jumped on the bed and curled up on Sebastian's pillow, even though he knew full well he wouldn't be permitted to remain there.

Sebastian gently smacked Gustav's bum to shift him, then undressed and got into bed. The sheets were cold, Gustav's belly when he stretched against Sebastian's side the only spot of warmth until his own body heat warmed the bed. Sebastian would have liked to go straight to sleep, but his mind had other ideas. As he lay in the darkness, his hand on Gustav's silky back, he tried to find a link based on what he'd learned so far, but, try as he might, he couldn't identify a common thread. The facts were like loose beads that rolled this way and that and would not form a necklace until they were strung together in a particular order, the circle made complete with the aid of a clasp.

Bertram Quince and his brother both worked for the railways and were in and out of King's Cross. Both men had been issued uniforms and caps that would display the railway's insignia, GNR. Gerald Quince's father-in-law owned a textile mill and there was a Birmingham connection. The victim had hidden an Albion Street address in her glove, may have come from Birmingham, and was called Helen, or something very similar. Sebastian supposed Hettie could look like Helen if written by someone who was agitated or felt rushed, but there had been only one tall letter in the middle of the victim's Christian name, and it hadn't been crossed, as a "t" would be. And if the victim was Hettie Quince, why would she follow her husband all the way to London when he was based in Peterborough and she could visit him there? Peterborough was closer to Birmingham than London.

At this stage, the questions had no answers, and the observations were a series of random facts that added up to more than coincidence and less than a theory. The world was full of coincidences that gained importance when one was able to tie them together to form a cohesive narrative, but, until he had tangible evidence, all Sebastian could do was file the information away. After all, what reason would either Quince have to murder the victim?

Sebastian's well-trained mind instantly supplied an answer. Quince had said that this was to be his first marriage, but he could have lied. By his own admission, he was now in his forties, and it was rare to find a man who had managed to avoid matrimony altogether, especially in his youth. It was possible that Quince had been married, and the arrival of his estranged wife would have put the kibosh on his plans to marry Mathilda Poole and appropriate the assets she had inherited from her late husband. Sebastian wasn't sure if he really believed Quince was the killer or if this theory was fueled by his instinctive distrust of the man.

As far as the other Quince went, if Gerald Quince's father-in-law had recently passed and he had inherited the mill, he might have decided to rid himself of a wife who'd sided with her father against him. It could be that he no longer cared for her and wasn't interested in a reconciliation, or perhaps he had met someone else in the course of his travels and might have started a relationship. The woman in the trunk had been wearing black, so it was possible that she was in mourning for her father.

And it was just as likely that she had no connection to either Quince. The railways employed thousands of men, all of whom wore a uniform and passed through London at some point, since London was a major transportation hub. To jump to unfounded conclusions and then try to fit the evidence into a theory was the sort of thing ignorant, power-hungry detectives did to get a conviction and move up the ladder of success.

And Sebastian had heard talk that the ladder might be getting another rung that would divide the inspectors into tiers of importance. Some men would give their eyeteeth to lord it over others and get that much closer to the top should Ransome's stint as superintendent turn out to be short-lived and an opportunity presented itself. Sebastian had no interest in throwing his hat in the ring or lobbying for a higher position, but he also didn't care to work for someone he didn't respect. The ideal situation would be to work for himself, but, until he decided to become a private inquiry agent, he had to put up with the rigamarole of departmental politics and refrain from taking sides should another shakeup become a distinct possibility.

Sebastian was still contemplating the benefits of working for himself when sleep overtook him, and he was finally able to rest. He dreamed that he was a conductor, and made his way down the length of the train until he came across an unattended trunk. The floor beneath was crimson with blood, and two men in uniform came at him from opposite ends of the train, presumably the Quinces.

TWENTY-TWO
FRIDAY, MAY 6

After a hurried and very early breakfast of oversalted kippers, under-salted porridge, and overcooked soft-boiled eggs, during which Bertram Quince grinned at Sebastian as if he were his long-lost brother, Sebastian set off down the street. It was still early enough that the lodgers at number thirteen should be in, probably at breakfast. He didn't know the landlady, but Mrs. Poole had mentioned her once or twice, mostly in negative terms. She liked to pass on neighborhood gossip over breakfast or at the dinner table and used it to fill the gaps when her lodgers failed to find a suitable topic of conversation. Silence hadn't been as much of a problem since the new lodgers had moved in, as Mr. Quince and Mr. Danvers more than made up for Sebastian's and Mr. Rushton's natural reticence and kept the conversation flowing easily and naturally throughout the meals. Sebastian reflected that this should be a lesson to him, and he should pay more attention since one never knew when totally random, even unwelcome information might become unexpectedly useful.

As he hurried down the street, he tried to dredge up what

Mrs. Poole had said about Mrs. Elmore. He couldn't recall most of her rants, but he did remember that Mrs. Poole had made it a point to cross the street when she saw Mrs. Elmore because she didn't think her respectable and had sneered at Mrs. Elmore's lodgers, calling them the dregs of society. Sebastian had assumed that this snobbery was meant to elevate her own profile and remind her lodgers how discerning Mrs. Poole was when choosing new boarders, but now he wasn't so sure. Perhaps Mrs. Poole really did know something damaging about the other woman and the state of her establishment. If more information was required, he would ask her, but at this stage Sebastian thought it best not to involve either Mr. Quince or Mrs. Poole in his inquiries. He might quickly lose control of the case if those two got wind that one of the lodgers might be a suspect.

Mrs. Elmore opened the door to Sebastian's knock and stared at him in wide-eyed surprise. She was about ten years older than Mrs. Poole, so in her mid-forties, a thin, wiry woman with leathery skin, small, gray eyes, and dark hair that was scraped into a tight bun. Her black-and-white gingham gown put Sebastian in mind of a heap of cold ash in the grate, and her apron was dusted with flour. She must have already started on her morning baking.

"No vacancies," Mrs. Elmore announced. "Especially for the likes of you."

"What like am I?" Sebastian asked, genuinely interested in the reason for her rancor.

"The police," the woman ground out. "If not for you lot, I'd still have a husband and a son."

Mrs. Elmore moved to slam the door in Sebastian's face, but he splayed his fingers on the door to keep it open.

"I'm sorry for your loss, Mrs. Elmore, but I'm in no way responsible for what happened to your family. And I'm not looking for a room."

"So, why are you here, then?"

"I need to speak to your lodgers."

"Why? What are they meant to have done?" Mrs. Elmore demanded, her eyes narrowing in suspicion as she released the pressure on the door.

She might resent the police but, if one of her lodgers was a thief or a rabble-rouser, it would be in her best interests to know the truth before she became embroiled in whatever they were up to and was found guilty by association.

"A woman's body was found in Paddington yesterday—" Sebastian began.

"So? What's that to do with us?" Mrs. Elmore cut across him.

"If you would allow me to finish."

"Go on, then," the woman said grudgingly. "And keep your voice down."

Sebastian's voice was already low, but he could understand why she wouldn't want the neighbors to overhear their conversation. The doors and windows might be shut, but people had a way of finding out anything that might be damning and passing it on, so the gossip spread like a contagion through the street. The information could cost Mrs. Elmore her livelihood, especially if resentful neighbors chose to embroider the facts.

"Perhaps we should talk inside," Sebastian said, and Mrs. Elmore immediately took his meaning. She nodded and stepped aside, but didn't invite him in. They stood nose to nose in the dim foyer, and Mrs. Elmore's gaze slid toward the door on the right, which had to be the dining room. Sebastian could hear low, masculine voices and the clink of cutlery as the lodgers enjoyed their breakfast.

"The woman that died had an address hidden inside her glove. Your address," Sebastian said, his voice barely above a whisper.

He chose not to tell Mrs. Elmore that the address could just as easily be that of Mrs. Poole's establishment, since the whole street would have been sure to hear by lunchtime that Mrs. Poole was harboring a murderer.

"What of it?" Mrs. Elmore asked. She tried to appear unconcerned, but there was a quaver in her voice that betrayed her anxiety.

"The victim might have been related to one of your lodgers. A wife or a sister," Sebastian said. "Surely they have a right to know if their loved one is dead."

He made it sound as if he were simply delivering sad news, not intending to question the lodgers with a view to isolating a suspect. Mrs. Elmore fell for the ruse.

"All right. They're at breakfast. You can talk to them in there."

She led him to the dining room, which was a bit shabby but looked clean and bright. The table was covered with a plain white cloth and set with mismatched crockery and two earthenware teapots. Four men sat around the table, half-empty plates of fried eggs and sausages before them. Sebastian noticed that each man had been given one piece of bread and there was no bread or butter on the table should they want more. He felt a twinge of appreciation for Mrs. Poole, who, even if she was a mediocre chef, at least wasn't stingy with bread, before addressing the men.

"Good morning," he said. "My apologies for interrupting your breakfast. I'm Inspector Bell of Scotland Yard. May I know your names?"

"Why are you here, and why do you need our names?" the youngest lodger asked. He was dressed in a porter's uniform and wore the belligerent expression of a man who usually had a bone to pick with someone.

"A woman was murdered at Paddington yesterday," Sebastian explained.

"Paddington's clear across town, mate," the youth

exclaimed. "We all work at King's Cross, so it's best you were on your way. Shall I draw you a map?" he taunted. "You seem to have rather a poor sense of direction."

The young man looked around the table, clearly expecting approval from the other lodgers, but only one man appeared to be mildly amused. The other two looked at Sebastian warily, having probably realized that he wasn't there by mistake.

"The victim had written out this address and hidden it among her possessions," Sebastian replied patiently, and waited for a reaction. The men stared at him in sullen silence.

"Names?" Sebastian asked again, once he'd taken out his notebook and pencil. "And occupations," he added, since the young man had said that they all worked at the terminus.

"Darren White," the oldest of the men volunteered. "I'm a train engineer."

"Peter Davis," the young man said. "Porter."

"Gordon McTavish," a red-haired man with a thick Scots brogue said. He was around forty, give or take a few years, and wore a short, thick beard that was a few shades lighter than his hair and appeared almost golden in the morning light coming through the window. His voice was low and gravelly, and Sebastian noted that his dark blue gaze was wary when it met his. "Porter."

"Seamus O'Connor," the fourth man said. He was of an age with McTavish and was obviously Irish. He had reddish-brown hair and a craggy face, the skin blotchy and reddened. "Fireman," he muttered.

"Thank you," Sebastian said. "I would like to speak to each of you in turn. Mrs. Elmore, may I use your parlor?"

"Have a choice in the matter, do I?" Mrs. Elmore grumbled under her breath.

"You do. I can take the men up to their rooms if you prefer."

"Nah," Mrs. Elmore replied. "I don't want you coming upstairs."

"All right. Who would like to go first?"

"I'm done with my breakfast, so I'll go first," Darren White said. "Finish up, lads."

The other three nodded and resumed eating, while Darren White followed Sebastian into the tiny parlor. The room was almost completely dark, so Sebastian walked over to the window and drew the curtains, allowing watery morning sunshine to dispel the gloom. The only furniture in the room was a worn brown settee and two tapestried chairs that stood around a faded braided rug. Mrs. Elmore didn't put on airs, like Mrs. Poole, who had a pastoral watercolor hanging above the fireplace and several gimcracks displayed on the mantel, and whose windows were hung with net curtains. Sebastian could see why she thought her establishment superior to Mrs. Elmore's and made sure everyone knew it.

Mrs. Poole hadn't taken on any foreigners since the late Herr Schweiger and said that they were sure to put off "discerning English gentlemen in search of genteel lodgings with a homey touch." She had used that exact phrase when advertising for new lodgers, and the words must have shot Mr. Quince through the heart like Cupid's flaming arrow. Or maybe it had been the price. For all her pretentions, Mrs. Poole had to remain competitive in a street that boasted two other boarding houses, and, in truth, no one who was familiar with London would be fooled by the word "genteel" when mentioned in the same sentence as Clerkenwell.

"How long have you lodged with Mrs. Elmore?" Sebastian asked once the two men were seated, Darren White on the settee and Sebastian in a chair across from him, notepad at the ready.

"Two years now. I moved in after I lost my wife. It's close to King's Cross, and I need someone to look after me."

"And does Mrs. Elmore do that?"

"She can be a bit gruff at times, but she's a decent cook,

keeps a clean house, and minds her own business. Can't abide a gossipy woman."

"Do you know anyone named Helen?"

"Not that I can think of. Why? Is that the name of your dead woman?"

"Where were you Wednesday night and Thursday morning?" Sebastian asked, ignoring the question.

"Right here. I got back just after six, came down for supper at seven, then went up at nine and didn't come down until breakfast. Mrs. Elmore can vouch for me."

Something in Mr. White's tone caught Sebastian's attention, and he fixed the man with a searching look. He had a feeling White had a soft spot for his landlady. Loneliness could make even the plainest woman seem beautiful and kind when she was the only one around.

Filing the information away, Sebastian thanked Mr. White and moved on to Peter Davis. He was something of a blowhard, but beneath the cocky exterior Sebastian saw a young man who was probably all alone in the world and had erected a hard shell around himself to protect the fragile boy within. Sebastian hadn't been so different at his age, when he'd come to London on his own and had yet to forge any meaningful friendships. He'd lived in a dingy room in Whitechapel, the only accommodation he could afford on his wage, and had pretended to be tough when all he'd wanted was to be back at the farm with Simian, where he'd feel safe and cared for.

"How long have you lived at this address?" Sebastian asked.

"Eight months."

"Where were you before?"

"I lived with my parents in Southwark."

"Why did you leave?"

"Needed my own space, and this is close to King's Cross."

"Where were you on Wednesday night, Mr. Davis?" Sebastian asked.

Davis shrugged as if he didn't care one way or the other what Sebastian thought of him. "I came back at seven, went straight in to dinner, then went to my room."

"You never left the boarding house?"

"No."

"What did you do in your room?"

"What's it to you?"

"It's a simple enough question."

"I read a penny dreadful I'd picked up at the terminus."

"You don't care for your fellow lodgers?" Sebastian asked.

Peter Davis seemed surprised by the question but answered honestly enough. "I neither like nor dislike them, Inspector. I'm around people twelve hours a day. I have to be helpful and polite and bite back sarcasm or an angry retort when people are rude and can't even be bothered to say thank you, much less tip me after I've helped them. I look forward to the few hours of solitude I get at the end of the day and enjoy them immensely."

"Do you know anyone named Helen?"

Peter shrugged. "There was a girl named Helen who lived in our street when I was growing up."

"Have you seen her recently?"

"No."

"Are you married, Mr. Davis?"

Peter Davis's eyebrows lifted in astonishment. "Would I be living here if I was?"

"You could be. Men often leave home when they can't earn an honest living, then send money to their families."

"I don't have a family, and I don't have a sweetheart, if that's your next question."

"It was."

"I'm not the marrying kind, Inspector."

"What kind are you?"

"I'm the kind that's content without female company, at

least for now. I'll be late for work if I don't leave now," Peter said, and Sebastian could see that he was genuinely concerned.

Davis's answers rang true, so Sebastian let him go. He wore a Great Northern Railway uniform but, unless his alibi didn't check out, Sebastian had no reason to suspect him. Not yet.

TWENTY-THREE

Seated across from Sebastian, Gordon McTavish looked strong and very fit, his bulk taking up nearly the entire settee that was meant for two people, three if they happened to be slight. McTavish wouldn't need a bodkin to kill a woman. His hand was large enough to close about the throat and crush the victim's windpipe. And he wouldn't have any difficulty killing a man either. Although a trolley would be useful, McTavish wouldn't have any trouble lifting the trunk or carrying it wherever he needed it to go. And the conversation with the Scot proved more interesting than with the previous two lodgers.

"Where are you from, Mr. McTavish?" Sebastian asked, opting for a friendly manner.

"Where do ye think?" McTavish replied sarcastically.

"I think Scotland, but I was hoping for a more precise location."

"Ballachulish."

Sebastian gave his best attempt at spelling the hometown in his notebook. "So, what brought you to London?"

"I fancied living in a cesspool filled with shite." When Sebastian didn't react and the silence had stretched on long enough for McTavish to become irritated, he said, "I needed work, and there was nae longer anything to keep me in Ballachulish. Sometimes ye just want to forget, aye? And the best place to do that is somewhere it's never quiet for tae long."

"Do you have any family?"

"Aye. I have a brother and a sister, both still in Scotland. I also have a son, but he's far away. I dinnae expect I'll ever see him again."

"Where is he?"

"North Carolina. Went with his mother when the conniving bitch left me for a smooth-talking Sassenach and followed him tae America."

"And what's your wife's name?"

"Catriona. My boy's name is Ian, if that helps ye any. And the bawbag she took off with is Joseph Pritchard."

"And your sister's name?"

"Morag. What's my sister got tae do with anything, Inspector?"

"Probably nothing," Sebastian replied. "Mr. McTavish, where were you on Wednesday night and Thursday morning?"

"Got back just after seven, had dinner, then went for a pint with Seamus O'Connor. We got back around midnight. Went to bed, got up at six, had breakfast, and was at work by seven."

"Which pub?"

"The Golden Fiddle," McTavish replied. "The publican is a friendly sort."

Which probably meant he didn't discriminate against patrons who weren't English or followers of the Church of England.

"And the publican will confirm this?"

"Aye," McTavish said with a shrug of his meaty shoulders. "He's got nothing to gain by shielding the likes of us." The Scot scoffed. "I didn't kill anyone, Inspector. If I was up for murder,

I'd have killed the son of a whore who stole away my wife and son."

"Maybe you did," Sebastian replied. "And that's why you're here. What better place to hide than in an English cesspool?"

"I like ye. Ye don't mince words. I reckon ye'd have made a fine Highlander."

"I'm not much for stalking or fishing. Don't have the patience."

McTavish laughed, a rich, vibrant sound. "And that's where ye're wrong, Inspector. No one does more stalking and fishing than a detective, and ye need to have loads of patience if ye mean to corner yer prey. And I think ye do."

Sebastian released McTavish and moved on to Seamus O'Connor, who had moss-green eyes and a mocking smile.

"Where are you from, Mr. O'Connor?"

"A small village outside Belfast. Ye wouldn't know it."

"And what made you come to London?" Sebastian asked.

Seamus O'Connor looked unbearably sad. "I needed a change, and I didn't have the means to get to America. Now, I know living among the English is not the best place to forget yer troubles, but I have a job, a decent place to live, and a few friends. For now, that is enough, so it is."

Sebastian could understand that. It had been enough for him for a long time, and his work and few good friends had sustained him until he felt strong enough to start again.

"Where were you on Wednesday night, Mr. O'Connor?" he asked.

"I came home, enjoyed a bowl of Mrs. Elmore's nearly meatless stew, then went for a pint with Gordon."

"Where did you go?"

"The Golden Fiddle."

"And how long did you stay there?" Sebastian asked.

O'Connor made a show of thinking. "I think Gordon and I left just before midnight."

"And were you together the whole time?"

The Irishman shrugged. "Not the whole time, no."

"How long were you apart?"

O'Connor paused and looked up at the ceiling, as if the answer was hiding in one of the spidery cracks in the plaster. "For about an hour," he said at last.

"Did Mr. McTavish leave the tavern?" Sebastian inquired.

"I really couldn't say since I went upstairs for a spell."

"Why did you go up?"

Seamus O'Connor gave Sebastian a flash of that mocking smile again. "I had to see about a lass."

"Meaning?"

"I've been keeping company with Colleen O'Shea. She's a barmaid over at the Golden Fiddle. She gets off at ten, so I made sure she got to her room safe like. I stayed for an hour, then let the poor lass get some sleep."

"Will Miss O'Shea confirm that?"

"Mrs. O'Shea," Seamus replied. "Her man's still in Ireland."

"I see. So you didn't see Gordon McTavish from about ten until eleven o'clock?"

"That's correct," O'Connor replied with a nod of affirmation.

"And what about yesterday morning?"

"We all had breakfast and went to work."

"Did you and Mr. McTavish walk to King's Cross together?"

"No. Gordon left first. He said he had something he needed to take care of before his shift."

"What about Mr. White and Mr. Davis?"

"They left just before I did. I saw them up ahead but didn't bother to catch them up. We're not all that friendly, if ye know what I mean."

"Do you know anyone named Helen?"

O'Connor paused to consider the question. "No, can't say that I do, Inspector."

"Thank you, Mr. O'Connor."

Once the men had trooped out the door of the boarding house, Sebastian double-checked their accounts with Mrs. Elmore, who confirmed everything they had said. Then he asked, "Has either Mr. O'Connor or Mr. McTavish left London for any length of time in the past year?"

"No. Why?"

"No reason," Sebastian replied as he turned to leave.

"So, which one of them was it that lost someone?" Mrs. Elmore asked. "None of them seem bereaved."

"I don't know," Sebastian admitted. "Does anyone else live here?"

Mrs. Elmore shook her head, and Sebastian realized that Helen might have had a connection to Mrs. Elmore and not one of the lodgers.

"Do you know anyone named Helen?"

Mrs. Elmore paled. "My sister's name is Helena. Why? Is that the name of the woman that died?"

"How old is your sister, Mrs. Elmore?"

"She's forty-nine."

Mrs. Elmore appeared to be bracing herself for bad news, so Sebastian hurried to reassure her. "The victim is around my age, so she can't possibly be your sister."

Mrs. Elmore breathed a sigh of relief. "Thank God for that. Helena is the only family I have left, and I would hate to lose her." The landlady's expression became purposeful. "I'm going to go see her right now. It's been too long since we've had us a nice chinwag."

Mrs. Elmore was already untying her apron and shepherding Sebastian toward the door. He thanked her for her assistance and left, turning his steps towards the Golden Fiddle.

TWENTY-FOUR

The tavern was located in Wharfdale Road, within walking distance of both the boarding house and the railway station, which probably accounted for the majority of the bar's patrons. The door was painted dark green, and the brick arch above bore a discreet sign, a fiddle standing in for the letter I in the name. The bar was still closed, but the publican was awake—his round face appeared in a window just above the sign when Sebastian banged on the door—and he reluctantly came downstairs. He wore a faded brocade dressing gown and leather slippers, and looked as bleary-eyed as one would expect a man who worked late into the night to look. He allowed Sebastian to come inside once he had shown his warrant card, but didn't bother to turn on a light or invite him to sit down.

"Your name?" Sebastian asked when the publican fixed him with an expectant stare.

"Brian Fenton. What's this about, Inspector?"

Sebastian explained the purpose of his visit and asked about Gordon McTavish and Seamus O'Connor, watching the publican's face carefully. Fenton's expression didn't change, which was a fairly good indication that he wasn't about to lie for the two men.

"Look, mate," he said groggily. "Yeah, I saw McTavish and O'Connor on Wednesday night. They're regulars. Do I know what time? No. Can I swear they stayed till last orders? Again, no. Do I think they're capable of murder? We're all capable of murder under the right circumstances, so make of that what you will."

"Seamus O'Connor said that he joined one of your barmaids upstairs from about ten until eleven o'clock. Did you see Gordon McTavish leave or come back while O'Connor was otherwise occupied?"

Mr. Fenton's expression seemed to say, *Didn't I just answer that, you daft sod?* but he took a deep breath and reiterated his earlier answer.

"I can't say for certain where McTavish was at any given time. The tavern was crowded, and after he got his drinks from the bar he disappeared into the crowd. He could have left and come back for all I know. I don't keep tabs on my patrons. As long as they pay for their drinks and behave in a civil manner, I have no reason to single them out." The publican moved toward the door. "Now, if you don't mind, I'd like to go back to bed. Alone, if that was your next question."

"Can I speak to Colleen O'Shea?"

"She's not here."

"Does she not live above the bar?" Sebastian inquired.

"She does, but she also works at the Caledonian Market. That's why she finishes at ten, so that she can get up at six and get going by seven."

"What does she do at the market?" Sebastian asked, genuinely curious.

Fenton sighed with exaggerated patience. "She sells beer. My boy drives her over with half a dozen kegs, and they stay till the beer runs out. That place is a goldmine," he added with a satisfied grin. "Have I answered all your questions now?"

"You have."

Sebastian stepped outside, and Fenton locked the door behind him. It would have been helpful to have a word with Colleen O'Shea, but Sebastian wasn't about to go to the Caledonian Market. It had opened only seven years before and had grown exponentially, overtaking Smithfield within the first few years. The open-air market was vast, and sold everything from cattle to furniture to household goods and coffins. By this time of the morning, it would be heaving with both vendors and buyers, and would already reek of overheated animals, sweating people, shit, and spilled beer. It could take hours to locate Colleen, and Sebastian didn't care to waste time on skirting bull pens and avoiding steaming piles of shit as he traversed acres of stalls. He had to get over to Holywell Street.

Until he was able to identify the victim, he was groping in the dark. To ask people if they knew a woman named Helen was utterly pointless since, even if they admitted to knowing someone by that name, that didn't mean it was the right Helen. The woman might not even be called Helen Owens. Her handwriting was so cramped, it was almost as if she'd had difficulty using her hand, which was odd since the collar in her sewing box had such neat stitches and Sebastian had not noticed anything wrong with her right hand.

And what about the G in the inscription? he thought as he hailed a passing cab and called out his thanks when the driver pulled over instead of proceeding to the nearest stand. Sebastian gave the man Zeke Robinson's address, then climbed in and settled against the worn leather seat, glad to have some time to analyze what he'd learned. If he was to go on the assumption that Helen had been intending to see someone in Albion Street, presumably her husband, then there were Giles Rushton and

Gordon McTavish, whose names started with the letter G, as well as Gerald Quince, whose wife's name started with H, and whose brother lived in Albion Street. Sebastian had seen Giles Rushton on the stairs when he'd come down to dinner on Wednesday, had yet to find out if Gerald Quince had been anywhere near London when Helen had been murdered, and had tracked Gordon McTavish to the Golden Fiddle.

At present, McTavish topped Sebastian's list of suspects. The Scot lived in Albion Street, worked for the Great Northern Railway, and was unaccounted for on the night of the murder. It would take longer than an hour to get to Paddington, kill the woman, and get back, but Brian Fenton couldn't alibi McTavish and Seamus O'Connor might have stayed with Colleen O'Shea longer than he'd thought. Or he could be lying, either to protect himself or his friend, or because he was the sort of man who liked to collect favors and call them in when it suited his needs.

On the whole, Sebastian got the impression that the two men were cannier than they let on and would have each other's backs in a city where they were viewed as foreigners and marginalized because of their Catholic faith. O'Connor and McTavish had answered Sebastian's questions readily enough, but in order to get to the truth he needed to isolate the facts and try to disprove their alibis.

If McTavish had left the Golden Fiddle as soon as O'Connor went up, or before, he could have conceivably got to the Great Western Royal Hotel, murdered the victim, and got back to the tavern before midnight. This gave him the opportunity and means, since he'd used a weapon he'd had to hand, but all this speculation was moot without a plausible motive. If Helen Owens had come from the Midlands or the north, how and where would their paths have crossed? Could the thistle carved into the handle of the bodkin signify a connection to Scotland?

Likewise, if McTavish had been on his way to the hotel to murder Helen, he probably would have brought a weapon and not relied on an implement from her sewing box. It wasn't very likely that the bodkin belonged to McTavish, since it was a tool used primarily by women and not the sort of thing a man who lived in a boarding house would happen to have on him. McTavish would then have had to come back in the morning to move the trunk from the storage room to the terminus, which would mean that he would have had to skip breakfast at Mrs. Elmore's in order to be seen at Paddington before eight. O'Connor had said that McTavish had left early to take care of an errand, but it would take him a long time to get to Paddington and back, and he would have been late for work if he started at seven.

And then there was Bertram Quince, who lived in Albion Street, was in possession of a porter's uniform, and was about to marry a widow who was very comfortably off. Quince would have a compelling motive if the victim was his wife and could destroy his chance of getting his hands on Mrs. Poole's boarding house and whatever other assets her husband had left her when he'd died. Sebastian only had Quince's word that his name was Bertram or that he had a brother who was a conductor with the Great Northern Railway. Quince was already using a pseudonym to publish his penny dreadfuls and could have easily invented a new name for himself to keep his wife from catching up with him.

It wasn't a crime or a confidence trick to use a nom de plume when publishing one's literary work, if Quince's penny dreadfuls could be classified as literature, but Sebastian didn't trust Quince—he hadn't done since the day Quince had moved in—and so he wasn't prepared to take anything he said at face value. It would be impossible to verify Bertram Quince's identity, but it wouldn't be too difficult to check if a Gerald Quince really worked for the Great Northern Railway and stopped at King's Cross on his route. There would be a log. Perhaps even a signature.

An idea suddenly presented itself, and Sebastian was annoyed for not thinking of it sooner. Quince and Owens could plausibly be mistaken for each other when sloppily written, and he already knew that the victim's handwriting had been barely legible. Was it possible that her name had actually been Helen Quince and that Sebastian's neighbor had tried to cleverly divert his attention by inventing a sister-in-law with a similar name? And did he then try to make himself more sympathetic by asking Sebastian to stand up as his best man? Perhaps the person the victim had been coming to see didn't live at Mrs. Elmore's establishment but slept under the same roof as Sebastian.

As the hansom crawled along, slowed by heavy morning traffic, Sebastian sighed with irritation and wondered if it might be faster to walk, then gave up on the idea and returned to his deliberations. Mr. Quince had been at dinner Wednesday night, and Sebastian had seen him at breakfast Thursday morning. As far as Sebastian knew, Mr. Quince and Mrs. Poole did not share a bed, so, once Mrs. Poole had retired, Quince could have easily slipped out. Mrs. Poole kept a spare key hidden behind a brick by the back door, so Quince could have let himself in without anyone knowing he'd gone out. If Sebastian had been in a deep sleep, Quince could have crept past Sebastian's room without him ever knowing. He could have also gone out straight after breakfast, which he took around six o'clock, and made it to Paddington by seven-thirty.

The only impediment would be the hotel, since Mr. Holden had said he locked the doors at ten. Still, it was possible that Quince had got to the hotel before ten o'clock, killed the woman, then brought down the trunk and got out through one of the back doors or through a window. Mr. Holden had admitted that he went to sleep in his office. He wouldn't have noticed if someone was prowling around or looking for a way out.

The next person Sebastian considered was Eugene Danvers. Danvers had joined them for dinner but had gone out to meet a friend for a drink afterwards, something he did several times a week. Danvers had many friends and frequently came home late, availing himself of Mrs. Poole's hidden key. Sebastian remembered that Danvers had eaten a hasty breakfast the following day. He had mentioned that he was in a rush to get to St. George's Hospital, where an operation he was particularly interested in had been open to surgical students. Sebastian knew from their conversations and also from working with Colin that a list of lectures and procedures was posted daily at the Royal College of Surgeons and the men could attend whatever lecture they wished, even if they weren't officially associated with the hospital. The more complicated surgeries usually took place early in the morning, when the surgeon was at his best and had the remainder of the day to monitor the patient after the procedure. Danvers often left early and returned late, since his hours weren't fixed like those of a porter who had to put in a shift.

Giles Rushton, meanwhile, had not joined them for dinner on Wednesday, which wasn't unusual, and had not been at breakfast on Thursday. Eugene Danvers had made a suggestive remark about his friend's whereabouts, joking that he had probably taken up with one of the nurses from the hospital, but Mrs. Poole had said that Rushton had asked for an early breakfast that morning because he had been invited to assist one of the surgeons at St. Thomas's in an operation and was eager to get to the hospital. He had left the house by six o'clock. Mr. Quince had confirmed this, but, if Rushton had lied, he would have had plenty of time to get to Paddington.

Sebastian sighed in frustration. Until Colin carried out the postmortem and was able to narrow down the time of death, all the alibis were virtually useless, and Sebastian couldn't definitively rule anyone out or in. However, even armed with Colin's estimate, the time of death was really just a guess, so Sebastian would still be working almost blind.

TWENTY-FIVE

"You should be in bed," Gemma admonished, but Colin shook his head stubbornly. He was the first one at the breakfast table that morning, a steaming cup of tea before him, his morning kippers no doubt already on the way.

"I feel much better," he insisted. "And Mabel tells me Sebastian has a fascinating new case."

"He does," Gemma replied, and relayed the facts. "I took the liberty of examining the remains," she added after a slight pause.

"Examining?" Colin's eyebrows rose halfway up his high forehead, making him look rather comical but also quite put out.

"I only looked the victim over," Gemma hurried to pacify him. "I didn't even undress her." *All the way*, she added inwardly. "The cause of death is obvious."

"Oh, is it?" Colin snapped.

His expression was painfully familiar. Gemma had seen its like many times, worn by doctors at Scutari after a lowly nurse had dared to express an opinion or question a doctor's orders.

Colin's sulky silence stretched on, so Gemma added, "I'm sure there's much to be learned from the postmortem."

"Indeed."

Gemma didn't think she should go into the other conclusions she had drawn from her examination, even though she'd slipped the notes into her pocket before coming down to breakfast in case Sebastian stopped by. Colin would see the body soon enough and make his own determination. She thought the conversation was at an end, but, judging by Colin's agonized expression, he had more to say and was probably trying to work out how to phrase his reproof in a way that would get his point across in a manner that was both effective and diplomatic.

"Gemma," Colin began, his gaze not quite meeting hers. "I respect your skill as a nurse and acknowledge your practical experience, but, to be frank, I take issue with you utilizing said experience to undermine me."

"Colin, I—" Gemma tried to interject, but Colin held up his hand.

"Please allow me to finish."

Gemma bit back what she was going to say and nodded. "Sorry," she muttered contritely.

"I do not object to you being present while I examine a body or perform a postmortem. In fact, I welcome your input, since you sometimes pick up on *minor* points I might otherwise overlook, but in future I would appreciate it if you didn't take it upon yourself to do a job you're neither qualified nor paid to do."

Gemma was stung by Colin's rebuke, but she could understand his irritation and knew she had to apologize. If she didn't, she could lose her job, her home, and Colin's friendship, which meant a great deal to her.

"I'm sorry. You're right. I shouldn't have examined the victim without asking for permission or waiting until you were available to supervise." Each word lacerated her throat like a burr as it left her mouth.

"Apology accepted," Colin replied magnanimously.

There seemed nothing more to say and they grew quiet, looking anywhere but at each other, the tension so thick one could cut it with the proverbial knife. Colin reached for his newspaper, while Gemma's gaze drifted toward the window, where a pigeon sat perched on top of a chimney pot of the house across the street. The stalemate was interrupted by Mabel, who brought Colin's kippers and fried eggs and Gemma's toast and soft-boiled egg.

"Thank you, Mabel," they said in unison.

Colin silently applied himself to his breakfast, while Gemma buttered her toast and sliced off the top of her egg. Her employer's nose was clearly still out of joint, but, although she had acknowledged that she had overstepped her authority, she wasn't sorry, not really. She was a trained nurse and had spotted several things she had thought were worth mentioning to Sebastian. She also didn't think that Colin was in any condition to conduct a postmortem, which took hours and required a considerable output of energy. She was still debating whether to say as much when the sound of knocking reverberated through the house.

"That will be Sebastian," Colin said. "He'll be anxious to hear the results of the postmortem."

Even as he said it, Gemma thought Colin realized the impossibility of completing the postmortem without help when he was only just recovering from a lingering illness. She was about to offer assistance when Mabel appeared once again.

"Mr. Danvers to see you, Mr. Ramsey," she announced.

"Danvers? What's he doing here?" Colin grumbled, then smiled ruefully. "It would appear I forgot to notify him that our session was canceled."

Colin pushed away his plate, gulped down the remainder of his tea, and followed Mabel into the foyer. Gemma remained where she was, nibbling on a slice of toast. She couldn't help but overhear the exchange between the two men as they walked toward the cellar door.

"I'm actually glad you're here, Danvers," Colin was saying. "I received a fresh corpse yesterday—a murder victim—and you can conduct the preliminary examination. And if I'm happy with what I see, I will let you take the lead on the postmortem. It will be excellent practice for you."

"On my own?" Mr. Danvers asked, clearly astonished by his unexpected progression from mere trainee to practicing pathologist.

"Why not? How does that sound?"

"It sounds like an incredible opportunity. Thank you, Mr. Ramsey. You won't regret this. I feel I'm more than ready."

"Yes, I believe you are. And even if you aren't, I will be there to guide you."

Gemma was glad Mr. Danvers was there to help. He was a pleasant and well-mannered young man and would defer to Colin, which would make Colin feel better about not being able to work on the victim himself. And it would be invaluable practice for the young surgeon. It was silly, really, that students were not permitted to learn by doing. To watch a trained surgeon perform an operation or a postmortem from their seats in the operating theater might be educational in a theoretical sort of way, but it was no substitute for practical experience. A training surgeon needed to hold a scalpel in his hand, feel the skin part as the blade sliced into the body, and apply the sheer physical strength needed to cut through the layers of fat and muscle until he reached the organs within.

But that first step wasn't enough to prepare the surgeon for the rush of blood that coated the hands and pooled inside the cavity if the patient was still living, or for the glistening slipperiness of the organs and bowels. As the surgeon removed the organs and plopped them into enamel bowls to be examined in due course, he was no different from a butcher who carved up a carcass and set aside the viscera to be cleaned and sold separately for use as sausage casings and pie filling. It took time and practice to attain a state of detachment and learn to focus on the work rather than the person in order to spot the defects that might otherwise get overlooked.

As she ate her breakfast in solitude, Gemma realized that she was still hurt by Colin's reaction to her admission, but there was no point in holding a grudge. Colin was more respectful of women than most men and had expressed his gratitude for Gemma's assistance on several occasions. Nurses so seldom got credit for their contribution, even in Crimea, where they had been expected to do considerably more than the dandified surgical students in London, whose hands were stained with ink rather than bodily fluids after watching an operation.

Gemma wasn't going to bring it up to Colin, but she knew more about the workings of the human body than someone like Eugene Danvers, whose knowledge came mostly from medical texts. She had assisted during operations that had not been scheduled in advance and executed in a measured, meticulous manner. The surgeries that had been performed at Scutari had been quick and brutal, and more often than not a last resort that ended either in death or fragile hope that often petered out like a tiny flame within a few hours of the procedure.

She could still recall the tile floor that had been slippery with blood and the awful smell of the operating theater as one patient after another was wheeled in and out, the surgeons moving like marionettes for hours on end without so much as a drink of water or a morsel of food. The corridors had been nearly impassable, blocked by bodies that either rested on gurneys or had been left on the floor, since there weren't enough cots to accommodate the incoming wounded. By the time the surgeons finished for the day, the operating room had resembled an abattoir, and both doctors and nurses had been numb with shock and fatigue and craved only the oblivion of sleep.

But Colin couldn't conceive of what Gemma had lived through, since his own experiences were limited to the dissections he had undertaken at his medical school in Edinburgh and the surgeries he had observed and performed at the hospitals in London. Frustrated as Gemma was by Colin's decree, she wasn't prepared to give up. There had to be another way to learn more about the woman in the cellar, and perhaps she might discover something important that would help to move the investigation forward.

TWENTY-SIX

Once she had finished breakfast, Gemma made her way upstairs to check on Anne, who was sitting up in bed, her hair wound into a thin, graying braid and her frilly nightdress covering every inch of flesh below the chin. Over the past few weeks, Anne's mental decline had grown more pronounced, and tasks that she had previously been able to complete unassisted had become more confusing and difficult to perform. As a friend, Gemma wanted to believe that Anne would get better and regain partial cognizance, but as a nurse she understood that Anne's illness was like a well-trained enemy that would proceed unchallenged and conquer her mind until she was left with the sensibilities and independence of an infant. But despite her advancing disability, Anne experienced moments of clarity that came at the oddest of times and lasted from mere seconds to several minutes, offering Gemma a glimpse into the woman Anne had been. This morning, she appeared to be experiencing one of these moments, and her gaze was clear and bright.

"I would like to go out today," she said, giving Gemma a

bullish look that usually meant she wouldn't be easily dissuaded.

"You're still unwell, Mrs. Ramsey. I think you need to remain indoors for one more day at the very least," Gemma replied patiently.

"No, I want to go outside. I don't expect I will see another May, Gemma dear, and I want to enjoy every moment of my last spring."

Gemma decided not to argue, even though she strongly opposed the idea of taking Anne outside so soon. At this stage, perhaps it was more important that Anne enjoy the time she had left rather than prolong that time by forcing her to stay in bed and making her unhappy. A short walk wouldn't do too much harm if Anne was properly dressed, and the sun was shining rather invitingly. It would also be advisable to break up the walk, in case Anne grew tired, and Gemma knew just the way to accomplish that.

"Would you like to call on Poppy, Mrs. Ramsey?" she asked.

"Poppy?" Anne asked, her gaze speculative as she tried to recall who Poppy was. Then her face brightened. "I can visit Rabbit."

Poppy Bright lived in a boarding house a few streets away and was usually at home in the mornings, since she worked the afternoon shift at an infirmary in Lambeth. Gemma and Poppy had known each other in Scutari and had recently reconnected, thanks to a case Sebastian had been investigating. The women saw each other every week, and Gemma was glad to have a female friend she could confide in and spend time with on her days off, since Sebastian wasn't always available and couldn't devote the entire day to her when he was. Gemma usually saw him in the afternoons, so she was free to visit with Poppy in the mornings.

Rabbit was the name Anne had given the little ceramic dog that was displayed on the mantel in the parlor of Poppy's boarding house. It was black and white, had a chipped nose, and reminded Anne of a dog she'd had when she was a girl. She cradled the dog lovingly whenever they visited Poppy, and whispered to it as she must have when she was a girl and had told her puppy her most precious secrets. Anne's older brother had used to call the dog Ratbag, which clearly still rankled, as Anne mentioned that fact every time she saw Rabbit.

"Yes, you can visit Rabbit, and I can have a nice chat with Poppy," Gemma said brightly.

"Can we get cake on the way home?" Anne asked eagerly. "I like the sponge with raspberry filling."

Gemma could never figure out why Anne remembered some things and not others, but perhaps her mind chose to focus on happy moments, and she clearly associated puppies and cakes with joyful childhood occasions.

"Of course," Gemma replied. "We can stop at the bakery and get some cake."

"Then I will come with you to visit Poppy."

Anne swung her legs out of bed, stood, and spread her arms, giving Gemma leave to help her dress. It took nearly an hour to get her ready, by which time Gemma was perspiring and would have liked to freshen up, but there was no time to waste, since Poppy would have to leave for her shift at the infirmary if they didn't hurry.

The walk took twice as long as it normally did, but when they finally arrived Poppy was overjoyed to see them and offered to make tea, while Anne settled by the hearth with Rabbit in her lap.

Once everyone was supplied with a cup of tea, Gemma finally got the chance to tell Poppy about the case.

"Does Inspector Bell have any leads?" Poppy asked.

Gemma sighed. "I don't know. I didn't see him today. I have an idea I'd like to follow up on, but I can't act on it until Mrs. Ramsey agrees to have a rest."

"What are you thinking?" Poppy asked, leaning forward, her dark eyes sparkling with curiosity.

"I was thinking that if the victim's body was left at Paddington in what could very well be her own traveling trunk, then perhaps she had recently arrived at Paddington. Sebastian questioned the staff, but, if Mr. Robinson could furnish me with a photograph of the victim, I could go to the terminus and show it to the porters and the ticket agents. Someone might recognize her."

Poppy nodded vigorously. "They might have helped her with her luggage."

"There's another possibility to consider," Gemma mused. "The victim might not have been alone. Perhaps she arrived in London with a companion, or someone might have been meeting her at the station."

"Even if a porter had seen her with a traveling companion, finding them based on a vague description would be like looking for a needle in a haystack."

"That's true, but it might tell us something equally important."

"Such as?" Poppy asked.

"If she traveled to London with a companion or if someone was meant to be meeting her, where are they now? Why have they not reported her missing? Are they the killer, or do they know who the killer is and had intentionally led the victim into a trap? Have they gone, or are they still in London, waiting to see what will happen? And might they come forward if they see a photograph of the victim, or will they keep to the shadows to ensure they aren't connected to the murder?"

"And you think you can find all this out just by speaking to a few porters?" Poppy asked, her doubt reflected in her eyes.

"No," Gemma admitted, "but it's a start. One thing I have learned from previous cases is that one clue leads to another.

Solving a mystery is much like unraveling a piece of knitting, albeit very slowly. One must find a loose thread and pull."

"I doubt your inspector will see it that way, and your day off is not until Sunday."

Gemma shook her head. "I mean to go today."

Poppy fixed Gemma with a grave look. "You must be careful, Gemma. You don't realize how fortunate you are to have such a good position. I make less, and I work six nights a week caring for dozens of patients."

"Have you heard about the nursing school Miss Nightingale is opening up?" Gemma asked. "Perhaps you should inquire about a position. I'm sure Miss Nightingale would welcome your expertise, and she knows you to be hard-working and reliable."

Poppy shook her head. "I don't care to teach, nor do I want to revisit our time in Crimea again and again. I have no regrets, and I made some good friends, but it's time to move forward. Would you consider applying if you were looking for a job?"

"Yes, I think I would, but only as a last resort."

Gemma fervently hoped she wouldn't have to look for another position once she left Colin's employ, but didn't want to presume that she'd have a future with Sebastian, not until things were settled between them and it was an absolute certainty.

"I would prefer to look after one person," Poppy said. "I know your patient can be difficult at times"—she cast a sidelong look at Anne, who was utterly preoccupied with the ceramic puppy—"but you have a comfortable home and an understanding employer who pays you a decent wage. That's as good as it gets for an unmarried, live-in nurse."

"Yes, I know," Gemma agreed, "and I hate to take advantage of Colin's good nature, but lately I find that it's simply not enough to be earning a living. I long for a sense of purpose, Poppy, and I need to see justice done. If this case is not solved, the killer will go free and will probably congratulate themselves on their cleverness while their victim rots in an unmarked grave."

"Perhaps you should leave the investigating to the police."

"There's no harm in asking a few questions. People respond differently to a woman than they do to a man. They tend to be more helpful."

Poppy sighed. "If you like, I can take Mrs. Ramsey home on my way to work and ask Mabel to help her to bed. That will give you a few hours, and I might get the chance to say hello to Colin."

She colored slightly, the telltale blush instantly revealing the depth of her feelings.

"Perhaps you can convince Colin to get some rest," Gemma suggested. "He's still unwell and could use the ministrations of an experienced nurse."

"Do you think so?" Poppy asked eagerly.

"Absolutely. I think he will be much more likely to listen to you."

"It's settled, then," Poppy said. "And how should I explain your absence?"

Gemma hated to lie, but Colin had made it plain that he disapproved of her sleuthing and thought she should leave murder inquiries to the professionals. He and Poppy were clearly in agreement on that score, and, given their quarrel at breakfast, Gemma knew she should tread carefully and not provoke Colin further.

"Tell him that I needed to collect a remedy Mary ordered for me."

Mary was Poppy's older sister, and she and her husband owned Harbor's Drugs, a chemist shop in Covent Garden.

Poppy raised a skeptical brow, then shrugged. "He is not likely to believe me, but all right. What is it that Mary has supposedly ordered?"

"I'm very fond of Constance's Creations," Gemma said. She

held up her reddened hands. "The hand cream does wonders for dry, chapped skin."

"Yes, I swear by it myself," Poppy replied. "Hold on." She left the parlor and returned a few moments later with a jar of hand cream. "Here, in case Colin requires proof."

"Thank you." Gemma stowed the jar in her reticule. The jar made it bulge unattractively, but she could hardly stuff it in her pocket or carry it in her hands. "I promised Anne a slice of sponge with raspberry filling."

"If she hasn't forgotten about it, we'll stop at the bakery on the way back," Poppy promised.

Gemma pulled out her coin purse and took out a sixpence, which she handed to Poppy. Poppy tried to wave the money away, but Gemma insisted she accept it. A slice of cake cost two pence, and she had to pay Poppy for the hand cream. Then she turned to Anne, to explain that Poppy would be taking her back, but Anne had fallen asleep, the puppy still clutched in her hands and her tea left untouched.

"Promise me you won't take any unnecessary risks," Poppy said as Gemma put on her bonnet and tied the ribbons before reaching for her cape.

"Do I ever?" Gemma replied, all innocence.

Poppy's skeptical expression said it all.

TWENTY-SEVEN

The businesses in Holywell Street had only just opened, but the shopkeepers were already doing a brisk trade. Passersby were perusing wares displayed on tables set up outside, and well-dressed gentlemen stealthily nipped into shop doorways as they searched for the most explicit images of nubile models. When Sebastian walked in, Mr. Robinson nodded in greeting and disappeared into the back room to fetch the photograph of the victim. When he returned, he handed Sebastian an envelope and invited him to have a look. The subject looked surprisingly lifelike, her gaze fixed on some point in the distance and a shawl draped over her shoulders to hide the blood soaked into the bodice of her gown. Gemma must have fixed her hair, and Mr. Robinson had cleverly applied rouge to render the skin less pale.

"I hope you're pleased with the result," the photographer said, clearly fishing for a compliment.

"Very. Thank you."

Mr. Robinson nodded. "Miss Tate was a great help. She is an excellent assistant."

"Yes, she is." *To me*, Sebastian added inwardly, and felt ashamed when he realized how proprietorial he sounded.

"I do hope you give me credit if the photograph is printed in the newspaper, Inspector. I can use the endorsement."

"I'll see what I can do." Sebastian took his leave and strode toward Half Moon Passage, which would lead him directly to the Strand.

He hadn't visited the offices of the *Daily Telegraph* since last December, when he had investigated the murder of Jacob Harrow, but he was sure the editor-in-chief would have no trouble remembering him. Marshall Lawrence was around seventy, but his mind was still as sharp as a tack, and his barbs just as likely to prick. The man was intelligent, ruthless, and entirely business minded, so to appeal to his humanity was a pointless endeavor. The only way Lawrence would assist the police was if there was something in it for him.

"Inspector Bell," Mr. Leslie, the clerk Sebastian had met on his previous visit, exclaimed with surprise as soon as Sebastian walked in. "What brings you to us this time?"

The large, desk-filled room was hazy with cheroot smoke, and several journalists abandoned all pretense of working and openly watched Sebastian, probably wondering if they should try to waylay him in case he was there to tell a sensational story.

"I would like to see Mr. Lawrence," Sebastian said. "He'll want to hear what I have to say."

"Wait here," Mr. Leslie said tetchily.

He strode toward the editor's office and returned a few moments later, smiling as if he had just performed a minor miracle. "Mr. Lawrence will see you, Inspector, but keep it brief. Time is money," he said with a self-satisfied smirk.

The expression smacked of the insolence that was often associated with Americans, who were made out to be hopeless mercenaries while the less-than-noble pursuits of their English counterparts were cloaked in rhetoric of duty and honor.

"Inspector Bell," Marshall Lawrence drawled when Sebastian walked in.

He looked exactly as he had the last time they'd met. The laurel of sparse white hair was neatly trimmed, his rheumy blue gaze was as piercing as ever, and a gold-framed monocle dangled from a chain suspended around the editor's neck.

"Good morning, Mr. Lawrence," Sebastian said with all the deference he could muster.

"Shut the door, Leslie. What can I do for you, Inspector?" Lawrence asked as soon as the door closed behind the departing clerk.

Sebastian removed his hat, took the proffered seat, and set the hat on his thigh, while the editor leaned back in his chair and surveyed Sebastian with a marked lack of interest. Sebastian took the photograph of the dead woman out of the envelope, laid it on the desk, and slid it toward the editor.

"Your bride, Inspector?" Lawrence sniggered.

Sebastian ignored the jibe. "This woman was found in a trunk at Paddington. She was stabbed through the heart with a bodkin."

"How dramatic. So, what would you have me do? I can only assume you're here to beg a favor."

"We don't know who she is, and no one has come forward to report her missing. I would like to issue an appeal to the public, asking for information."

"What else do you know?"

"Is it not enough that she was murdered and stuffed into a trunk?"

"If I print a portrait of everyone who met with a sad end, my paper will be reduced to a catalogue of post-mortem photography. And as much as the average reader enjoys macabre murders and salacious gossip, they rely on the *Daily Telegraph* to counterbalance the scandalmongering and not fall headlong into the cesspool of filth and scandal that the other publications usually fish in."

Lawrence's gaze slid toward the door. "Unless you have something attention-grabbing to offer, I will wish you good day, Inspector."

Sebastian returned the photograph to its envelope and left without bothering to say goodbye, walking past the desks of the reporters, who no longer seemed interested.

The *Illustrated London News* was the next logical choice. There were several other newspapers he could approach, such as *Lloyd's* and *Reynold's Weekly*, but they couldn't rival the circulation of the *News*, which was in the hundreds of thousands. Problem was, that this week's edition was already typeset, and the next edition wouldn't hit the streets until the following Saturday. Much could happen before then, but Sebastian had little choice. He would deliver the photograph to the editor of the *News*, but, since the offices of the newspaper were near Fleet Street, in Crane Court, it would make sense to stop by the Yard first so he wouldn't have to traipse back afterwards. He needed a word with Ransome.

TWENTY-EIGHT

Gemma had never been to Holywell Street and was surprised to discover that it didn't look any different from other shop-lined London streets, at least from the outside. Risqué merchandise wasn't openly displayed in the bow windows, and disreputable transactions were conducted much like regular purchases, with nothing untoward to catch the eye of passersby as goods and money changed hands. She was surprised to see several ladies stroll past, most of them accompanied by gentlemen who led them into the shops. Gemma had never seen the sort of photograph that was said to be sold in Holywell Street, nor did she care to, but she was curious about whether the ladies were aware of the clandestine nature of the street's trade or simply followed their husbands into what they thought were respectable bookshops.

Gemma glanced at the crescent moon sign that was mounted above a dank passage and hurried past. The moon's disdainful glare seemed to be judging her, and she felt a twinge of guilt, not for strolling down the infamous street but for deserting her post and relying on Poppy to get Anne home. She wasn't so deluded that she didn't realize she was in the wrong, and she would freely admit that Colin had every right to be angry. He'd recently accused her of becoming addicted to danger, but he had been way off the mark.

Gemma didn't crave danger. She wasn't that foolish, especially not after her run-in with an unrepentant killer who'd nearly gutted her the last time she'd become involved in one of Sebastian's investigations. She understood the ramifications of her decisions and accepted the consequences of her actions. But come what may, she could no longer spend her days looking after the needs of a demanding patient without feeling like life was passing her by. Emotionally and intellectually, she needed more—a sense of accomplishment and the knowledge that she was putting her talents to good use. Perhaps that sounded vainglorious and unladylike, but she had tasted the forbidden fruit of validation and triumph and could never unknow how wonderful it felt to make a contribution that resulted in justice, not only for the victim but also the people who loved them. She would explain her reasons to Colin and offer to make it up to him and Anne, but, since she'd already taken the time, she intended to put it to good use.

Having finally found Mr. Robinson's shop, Gemma pushed the door open and walked in. It took her a moment to collect herself in the face of so much recorded death, but she tore her gaze from the walls and smiled at Mr. Robinson when he approached her, his surprise evident.

"I didn't expect to see you again so soon, Miss Tate," he said with an answering smile. "If you are looking for Inspector Bell, he's come and gone. Or have you come on a more personal errand?"

"Have you developed the photographs of the victim? I need one," Gemma said without preamble.

Mr. Robinson seemed confused by her request, and when he replied his tone was impatient. "I just told you, I gave the photograph to Inspector Bell. I can only print one image from each plate."

"But you took two photographs," Gemma said.

"The first image was too dark, and Inspector Bell had specified that the photograph was intended for a newspaper appeal. It would be impossible to make out the woman's features once the image was reproduced during the printing process."

"I won't be reproducing the photograph," Gemma replied.

"Then what do you need it for?"

"For the purposes of identification."

Mr. Robinson regarded her with suspicion. "No doubt your intentions are noble, Miss Tate, but I tend to feel protective of my subjects, particularly when there's no one left to speak on their behalf. To show the image around would be a violation of the victim's privacy."

Gemma bristled. "You had no problem taking a photograph for the purposes of mass reproduction. Surely that's a greater violation than showing the likeness to a few people who might have seen the woman shortly before she was murdered."

Realizing he had blundered, Mr. Robinson slid off his high horse and tried a different tack. "Inspector Bell paid for only one photograph."

"I will pay you," Gemma snapped.

The man would discard the plate anyway—Gemma didn't think there was a way to reuse it—but she was happy to compensate him for his time if he needed to develop the image and for the paper he would use to print it.

"You're a determined young lady," Mr. Robinson said. "And a foolhardy one. Poking around in other people's affairs is a dangerous business and should be left to men."

"Will you sell me the photograph or not?" Gemma's patience and the time she could devote to this errand were quickly running out.

"Two shillings."

Gemma handed over the coins and snapped her bulging reticule shut as Mr. Robinson slid the coins into his pocket. He walked away without another word and disappeared through a door in the back wall. Gemma didn't want to look at the pictures on the walls while she waited, but her gaze strayed to the images of its own accord, a sob catching in her throat as she glimpsed a fair-haired little girl whose coffin was held upright by her parents. Their grief was etched into their faces, and their loss echoed in Gemma's heart and settled heavily in her chest. She longed for a child of her own, but was she prepared for the risks involved?

A spinster could never lose a child or mourn a husband. An unmarried woman lived in a cocoon of emotional detachment, concerned only with her own trials and immediate needs. It was a barren existence, but in some ways also a safe one. To marry and have children was to open oneself up to the risk of loss and untold suffering—but also to immeasurable joy, Gemma reminded herself as she turned her back on the image. She was terrified of losing more people she loved, but she was more afraid to live a life of spiritual solitude, missing out on life's greatest gifts and the depths of feeling only having a family could guarantee.

Mr. Robinson returned a few moments later, the photograph in his hand. He must have printed it already, and Gemma could see why it wouldn't work when reproduced. The image was too dim, and someone would have to look very closely indeed to make out the woman's features, but Gemma thought it would serve her purpose nonetheless. Mr. Robinson held out the photograph, and she accepted it with thanks.

"Best of luck with your endeavors, Miss Tate," Mr. Robinson said. He seemed pleased to have sold an otherwise useless photograph and eager for Gemma to leave, which she did as soon as she stowed the photograph in her reticule.

Paddington Station was miles away from Holywell Street,

and it would take time to reach the terminus, especially at midafternoon. It would be quicker and easier to find a hansom in the Strand, since Holywell Street was too narrow to allow for extensive commercial traffic; Gemma hadn't seen a single cab the entire time she had been there. She strode toward the off-putting moon sign and hurried through the dark, smelly passage beneath, grateful to emerge on the other side without getting accosted by some ruffian who might think it a good place to harass a woman on her own.

When she finally found the cab stand and settled in for the ride in the creaking vehicle that had been first in line, progress was excruciatingly slow. The streets were congested with dray wagons, private carriages, and an omnibus that lumbered down the street and pulled over at every stop. Traffic was further slowed by tiny, bedraggled crossing sweeps, who darted into the road, their bare ankles flashing and their birch brooms at the ready as soon as a horse did its business in the street and a pile of muck needed to be cleared away. They had no fear of getting trampled if an oncoming conveyance failed to stop, since the alternative was more frightening. If they didn't sweep, they didn't eat, which rendered the risk acceptable—a sad fact of modern life, in which orphaned children had to live on the streets and risk their lives for a crust of bread since no one cared if they lived or died.

Gemma averted her gaze when the cab crawled past the offices of the *Daily Telegraph*. The building and the omnibus stop that was just down the road would forever remind her of Victor and his horrific death. It had been one of the worst days of Gemma's life, and, even though Victor's killer no longer drew breath, she didn't feel either vindicated or less bereaved. Her official period of mourning was coming to an end, but no amount of time would heal the wound that had been inflicted that day. She thought of her twin every day and frequently held conversations with him in her head. That was the thing about knowing someone so well—one instinctively knew how they would respond, as if one were psychic and could summon the person's spirit.

In fact, Gemma had a fairly good idea what Victor would say to her now. He would implore her to call out to the driver and ask him to turn the cab around and return to Blackfriars, not only because she bore a responsibility to Colin and Anne, but because he would want to keep her safe. Victor would beg her to leave the investigation to the professionals and focus on work that was appropriate for an unmarried woman. And if she had known Victor, who had been surprisingly practical despite his idealistic nature, he would also tell her to make herself indispensable to Colin and build a life with a man who was kind, noble, and safe.

But Victor had never met Sebastian, Gemma thought with an inward chuckle, so any comment that sprang to mind would be one of her own inventing. If Victor had met him, Gemma was sure he would admire and respect Sebastian as a friend, but would probably warn her to keep her distance and consider her future and reputation. And he would be doing the right thing as her brother and her guardian. She would expect nothing less.

Victor had been shocked to the core when Gemma had announced that she would be going out to Crimea. He had tried to reason with her, frighten her, threaten her, and guilt her into giving up on her foolishness, but in the end Gemma had accompanied Florence Nightingale and the other brave women who'd answered her call, and Victor had accepted her decision because he'd loved her and would have never allowed a disagreement to come between them. He had even joined Gemma in Crimea in his capacity as a reporter, and they had met whenever they could in a place that was unpredictable and hostile and reminded them every day how lucky they were to be alive and have each other.

I would learn to love Sebastian if he made you happy, Gem,

Victor said in her head, his beloved voice nearly bringing Gemma to tears. *I would only ask that he keep you safe. Will he do that?*

"He will," Gemma said, and realized that she'd spoken out loud. *He will keep me safe, Victor*, she repeated silently. *He loves me.*

You shouldn't have to prove your worth to him, Victor argued.

Gemma wanted to rail at the voice inside her head, but she wasn't oblivious enough to believe that all she cared about was justice. She supposed if she were completely honest, she also hoped to show Sebastian that she could be his partner in all the ways that mattered. She wanted him to view her as a helpmeet, not just some helpless woman who needed to be guided and protected from the world around her. Sebastian had reason to worry and would never completely recover from the tragedy that had shaped the past few years of his life, but she wasn't Louisa. Gemma had been to war, had seen death in all its grim forms, and understood all too well what human beings were capable of. She had also come to understand that there could come a day when she might have to protect herself, and it was time she learned how to use the gun Sebastian had given her. When she had held it in her hand, she had felt like a vigilante and could almost imagine that she was an agent with the Pinkerton Detective Agency that Sebastian had told her so much about.

Gemma didn't think Sebastian was still thinking of leaving, but she couldn't help but worry that his long-standing plan to go to America held the sort of appeal only a cherished fantasy had the power to do. America was the Promised Land, a clean slate, and Gemma could understand Sebastian's reasons and easily imagine him in a place where he wouldn't be bound by convention or have to report to some puffed-up bureaucrat when he could be his own man and defer to his own judgment without fear of repercussions or instant dismissal. She was certain the only reason Sebastian had chosen to remain in England was because he didn't want to leave her, and she was desperate to show him that she was worthy of the sacrifice, even though he had never asked her for anything other than her regard.

Gemma felt a thrum of excitement when the cab glided past the entrance to the Great Western Royal Hotel and turned the corner, where it joined the line of cabs waiting to enter the terminus. When she reached into her reticule to get the fare for the cab, she ran her fingers over the folded photograph. This was her investigation now, and she intended to do everything in her power to move it along.

TWENTY-NINE

The terminus was heaving, and, when Gemma alighted at the cab stand between Platforms 5 and 6, she needed a moment to get her bearings. It had been a long time since she had been inside a train station, and the acrid smells of burning coal, machine oil, and hissing steam took her back to the day she had taken the train to Portsmouth, where she'd boarded a ship bound for Crimea. She had been excited and terrified and had wondered if she had made a dreadful mistake when the ship had begun to move, the distance between the frightened nurses and the shore growing wider by the minute.

"Lady, get out of the way," a gruff voice shouted, and a man who had climbed out from a cab that had pulled up next to her pushed past her, his shoulder nearly knocking her off balance.

Her reverie interrupted, Gemma moved away from the cab stand and headed toward the crossing that led to the other platforms. It offered a good view of the terminus, and she took it all in, a little overwhelmed by the hustle and bustle of the station. Two trains were currently boarding, one at Platform 1 and the other at Platform 3. Porters hurried along, their trolleys heaped with luggage, as they followed the departing passengers and helped them load their cases onto the train.

On Platform 2, a woman of middle years wearing a fox stole and a thick rope of pearls around her neck was berating a young porter. The poor man looked like he was about to weep. Looking closer, Gemma realized he had dropped the lady's portmanteau and must have scratched it against the wheels of the handcart. The porter's face was flushed with embarrassment and he apologized profusely, all the while staring into the lifeless face of the fox that rested on the woman's heaving bosom and appeared to be glaring at him.

Gemma thought she would start at the booking office and made her way toward the front of the terminus, where two newsboys were quickly going through the dwindling stacks of the morning editions of their papers, and a lad of about ten was calling out to passersby to check out the most recent publication of *Murder at the Apollo*. It was the same edition as the one Gemma had found in the victim's pocket.

Several vendors were positioned by the entrances, selling everything from penny pies to sweetmeats. The porters made a halfhearted attempt to get them to leave, but Gemma supposed they could understand the need to make a living, and who better to pitch their wares to than hungry, thirsty people, who had either just arrived or had some time to kill before their train was ready to depart and were eager for something to eat or read? There was a palpable sense of anticipation and excitement that identified the departing passengers, and Gemma couldn't help but think how exciting it would be to go on a trip.

She would settle for a few days at the seaside—time to read, walk on the beach, and dream as she looked out to sea. Of course, Sebastian immediately intruded on her fantasy, and she pushed it aside lest she get distracted from her purpose and stand there mooning over the possibility of spending time together, completely free from the demands of new cases and

Gemma's daily duties. Her face grew warm as she imagined the intimacy they would enjoy if they were married and truly alone together for the first time, and she dragged her mind back to the task at hand, refusing to get carried away on a wave of longing.

Once she spotted the sign for the booking office, Gemma hurried her step, eager to get started. She thought that perhaps the victim had stopped in to reserve a return ticket. That would be quite fortuitous, since the clerk would likely know her name and maybe even her home address, or at the very least the return destination. Gemma waited in line for what felt like an eternity, only to be told that no one who resembled the woman in the photograph had come by in the past week. Gemma asked if there might be another booking agent, but the clerk assured her that he was the only one and he would have remembered.

Leaving the booking office, Gemma traversed one platform after another, asking anyone in uniform if they had seen the woman, but made sure to avoid Barnaby Lang, the boy who had delivered the body to Colin's cellar, in case he decided to inform the station manager that she was questioning the staff. The porters shook their heads, smiled apologetically, and hurried away, too busy to take the time to speak to her properly. No one bothered to ask why Gemma was inquiring after the woman, so she decided not to explain. There was little point if no one recognized her. And why would they? There was a constant stream of passengers, so, unless the victim had drawn their attention in some way, the porters were hardly likely to pick her out from a sea of female faces whose features were obscured by bonnets and framed by ribbons and curls.

Gemma had quite despaired of finding anyone who recognized the victim until she asked an older gentleman in a porter's uniform, who had been strolling along Platform 4 and had inquired if she needed assistance. He peered at the photograph for an inordinate length of time, his graying eyebrows furrowing beneath the visor of his cap as he examined the image, and

Gemma appraised him for lack of anything else to do while she waited. The porter had a florid face, bracketed by graying mutton-chops that were bridged by a thick moustache that obscured his upper lip. His belly strained against the buttons of his navy waistcoat, and his cleanly shaven chin looked very pink against the white of his shirt collar.

"Yes," he said, drawing out the word. "I do remember her." He nodded in affirmation. "She arrived on Monday, on the 1:47 from Oxford. She had mentioned that she'd traveled from Birmingham."

He went quiet, so Gemma tried again. "What do you recall about her?"

The man removed his cap, scratched his balding head, then put the cap back on, drawing Gemma's attention to the letters stitched into the patterned band that encircled the cap. *GWR*.

"The lady was flustered," the porter said. "Someone was meant to meet her, but they didn't show. She just stood there, looking frantically about her. I approached and asked if I might be of service, and she said she had nowhere to go and asked if I could recommend affordable accommodation. I directed her to the Great Western." He gestured toward the hotel entrance. "I assured her that they had reasonably priced rooms for single travelers, but she was worried that as a single woman she would be turned away. I told her that wouldn't be a problem, and she was most grateful." The porter puffed out his chest with importance, and Gemma could see that he relished his position of authority and had been glad to help.

"Are you a relation?" the man asked, peering at Gemma suspiciously now that he'd realized he'd volunteered information about a passenger to a complete stranger.

"No, I'm not," Gemma replied. "But the lady in question was meant to start a nursing position and never turned up." She hated to lie, but had the feeling the porter wouldn't tell her anything else unless she was able to offer a plausible explanation for her curiosity.

"At St. Thomas's?" the porter asked, his brows furrowing again.

"Erm, yes," Gemma improvised.

The man nodded. "She did ask where the hospital was located."

"Did she mention who was supposed to be meeting her? I didn't think the hospital had sent anyone."

"I got the impression it was her husband, but I don't suppose it would be, not if she was here to work."

"What made you think it was the husband?" Gemma asked.

She was deeply grateful for the porter's powers of observation. He had already revealed more than she had expected to learn from a mere sighting of the victim, and she hoped he had a few more morsels of information to impart.

"The lady wore a wedding band on a string around her neck, and her hand kept going to it, as if for reassurance." The porter sighed. "Now that I think on it, she was probably widowed. That would explain the widow's weeds and the ring on a string. If she had still been married, the ring would be on her finger."

"Yes, I believe she was recently bereaved," Gemma confirmed. She had to be, so that was an honest enough statement. "Did she say anything else?"

"No."

"And did she have any luggage?"

The porter shook his head. "Just a valise and a reticule that she clutched to her middle. I expect she was fearful of being robbed. Maybe that's why she wore the ring around her neck. She could hide it then. The reticule was quite lovely," he went on. "Black velvet with a steel frame embossed with flowers. My wife would kill for one like it." His cheeks reddened when he realized how that must have sounded. "Begging your pardon, ma'am. It was just a turn of phrase."

Gemma suspected the porter knew all about the murder, as everyone who worked at the station was bound to, but, since the story had yet to make the papers, he wasn't indiscreet enough to mention it, especially to a lone woman, who might swoon with fright. He seemed a sensible man and keenly aware of the fears a woman on her own might be plagued with. No doubt he had encountered plenty of travelers like Helen in his work, ladies who were frightened and alone and looking for a man they deemed respectable to guide them.

The porter gazed down at Gemma with sympathy. What with her mourning attire and reference to nursing, he had probably pegged her as a sad, bereaved spinster, who'd been sent on an errand no one else had time for. This suited Gemma just fine since he seemed to have an innate sense of chivalry that made him eager to help.

"Is there anything else you can tell me?" Gemma cried as the porter turned to leave.

A smoke-belching locomotive had appeared in the distance and seemed to be approaching very quickly. In a few moments, the platform would be swarmed with people, and the porter would need to get about his work. Gemma thought he had probably told her everything he knew, but the description of the reticule didn't quite square with the rest of Helen's things. Perhaps it had been a gift, or maybe Helen had been fashion-conscious before life had robbed her of her husband and shrouded her in mourning attire. She had appeared to curl her hair, which was a small vanity at a time when she was meant to look drab.

The porter's eyes widened, as if he suddenly remembered something important. "She had an accent," he exclaimed, clearly pleased to have recalled this vital detail. "I could hardly understand her at first." He smiled ruefully. "Had to ask her to repeat herself twice before I was able to grasp what she was saying."

"What sort of accent?" Gemma was quick to ask.

"A Highland burr," the man replied proudly. "Worked with a lad from Aberdeen in my younger days, so I was able to place it."

Gemma was about to thank the man and take her leave, but then recalled the question that had sprung into her mind when he'd taken off his cap. "Do all the porters wear the same uniform?"

"Yes."

"What about at the other stations?"

"Well, I expect the insignia is different," the porter said, "but otherwise, I would think their uniforms look much like ours."

"Thank you," Gemma said, but the porter had already turned away, his attention on the whistle blowing as a train chugged into the station. The engine was puffing steam as the train slowed to a crawl and then came to a stop with a metallic screech.

Gemma walked briskly toward the cab stand and climbed into the first available conveyance, praying all the while that there wouldn't be too much traffic on the way back. The cab exited into London Street, then turned into Praed Street, which thankfully wasn't too congested. As the cab moved toward Blackfriars, Gemma sat back and considered what she'd learned. She very much wanted to speak to Sebastian, but she wasn't likely to see him today, and she hoped the information would still be relevant when he called on Colin next.

THIRTY

When Gemma got back, the house was quiet, the ground floor seemingly deserted. She went up to her bedroom, pulled off her gloves, hung up her cape and bonnet, and stowed her reticule and the jar of cream in a dresser drawer before patting her hair into place and going down to the kitchen. Mabel was putting the finishing touches on a meat pie she was making for dinner, and went on with her work after she had nodded to Gemma in greeting.

"I quite despaired of seeing you this afternoon, Miss Tate," she said, her gaze turning speculative, before she returned her attention to the pie.

Mabel was no fool and had surmised that Gemma had been doing something in aid of Sebastian's investigation. The maid didn't judge, but she liked to be taken into Gemma's confidence and feel included, since her days didn't offer much in the way of entertainment, and she spent most of her time either in the kitchen or the laundry and was bone-weary by the time she finally trudged upstairs at night.

"I'm sorry I took so long. Is Mrs. Ramsey all right?" Gemma asked.

"Sleeping like a baby," Mabel replied. "Miss Bright brought her back and helped her to bed, since Mrs. Ramsey didn't want her luncheon. She was muttering something about cake, and I could have sworn her nose was sprinkled with powdered sugar."

"What about Mr. Ramsey?" Gemma hurried to inquire.

Mabel scoffed. "Still in his dungeon. I brought him a cup of tea and a sandwich around noon, but he hasn't budged from his stool all afternoon."

"And Mr. Danvers?"

"Slaving away under Mr. Ramsey's command. The poor lad must be ready to drop with exhaustion," Mabel said disapprovingly. "I offered to bring him a sandwich as well, but he waved me off. He was elbows deep in that poor woman." Mabel wrinkled her nose in disgust. "Can't for the life of me understand why someone would choose to do that for a living."

"Does Mr. Ramsey know Poppy was here?" Gemma asked, her voice quavering with trepidation.

Mabel shook her head, and her mouth quirked in amusement. "She was so disappointed, the poor love. Wanted to see Mr. Ramsey, no doubt, but I thought it best not to tell him that you had left Mrs. Ramsey in her care. I would trust Miss Bright with my life, but why give Mr. Ramsey cause for concern?" Mabel said diplomatically.

"Thank you, Mabel. You're a star." Gemma had been preparing for a lengthy diatribe and was grateful to be spared the reprimand she knew she richly deserved.

Mabel cut her eyes at Gemma. "You watch yourself, Miss Tate. I don't have to ask to know what you've been up to."

"And how do you know that?" Gemma asked, smiling despite herself.

"I wasn't born yesterday, was I? I see the gleam in your eye, and it will get brighter still if a certain inspector darkens our door."

Gemma felt heat rise in her neck and spread to her cheeks. "Am I so transparent?"

"You are to some." Mabel shook her head and chuckled. "Maybe to all. You light up when you see him, and there's an answering flame in his eyes." She sighed heavily. "I only wish I could find a man who'd admire me so."

"Your time will come."

"Will it?" Mabel asked testily as she passed a brush dipped in beaten egg over the top of the pie. "How am I to meet a suitable man when I hardly leave the house?"

Gemma tried to suppress a grin, since she knew Mabel to be exaggerating the hopelessness of her situation. "I know for a fact that a certain coachman is very sweet on you."

Mabel's eyes lit up. "Do you really think so, Miss Tate?"

"I know so. I could be wrong, what with my eyesight not as sharp as it used to be," Gemma joked, "but I could have sworn I saw you two chatting by the neighbor's carriage house just yesterday evening."

"You're right, Miss Tate, your eyesight is not as sharp as it used to be," Mabel said with a coy shake of her head. "That wasn't me talking to Jacob, because that would be improper."

"No? There must be another maidservant who looks just like you living in this street," Gemma said.

"Must be," Mabel replied, grinning openly now. "Jacob is a handsome man, isn't he, Miss Tate?"

"I should say so, and he has lovely manners."

"He does. But I shouldn't go mooning over him or he'll lose interest."

"And why would you think that?" Gemma asked.

"My granny warned me never to let a man know he's won my affections. She said they enjoy the chase too much to be happy when it's done."

Gemma was considering how to word her reply in a way that wouldn't be disrespectful to Mabel's granny but urge her all the same not to listen to such outdated advice, when there was a knock at the door. Mabel reached for a towel, but Gemma held up her hand.

"I'll get it."

"Thank you, Miss Tate. I have to start on the potatoes as soon as I get this pie in the oven if I hope to have them ready in time for dinner."

Gemma left Mabel to it and hurried to the foyer. A man she had never met before stood on the step, his gaze alighting on her eagerly when she opened the door.

"Good afternoon, ma'am. I was wondering if I might have a word with Mr. Ramsey."

"Is Mr. Ramsey expecting you?"

Gemma thought he was probably a new student, come for practical instruction. Colin's pupils came and went, most men only taking a few private lessons before they felt ready to move on to the next step in their training. This gentleman was a few years older than the others, but some people decided to change professions or to improve on the skills they already possessed in order to command a higher salary or find more satisfactory employment at one of the better-regarded hospitals.

"No, he isn't, but perhaps he can make an exception." The man smiled, but the smile held no warmth and didn't reach his eyes. Gemma thought him off-putting.

"I'm sorry, but Mr. Ramsey is not receiving today. If you would like to leave a message, I would be happy to pass it on."

The man shook his head. "I need to speak to him in person. Perhaps you can tell him I called."

"Of course."

He took out a card and handed it to Gemma. It was very plain, printed on inexpensive paper and devoid of any embellishment. "I will try again tomorrow afternoon. I hope he will be able to see me then."

"I can't promise anything," Gemma said. "I'm not privy to his schedule."

The man nodded. "Perhaps I will write him a letter or seek him out at the Royal College of Surgeons."

"That would be wise."

Gemma read the name on the card once the visitor had turned away and she had shut the door.

Giles Rushton. Surgeon. St. Thomas's Hospital.

She had heard the name before. Sebastian sometimes mentioned his fellow lodgers in the course of their conversation. Gemma considered going down to the cellar to tell Colin he'd had a visitor, but Anne's reedy voice calling from the floor above stopped her in her tracks. She would speak to Colin later, she decided as she hurried upstairs.

THIRTY-ONE

The duty room at Scotland Yard was still quiet, which was normal; the action generally picked up in the evening, particularly on Fridays and Saturdays, when men who should have held on to their wages and gone home to their wives found their way to taverns and public houses and either drank themselves into oblivion or got just enough liquor in them to fuel their anger and fire up their sense of injustice. When brought to the forefront, these feelings usually resulted in violent brawls over unintended slights, grave bodily injuries that all too often ended in loss of life, and a ride in a police wagon, the miscreants' final destination the cells at Scotland Yard. And then there was the usual stream of prostitutes who'd been beaten to within an inch of their lives by nasty punters, outraged dandies whose pockets had been picked and their purses snatched, and respectable-looking ladies and gentlemen whose faces were gray with fear and whose hands shook as they wrote out the names of missing loved ones and their last known whereabouts.

Sergeant Meadows was at his post, his gaze following Sebastian as he walked through the door. "Good afternoon, Inspector Bell."

"Good afternoon, Sergeant."

"Pleasant weather we're having," Meadows remarked. "I thought for sure it was going to rain."

Sebastian didn't have time to talk about the weather, though he had to admit that it was a fine day, and he would have loved to take Gemma for a walk in one of London's many parks; but seeing her privately would have to wait. He had a case to solve, and the more time passed the faster the trail cooled. By next week, he'd have no hope of learning anything about the victim unless the public appeal threw up something definite.

"Did anyone report a missing woman last night or this morning? Around thirty, dark hair, blue eyes, a bit stout."

"None that fit your woman's description," Sergeant Meadows replied without bothering to check. "Only one new report since you asked the last time, and it's for a girl of twelve."

"Where is everyone?" Sebastian asked when he realized that none of the constables were about.

"We're short-handed today. Constable Putney had to attend a funeral. Constable Hammond had to leave early on account of a severe bout of indigestion. I told him not to buy eel pies first thing in the morning since they were bound to be left over from the day before, but would he listen? Of course not. And now he's shi—"

"What about Constable Bryant and Constable Forrest?" Sebastian cut across Meadows. "Are they about?" He had to agree with Sergeant Meadows about the freshness of the pies but wasn't interested in hearing the details of Hammond's gastric distress.

Meadows shook his head. "Constable Bryant is out with Inspector Warren, and Constable Forrest tripped over a drunk and twisted his ankle. The super has him on filing duty, and a good thing it is too. The files are in utter disarray, what with everyone rooting through them and then sticking them back into the cabinets willy-nilly. I was just saying to

Superintendent Ransome that we need to implement a better system."

"Indeed, we do, Sergeant. Is Ransome available?"

"He should be. I just brought him a cup of tea and a slice of cake my wife baked for the men. She's a rare baker, my missus," Sergeant Meadows said proudly. "I'd offer you a slice, but the lads fell on the cake like vultures on a fresh corpse. A new recipe that calls for orange peel. Difficult to obtain in May, oranges not being in season, but my Molly dries peel all winter long and then uses it over the rest of the year."

"That's remarkably resourceful," Sebastian replied, and wished the sergeant would have saved him a slice of cake. He was hungry. "Do save me a piece next time."

"I never know when you're coming in, Inspector Bell," Sergeant Meadows said, sounding affronted. "And I can hardly refuse the super a slice when he's sniffing the air like a bloodhound and asking why it smells like fresh oranges."

"No, of course not," Sebastian agreed.

He cut across the duty room and headed to Ransome's office. The door was open, Ransome in the act of composing a missive that was clearly giving him trouble. Several lines had been crossed out, and there were scribbled notes in the margin. An empty plate and teacup had been pushed toward the back of the desk, and the office still smelled delicately of oranges and strong tea. Ransome set his pen on the ink tray and looked up as soon as Sebastian knocked on the doorjamb and approached the desk.

"Take a seat, Bell."

"How was the party?" Sebastian asked once he'd taken off his hat and unbuttoned his coat and was comfortably seated.

He belatedly realized that he probably shouldn't have asked about the anniversary celebration. He still thought of John Ransome as his equal, another detective he could confer with when he stopped in at the Yard, but Ransome was now his superior, and, even though he had confided in Sebastian, it was best not to quiz him about his personal life.

"Unexpectedly fruitful," Ransome replied, but didn't elaborate. He'd probably had the same thought and had decided he didn't care to divulge any information that would put them on an equal footing. "Any progress on your case?"

"Not a whole lot," Sebastian was forced to admit. "I have a photograph of the victim, but the *Telegraph* won't print it. My only other option is to take it to the *Illustrated London News* and wait a full week for results."

Ransome tut-tutted. "By the time you have a lead worth pursuing, the killer could be long gone. They might be gone already. Have you considered that? The culprit could have delivered the trunk to the station and boarded an outbound train, disappearing in a puff of smoke. Poof!" Ransome made a hand gesture worthy of an illusionist.

"Yes, they could have, but even if the killer is long gone the least I can do is confirm the woman's name. Someone out there must be missing her. They deserve to know what happened and the chance to bury her."

Cocking his head to the side, Ransome considered the situation. "Let's be frank," he said after a moment's deliberation. "There are probably only two people besides her kin, if she has any, who really care about what happened to this woman—you and whoever killed her. The public has no interest in some country bumpkin whose decision to travel to London ended in tragedy, but what they do care about is their safety. This city relies heavily on the railways and the service they provide. The railways are like veins that carry blood to the heart so that it can keep on beating."

Ransome looked immensely proud of this analogy, and Sebastian thought that he might have heard the phrase and repurposed it for his own ends.

"If travelers don't feel safe at a railway terminus and if they think their women cannot be left unattended, that's a problem for the police service since we don't have the resources to man the stations and must rely on the porters to do the job," Ransome went on. "It's up to us to make the public feel safe in a city that's far from it."

Sebastian drew in a sharp breath. It almost sounded as if Ransome wanted to sweep the case under the carpet and claim that it was for the greater good.

"What exactly are you saying, sir?"

"We either need to apprehend the culprit quickly and inform the public that we have saved the day, or keep mum and work a case we can solve." Ransome had the decency to look ashamed and attempted to explain himself. "I can't afford to become mired in failure, Sebastian. I'm new to the job, and there are still those who question my appointment and believe I was promoted because of my personal connection to Sir David. They would like to see a more senior man at the helm and only need an excuse to give me the sack."

Ransome's moment of vulnerability passed as quickly as it had come, and he fixed Sebastian with a flinty stare. "You have until the end of Saturday. If you don't identify any viable leads by then, move on."

Sebastian felt a stab of anger at this pronouncement, but he couldn't blame Ransome. His concerns were valid. There had been talk of nepotism from the first, and, even though Ransome had transferred a few of his more vocal opponents to other stations, there were still those at Scotland Yard and beyond who'd be glad to see him fail. After careful consideration, Sebastian had backed Ransome's appointment, and would hate to see him supplanted by some puffed-up bureaucrat. Ransome would be good for the Yard and supportive of the men, but first, he needed a chance to prove himself.

Tamping down his irritation at the unreasonable time constraint, Sebastian turned his mind to practicalities. He could no longer afford to wait for next Saturday's edition of the *Illustrated London News* to identify the dead woman; he needed to outline a more immediate plan of action.

"It's imperative we check with the other stations," Sebastian insisted, even though Ransome had refused to spare the manpower before. "Someone might have reported the victim missing by now."

The information would save time and the cost of an appeal, although Sebastian highly doubted he'd be able to find anyone willing or able to run an appeal tomorrow. After that would be too late since he wouldn't have enough time to investigate any leads the inquiry might throw up.

"No one is available," Ransome replied gruffly. "I intend to address the shortage of constables at my next meeting with Sir David, but just now I can't spare anyone."

"Then I will have to do it myself and check with the divisions most likely to have taken down the report."

"And how will you determine which ones to call at?" Ransome asked. He seemed genuinely interested, his gaze speculative as if he were making a note of Sebastian's reply.

"Based on the woman's attire and physical appearance, I don't think she was of noble rank, but neither was she someone who was likely to reside in the slums. I will start with the middle-class neighborhoods and work my way outward. If someone knew the victim or had been expecting her, they are bound to realize something must have happened to her by now."

"There are seventeen divisions, Bell," Ransome reminded him. "And there is always the possibility that this woman was a nurse or a governess or even a cook who had just arrived in London to take up a position with a new family."

"So what do you suggest?" Sebastian snapped. Ransome had tied his hands and his observations weren't helping.

Ransome sighed heavily and shook his head in evident disbelief. "Before I accepted this position, I had no idea what it took to keep to a budget, but now that's all I think about. Every piece of paper, every bottle of ink, every tin of tea chips away at the funds I can allocate to fighting crime. To waste the time of an experienced detective on an errand a clever child can undertake is a criminal waste of resources." He nodded as if he had come to a decision, then opened the bottom drawer of his desk and took out a strongbox. Sebastian thought this was Ransome's private stash, the funds not part of the petty cash disbursed by Sergeant Meadows.

The superintendent unlocked the box with a key he extracted from a shallow drawer at the center of the desk, took out several coins and laid them on the desk. "Give this to Constable Forrest and ask him to check with the stations you think the most likely to have received the report. He has a sprained ankle, but he won't come to too much harm if he hops from the curb to the door of the station and back again. Tell him to have the cab wait for him so he doesn't have to find a new one after every visit. He's witless enough to do just that," Ransome said without rancor. "He's a good lad, Forrest, and always eager to help, but he has much to learn about efficiency, as do we all, apparently." Ransome sighed again, as if the responsibility of leadership weighed heavily on him. "I will have a message sent to your lodgings if Forrest comes back with anything useful. In the meantime, pursue your own investigation, and let's see where it takes us."

"Thank you, sir."

Having carefully instructed Constable Forrest—who was as excited as a playful puppy to escape filing duty and get out in the field—on where to go and what to ask, Sebastian stepped outside into the glorious May afternoon. It was after three o'clock, and the daytime shift at the Great Western Royal Hotel ended at four. Even if he left immediately and didn't encounter heavy traffic on the way to Paddington, he might not arrive at the hotel until after the daytime staff had already gone. It wasn't ideal, but he would have to speak to them tomorrow.

In the meantime, he would find something to eat, then head over to Fleet Street. Perhaps he could find a printer who could make up leaflets with a portrait of the dead woman that Sebastian could distribute in and around Paddington. He briefly considered stopping by Colin's house but saw no good reason to detour to Blackfriars, since Colin was ill and not likely to have started on the postmortem. With any luck, he would feel better tomorrow.

For now, Sebastian had to rely on the information provided by Gemma. She wasn't a surgeon and couldn't speak to the victim's internal injuries, but she had sufficient medical expertise to draw judicious conclusions based on her external examination of the body. The picture wasn't complete by any means, but it was better than nothing.

Sebastian did think he should pay a visit to King's Cross now that he had some time to spare. It was a fair distance from there to Paddington, but it was too much of a coincidence that both Quinces and Gordon McTavish should have a connection to the Great Northern Railway and be in possession of uniforms that could be used to effectively disguise their identities. No one looked at porters or conductors too closely. They were faceless, nameless men, identified by their uniforms.

Likewise, few people bothered to check the insignia on a porter's cap, simply assuming that they were to be trusted, much like a bobby. Bertram and Gerald Quince would be easily overlooked if they walked into Paddington Station, but Gordon McTavish would stand out, due to both his size and his accent. Sebastian would need to question the porters at Paddington again now that he had a photograph of the woman and knew that the porter in question might have come from King's Cross, but, since he wouldn't be returning to Paddington until morning, he would start with the staff at King's Cross.

He had to confirm Bertram Quince's claim that he had left his position at the terminus and check when was the last time Gerald Quince had a stopover in London. He also wanted to verify McTavish's alibi. No one could vouch for his whereabouts for the entire time he claimed to be at the Golden Fiddle, but someone would have noticed if McTavish was late to work on Thursday, or if he had left early on Wednesday. Jory Dixon said he'd heard an argument coming from room four thirty-seven while he was with Polly, but the young man would have been understandably distracted and might have heard voices that had come from a room on the other side, room four thirty-three, or even from a room across the corridor.

Without a more accurate time of death, Sebastian couldn't rule out that the victim was murdered earlier in the day. The killer could have then returned to the hotel the following morning, loaded the trunk onto a trolley, and wheeled it into the terminus once the station opened and the trains started running. McTavish or Quince could have easily done just that after showing their faces at, or before, breakfast. No one was likely to have noticed if they had gone out. Mrs. Elmore and Mrs. Poole would have been in their kitchens, getting the ranges going and starting on breakfast, and the lodgers would still be in their rooms, waking up and getting ready for work. Sebastian could hold off on leaving the photograph with a printer and show it around at King's Cross. The victim had been staying at Paddington and was found at the station, but that didn't mean she hadn't come to King's Cross if that was where her man happened to work. Perhaps someone had seen her.

Having settled on a plan of action, Sebastian was about to purchase a pie from a street vendor, then recalled Constable Hammond's predicament and decided to take the time to eat at a nearby public house instead. Once he'd wolfed down a mutton chop served with boiled potatoes, he paid the bill, and was on the move once again in less than an hour.

THIRTY-TWO

Sebastian arrived at King's Cross just after five o'clock. At this time of day, most passengers were exiting rather than entering the station, since fewer long-distance trains departed in the late afternoon. Travelers didn't care to arrive at their destination after night had fallen and they became easy—or, more accurately, easier—prey for pickpockets and unscrupulous cab drivers. Anyone in possession of a purse or any visible valuables was a target.

Now it was still light out, sunset nearly three hours away. Sebastian loved the long spring days that culminated in the summer solstice, when the sun set so late that there were only a few hours of darkness until it rose again. The world always seemed more benevolent during the daylight hours, even to a copper who knew safety to be an illusion.

Unlike the elegant façade of the Great Western Royal Hotel that served as the main entrance to Paddington, the area in front of King's Cross resembled an open-air market. Even this late in the day, it was thronged with passengers, animals, and wooden crates. There were wagons and carriages of all shapes and sizes, both loading and unloading people and freight. An omnibus had just arrived and, after a few people got off, new passengers climbed aboard, several people scaling the short stairs at the back to get to the upper level, where they could sit on benches affixed to the roof and enjoy what was left of the fine weather as they trundled toward their destination.

There were at least a dozen vendors who either occupied a particular spot or moved through the crowd, their trays slung around their necks with leather belts as they called out their wares, which were mostly foodstuffs. A young woman selling buns was doing a brisk trade, and an older woman had just arrived with a tray of steaming pies. She was swarmed by customers, unlike a sour-looking older man who was selling sheep's trotters that were beginning to stink after hours in the sun.

A scrawny newsboy was positioned just beneath the clocktower, a thick stack of newspapers before him and one in his hand, the front page clearly visible to anyone exiting the station. A small girl, who was dressed in a threadbare frock and shabby shoes that looked to be too small for her feet, sat on the ground behind him, her back against the wall. The child was terribly pale, her forehead looked clammy, and greenish mucus crusted her nostrils. Her eyes were partially closed with either illness or fatigue. Probably both.

Sebastian hoped the children had someone waiting for them at home, but, given their tatty appearance, he didn't think that was likely. They probably lived on the streets, and the only way the boy could keep them fed was if he kept his little sister with him while he worked. If he left her at an orphanage or a workhouse, they would probably never see each other again, and the siblings would lose the only family they had left.

It was a sad reality, one that Sebastian came face to face with quite often and could do nothing about. But he could make sure the children got a hot meal tonight. He approached and held out a shilling to the little girl, who snatched it from him with a grubby hand. The boy turned to thank him, and Sebastian saw the headline of the evening edition. The bold, black type of the *Telegraph* practically screamed:

Murder at Paddington
Mystery Woman Stabbed Through the Heart

"Damn you, Lawrence," Sebastian ground out as he walked past the startled newsboy and entered the station. He hadn't really expected anything else. He'd say that Lawrence had the moral code of a baboon, but that was unfair to the baboon, who probably lived by its own code of honor.

Inside the terminus, late-afternoon sunshine streamed through the glass dome and bathed the station in golden light. Although King's Cross wasn't too different from Paddington in its general layout, there were currently only two working platforms, numbered 1 and 8, and the tracks in between were being used for carriage sidings. This meant there were considerably fewer porters, but Sebastian decided not to waste time speaking to the men, who were all busy. A train had just arrived at Platform 8, and the porters surged in that direction to help as the passengers began to disembark.

Sebastian headed to the office of the station manager, which was midway down the first platform. When he entered, the manager was reading the paper, but he immediately set it down and turned to face Sebastian. A discreet brass nameplate proclaimed him to be Mr. Fish and there was something about his droopy lids and the cast of his mouth that reminded Sebastian of a flounder.

"How may I be of assistance, sir?" Mr. Fish asked wearily.

"Inspector Bell of Scotland Yard. I need to ask you a few questions."

"If you're here regarding that railway murder," the manager said as his eyes slid toward the *Telegraph*, "then I'm afraid you have the wrong terminus."

Sebastian let the dig slide. He wasn't in the mood to argue with this tired, bored-looking clerk.

"Mr. Fish, do you keep a record of conductors that put in at King's Cross on any given day?"

"No. Why would we?" Relenting a bit, Mr. Fish added, "There's a record of every train and the time it arrives and departs but not of any specific individual aboard. Do you know which train your man arrived on and from where?"

"I don't. All I have is a name."

"And what is this man meant to have done?"

"He might have information pertaining to a murder inquiry."

Mr. Fish's eyelids lifted a fraction of a millimeter. He was clearly curious. "Whose murder?"

"The one you were just reading about."

"But that happened at Paddington." The eyes were fully open now, the pale gray irises the same color as the office walls.

"It did, but the victim might have had a connection to someone who works at King's Cross, and a porter wearing a Great Northern Railway cap was seen at Paddington."

"Who was it?" Mr. Fish cried.

"I don't know. He may be an employee or even a visiting conductor."

"I don't claim to know every railman who comes into my station, but I am familiar with a good number of them. Who is this man you need to question?"

"Gerald Quince. Know him?" Sebastian asked and almost expected the manager to tell him that he'd never heard of the man.

"I do, as it happens, but not well," Mr. Fish hurried to clarify, lest Sebastian think him an accomplice.

"When did you see him last?"

Mr. Fish thought quickly. "Wednesday. He arrived on the 1:17 from York. We had a brief exchange."

"What about?"

"Mr. Quince asked that the station lad find him a cab."

"A cab to where?" Sebastian asked.

"St. Thomas's Hospital."

"Why did he need to go to the hospital?"

"I think he might have been ill. I instructed one of the porters to assist him."

"Which porter?"

"Mr. Gill."

"I need to speak to him," Sebastian said.

"Mr. Gill is not in today," Mr. Fish informed him.

"Do you have an address for him?"

"I do not."

"Do you not keep a record of your employees?"

"I do, but Mr. Gill recently moved to new lodgings, and I have been remiss in asking for his address."

Giving up on Mr. Gill for the moment, Sebastian asked, "When did Quince return to King's Cross?"

"I don't know."

Sebastian's exasperation mounted. This man was either utterly useless or being intentionally obstructive. He thought it was the former. Everything about the manager spoke to his apathy.

"*Did* Quince come back?" Sebastian snapped.

"I didn't see him with my own eyes, but the train bound for York departed at three-fifteen."

"Is there anyone here today who can confirm he boarded the train?" Sebastian ground out. He was seriously tempted to throttle the man.

"If he didn't, departure would have been delayed until

either Mr. Quince turned up or another conductor was found to take his place," Mr. Fish said.

"I would like to speak to Mr. Quince. When will he be back?"

"I'm really not sure." The apathy was replaced by a chuckle of amusement. "He's not the only conductor to service that route, Inspector."

Sebastian nearly growled with frustration. If Quince had been in any way involved in the murder, he could be gone for good if he had decided to jump the train in York and continue on to Edinburgh.

"What about his brother? I trust you know Bertram Quince?" Sebastian asked.

"Of course, but he's no longer employed by the Great Northern Railway."

"He resigned?"

"He was dismissed."

"On what grounds?" Sebastian asked, wondering if Quince was keeping secrets or had been too embarrassed to tell Sebastian the truth of what had happened.

"I don't know if you're aware, Inspector, ah, *Bell*," Mr. Fish said with a smirk that seemed to imply that clearly he had made the connection with Sebastian's name, "but Mr. Quince fancies himself an author. He has written a number of penny dreadfuls, which I'm told have enjoyed a measure of success. I even allowed issues to be sold right here at King's Cross, since I did not see this as a conflict with Mr. Quince's position as a porter. In fact, I applauded his ingenuity."

Sebastian highly doubted that Mr. Fish had ever applauded anyone else's success, but he kept the thought to himself. "What changed?"

"I received a number of complaints from individuals I could ill afford to antagonize, in which the persons concerned not only claimed, but had shown me proof, that Mr. Quince had turned them into characters in one of his stories."

"Surely he changed the names."

Quince had openly admitted to the lodgers at Mrs. Poole's that he mined King's Cross for inspiration and that his characters were at times inspired by real people, but Sebastian hadn't thought he would be daft enough to make the connection so obvious. But then again, the thinly veiled references to Sebastian and the murder at the Orpheus Theatre suggested that Quince was more careless than Sebastian had first assumed. It seemed Quince had wrongly imagined his nom de plume would keep him safe from accusation.

"He changed the names," Mr. Fish confirmed, "but they were too close to the original to effectively obscure the connection. The most obvious instance was in *The Revenge of Boudica*, which was published last month." The manager sighed with his entire bulk. "Mr. Quince appears to have bought into the harebrained suggestion that, because this area was previously known as Battle Bridge, this was the site of the final battle between Boudica and the Romans. He went so far as to suggest that she's buried beneath the terminus. Never heard such nonsense in my life, and as far as I know there's absolutely nothing of note to support this balderdash, but, like I said, Quince does fancy himself a writer and therefore doesn't feel that his works should be based on fact."

"What was it that was so offensive?" Sebastian asked.

He hadn't read any stories written by B.E. Ware, aside from the one in which he himself had been mentioned, but found that he was amused and a little bit impressed by Quince's ingenuity. People liked their legends, and most folklore had little to do with fact. To suggest that Boudica's remains rested beneath King's Cross was actually a rather clever idea, and, as Mr. Fish had pointed out, it was fiction and intended to entertain.

Mr. Fish's lips quirked with what had to be mirth.

"Mr. Quince renamed the Earl of Shaftsbury the Earl of Shatsbury. The fictional earl soils himself when confronted by what he thinks is the ghost of the warrior queen. Such a parallel is not only obvious, but also quite insulting to a personage of such stature."

"Anyone else?" Sebastian asked.

"Yes. In the same publication, the Duchess of Devonshire—who happens to be rather corpulent—was turned into the Duchess of Divan. That would not be terribly offensive if the character in question was not met at the station by two strapping footmen who carried her off in a sedan chair, which they then loaded into a specially modified conveyance so that the duchess would not have to navigate unstable steps and maneuver her bulk into the carriage. In the story, the bearers are so petrified by the specter of a stampeding elephant that they drop the chair, and their mistress dies of an apoplexy as she tries to crawl to safety."

"I see," Sebastian muttered.

He wasn't sure if Quince was unapologetically brazen or epically stupid, and decided it was probably a bit of both since the comparisons really were too obvious to ignore, as they had been in the case of Inspector Knell, who had at least acquitted himself admirably and not soiled his trousers.

"Mr. Quince thought he could get away with his uncensored observations because he published his rag under a pseudonym," Mr. Fish continued, "but everyone who works at this station is privy to his secret. I think someone intentionally brought the complainants' attention to the passages in question. I had no recourse but to sack the man."

"Has Mr. Quince returned his uniform?"

"Not yet. We ask that the uniforms are cleaned before they are returned. I expect Mr. Quince will bring it back next week. Is that all, Inspector?" Mr. Fish inquired, his expression hopeful. It was nearly six o'clock, and he no doubt wanted to get home.

"Just one more thing. Do you keep a record of employee attendance?"

"Of course. How else can I dock their wages if they fail to show up for work?"

"Would you notice if someone came in late or left early?"

"If you're referring to Bertram Quince, then I must disappoint you on that score. He was always very punctual and never left before his shift ended."

"I was more interested in Gordon McTavish."

"McTavish?" Mr. Fish exclaimed. "What's he got to do with this?"

"Just answer the question," Sebastian snapped. He was in no mood to explain, and the man was grating on his last nerve.

"Gordon McTavish is generally on time."

"Was he on time Thursday morning?"

"If he wasn't, no one reported it to me."

"Is there anyone here who can verify McTavish's whereabouts on Wednesday night and Thursday morning?"

"Seamus O'Connor. Those two are as thick as thieves."

"Is there anyone else?"

"You would have to check with the men. Now I'm afraid I cannot afford to dally. A prior engagement, you understand."

Sebastian didn't bother to thank the man and walked out of the office, allowing the door to slam behind him. He questioned several porters, but no one could say for certain if Gordon McTavish had left early Wednesday evening or arrived late Thursday morning. Sebastian got the impression that they liked the man and didn't want to shop him to the police, especially when McTavish was there, watching Sebastian as he went about his work. Or perhaps they were just afraid. Gordon McTavish could probably take on any of them with one hand tied behind his back and win.

The clock in the tower chimed half past six when Sebastian finally left the station. Even though Mrs. Poole's boarding house was within walking distance, and he could be home by seven, he felt an overwhelming desire to see Gemma. It was almost a physical ache, and, after a moment's hesitation, he hailed a cab and instructed the driver to take him to Blackfriars.

THIRTY-THREE

When Gemma opened the door, she looked as tired as Sebastian felt, and there was something else that briefly flashed behind her eyes. Perhaps a spark of guilt? The momentary awkwardness was quickly replaced by pleasure, and she smiled up at him, her eyes glowing with affection.

"How are your patients?" Sebastian asked once Gemma had taken his coat and hat and had invited him into the parlor.

The room seemed strangely empty without Anne, who liked to sit by the window and watch the world go by until it grew too dark to see. Colin wasn't there either, which was a good indication of how things were progressing. He rarely retired this early and never missed an opportunity to speak to Sebastian when he called by, even if Sebastian was there to see Gemma. Colin saw himself as Gemma's protector and thought he should act as chaperone in lieu of a father or a brother, who would ensure that nothing improper took place between the unmarried couple. Sebastian thought it ludicrous but didn't raise the issue with Colin. His friend was doing what he thought was right, and, since they were meeting in his house, they had to respect his rules.

"Would you like a drink?" Gemma asked once Sebastian had sat down in the chair Colin usually occupied.

"Yes, please."

He knew he probably shouldn't, but he was tired and cross, and one drink wouldn't hurt. Gemma poured a tot of brandy from a decanter on the sideboard and handed Sebastian the glass. She was about to sit down, then reconsidered and returned to the sideboard. After pouring a small sherry for herself, she settled across from Sebastian, and breathed a sigh of relief at being off her feet.

"Colin refused to rest and carried out the postmortem with the help of Eugene Danvers," Gemma said, answering Sebastian's question as if no time had passed since he'd asked it.

"Has he shared the results?"

Gemma shook her head. "He was exhausted and retired immediately after Mr. Danvers left. A Mr. Rushton came by in the afternoon," she added as an afterthought. "He left his card." She pulled the card out of her apron pocket and handed it to Sebastian. "Is this the Mr. Rushton who lives at Mrs. Poole's? I wasn't sure."

Sebastian looked at the card. "Yes, it is. I didn't realize he was one of Colin's students."

"I've never seen him here before."

"What did he want?"

"He asked to speak to Colin, but I told him Colin was unavailable."

"Did you tell Colin?"

"Yes, when he and Mr. Danvers finally came upstairs. He knew who Mr. Rushton was but had no idea why he wished to speak to him."

"It is curious, I'll ask him when I get home," Sebastian said.

"The visit might have nothing to do with the case," Gemma said. "Perhaps he's interested in additional instruction or wanted to consult with Colin on a case. I expect they know each other from the Royal College of Surgeons. It's like a secret club where everyone knows everyone, at least by sight," she added with a smile.

"Does Colin spend much time at the RCS?"

"How do you think he finds new students?" Gemma replied.

Sebastian had never asked how Colin came by his students. He had assumed that Colin placed an advertisement in the paper, but realized now that the Royal College of Surgeons was probably the best place to find young, eager students who had the desire and the means to pay for private sessions.

Their conversation was interrupted by Mabel, who entered the parlor and greeted Sebastian with a friendly smile. "Hello, Inspector. I thought I heard your voice."

"Good evening, Mabel. I trust you're well?"

"Run off my feet is what I am," Mabel replied grumpily. "Mr. Ramsey would like his supper on a tray, and Mrs. Ramsey is refusing to eat fish. Says she has a hankering for fricandeau of veal with spinach." Mabel huffed. "I don't even know what that is, but I expect it's something fancy and French that she tried years ago at some supper party but thinks it was just last week," she went on with a shake of her head. "I would make it for her too, if I thought it would make her happy, but by the time I find a recipe and purchase the ingredients she will have forgotten all about it."

"I'll speak to her," Gemma said, and started to rise, but Mabel shook her head.

"She asked for soup instead. I'll see that she's fed, Miss Tate. You take a moment. You've earned it."

"Thank you, Mabel," Gemma said, clearly relieved not to have to trudge upstairs and engage in a lengthy discussion with Mrs. Ramsey, who'd probably forgotten all about both the fricandeau and the soup.

Growing up, Sebastian had always thought that death was

the worst thing that could happen to a person, but since coming to London and joining the police service he'd had reason to change his mind. He'd seen the bodies of victims who'd died after prolonged suffering and thought they had probably longed for death rather than endure another moment of pain. Anne Ramsey was not suffering in any physical way, and she was loved and cared for, but, watching memory and reason desert her more each day and knowing what the eventual outcome would be, Sebastian thought that he would rather endure hours of agony if he could die at the end of it rather than be subjected to this slow, torturous loss of oneself. Who was he without his mind and his ability to reason? He knew that a life in which all that was left to him was food and sleep would not be worth living.

Colin put a brave face on it, but Sebastian knew he was suffering. He was an only child and had lost his father a few years ago. They had all suffered terrible losses, but knowing that others were suffering too did not make one's own tragedy any easier to bear. Sebastian hoped for Colin's sake that he would not waste his chance to find happiness. He was aware that Colin had feelings for Gemma, but Gemma was spoken for, and Colin had to emerge from his cellar dungeon and find a woman of his own, or time would pass him by and he would wind up a sad, lonely old man.

It wasn't Sebastian's place to advise Colin or point out that a lovely, capable young woman had her eye on him. Colin had to recognize the opportunity for himself; but perhaps Gemma would give him a slight nudge if he failed to make his move and acknowledge Poppy's interest.

"I trust you have no objections to fish pie, Inspector?" Mabel asked, interrupting Sebastian's thoughts.

"Not as a rule, no," he replied.

"Then please join me for dinner," Gemma said.

It wasn't really her place to invite guests to dine since, technically, she was just a step above Mabel in the hierarchy of the household, but Colin wouldn't mind, and Sebastian knew how much Gemma hated to eat alone. It reminded her of the weeks following Victor's death, when she had been left alone in the house they had shared. Lonely days followed by lonely nights, when she'd fretted about the future and thought she would spend the remainder of her days living in some mean boarding house or as a half-servant in a live-in position. Not everyone was as democratic as Colin and invited their parent's nurse to dine with them as if they were a member of the family. Supper on a tray was the norm for nurses and governesses, followed by lights out if they had used up their daily ration of coal and the room was growing drafty and cold.

Sebastian wanted to reassure Gemma that she would never be alone again, but he was in no position to make such an oath. All he could safely promise was today, and tomorrow. And hopefully a long time after, but he'd seen enough to know that life was cruel and unpredictable and that men like Mr. Robinson would never run out of customers.

"Thank you, but I'm afraid I can't stay. I made plans to meet Simian at Mrs. Poole's," Sebastian said when he realized Gemma was still waiting for an answer.

"Surely you don't mean to dine at the boarding house," Gemma said, looking disappointed and a little bit horrified.

"Mrs. Poole probably made boiled cod again," Mabel muttered under her breath.

"How did you ever guess?" Sebastian quipped.

Gemma made a face. "Can she not think of something more palatable?"

"I'm not sure her imagination stretches very far when it comes to food," Sebastian replied.

"Mr. Quince is either a very brave man or a very foolish one," Gemma joked.

"Truer words have never been spoken," Sebastian replied,

recalling what he had learned from Mr. Fish. "I will take Simian out, or he will never speak to me again."

"What about Gustav? Will you leave him to fend for himself?" Gemma asked. It was endearing the way she always worried about the little rascal.

Sebastian did feel a bit guilty about Gustav, who was probably prowling the rooms as he waited for Sebastian to come home, but the cat would have to wait. He was hardly starving, since Mrs. Poole had been letting him out during the day so he could hunt for mice and help her keep her establishment rodent-free—or nearly rodent-free, since there was probably not a house in London that didn't have some vermin.

"Mrs. Poole promised to give him a piece of cod," Sebastian replied, and Gemma smiled, pleased that Gustav would get his due.

They both turned and looked at Colin in surprise when he appeared in the doorway. He seemed tired and a bit pale, and had clearly been in the process of getting ready for bed, being in his shirtsleeves, his collar open at the neck and his waistcoat unbuttoned. He didn't normally walk about in a state of near undress, but he was clearly unwell and unaware of how disheveled he appeared.

"Colin, won't you sit down?" Sebastian asked, and made to stand up, but Colin shook his head.

"Don't get up on my account. I'll sit here." He lowered himself heavily into the nearest chair.

"How are you feeling?" Sebastian asked.

"I'm much improved; just tired. I was for my bed when Mabel mentioned you were here, so I thought I'd share the results of the postmortem. I know you've been waiting, and I didn't want to hold you up any longer."

"Were you able to complete it?"

"Yes, but Mr. Danvers will come back tomorrow to help me close the body. He had to rush off. A previous engagement. I think he's going to propose to Miss Chandler any day now," Colin said with a melancholy smile. "I've never met the young lady, but I know her father, and he's a good man. Upstanding," he added. "Eugene couldn't marry into a better family, and that means a lot when one has no living family of one's own. Mr. and Mrs. Chandler will treat him like a son."

"I'm sure it won't hurt his career prospects either," Sebastian said, reflecting on what an advantageous marriage had done for Ransome.

"I assure you, Mr. Danvers can hold his own in the operating theater. He conducted the postmortem almost entirely on his own. I simply gave him a few pointers and helped him to analyze the evidence. He was calm, professional, and detached, which a good surgeon needs to be. Self-doubt can lead to mistakes and a feeling of panic, and can ultimately result in the death of the patient. I think Mr. Danvers will make a fine surgeon. In fact, I intend to give him a recommendation that will weigh heavily in his favor when he applies for a permanent position."

"That's very kind of you," Gemma said stiffly, and Sebastian thought Colin looked tense when he turned to answer her.

"It's nothing of the sort. It's based entirely on merit. I always acknowledge people's hard work and practical experience."

"I never meant to imply you didn't," Gemma replied and looked away.

"How well do you know Mr. Rushton?" Sebastian asked. "Gemma tells me he called earlier."

"I only know him by reputation. He's a competent surgeon. If anything, I expect you know him better. Doesn't he live with Mr. Danvers at Mrs. Poole's?"

"He does, but we're not what you'd call friends."

"I don't think he has many friends. Mr. Danvers probably took him under his wing. He's the sort to attract brooding loners. I wager Mr. Rushton is too intense to make lasting social connections easily."

Sebastian nodded. Mr. Rushton certainly was that, and Sebastian felt a twinge of sympathy for the man. People tended to think Sebastian was too intense as well, and some kept their distance, put off by his unflinching honesty and refusal to conform. It was those qualities that would keep him from attaining a higher position in the police service. One had to be willing to play the game, but Sebastian simply wasn't interested in winning at arse-licking.

"The postmortem," he prompted Colin, who looked like he was about to fall asleep.

"Oh, yes. Sorry. Nodded off for a moment there." Colin cleared his throat and began. "The victim was in her late twenties or early thirties. I can't give you a more accurate time of death," he said apologetically. "By the time I got to her, it was too difficult to narrow down a plausible window. She was most likely murdered on Wednesday night rather than Thursday morning."

Sebastian nodded. He was disappointed, but he had to work with what he had.

"At first glance, Mr. Danvers and I deduced that she had recently given birth, and we strongly suspected that the child was either stillborn or died shortly after birth. Her breasts were bound, presumably to stop lactation, and her abdomen was still distended."

Gemma nodded, as if she had already known as much. "First glance?" she asked.

"The belly was distended for quite a different reason," Colin said, and cast a pointed look in Gemma's direction.

"Oh?" she said. "What else would cause a woman to have a distended abdomen shortly after delivering a child?"

"Once Mr. Danvers opened her up, we discovered a sizable tumor in her womb. It measured nearly five inches, and, although I can't be certain without the benefit of microscopic analysis, I believe the growth was malignant. Mr. Danvers was quite shocked. He'd never seen a tumor up close and insisted on dissecting it to study it more closely."

"Would the cancer infect the baby in utero?" Gemma asked.

"I suppose it's possible, since the mother's blood nourishes the fetus, but, even if it didn't, the tumor would still crowd the infant and prevent it from developing normally, especially if the victim continued to lace her corset tightly and left the growing child no room to move. However, the tumor may have become larger after the victim delivered, and the child might have been developing typically." Colin sighed. "It's difficult to tell precisely how long ago the victim gave birth due to the presence of the tumor and the postnatal-like symptoms it might have caused."

"Would the cancer have killed her?" Gemma asked.

Colin nodded. "If the growth was indeed malignant, then the poor woman probably didn't have too much time left."

"Were you able to find anything that shed light on her murder?" Sebastian inquired.

"She had bruises on her neck and wrist, so an altercation must have taken place, but I didn't notice any defensive injuries," Colin said. "I expect the mortal blow came as a surprise. Have you been able to discover her name?"

"I saw her signature in the hotel register, but the full name was difficult to make out. She had terrible penmanship."

"I believe I know the reason for that," Colin supplied.

"Was her right hand deformed?" Gemma asked. "I didn't notice anything amiss when I helped Mr. Robinson pose her for the photo."

"There was nothing wrong with her right hand except that she was most likely left-handed. Individuals who naturally favor the left are forced to write with their right hand, which sometimes makes their handwriting difficult to read, especially if they don't write on a regular basis. I don't know if you know this," Colin added conversationally—he seemed a little more animated now, his fatigue forgotten in the face of his discoveries—"but *sinister* is Latin for left. Leftism is seen as a stigma and a sign that the person is somehow unnatural. At one time, it was even believed to be proof of witchcraft."

"Why am I not surprised?" Gemma muttered under her breath. "And probably only in women."

"I don't think too many men were accused of being witches," Colin replied. "Still, it is an oddity, if not necessarily proof of moral deficiency."

"How could you tell she was left-handed?" Sebastian asked.

"Her left hand was considerably more workworn, so I suspect she used it as her primary hand in everything but writing."

"Which would explain why her stitching was so neat while her handwriting was barely legible," Sebastian said.

"That's right," Colin said. "She would have used the hand she was most comfortable with. I noticed more wool particles caught in the hair on the left side of her head. I expect she used her left hand to card wool and hadn't washed her hair since. Oh, and that reminds me. The victim had a hair caught beneath the fingernail of her index finger of her left hand."

"Could have been her own," Sebastian said. "She would have used her left hand to tidy her hair, wouldn't she?"

"It wasn't hers," Colin replied. "The hair was smooth and reddish, and it didn't have a root follicle."

"What does that signify?" Gemma asked.

"I don't believe she tore the hair out. It probably came away when she touched it because it had already fallen out."

Sebastian filed that tidbit away, then asked, "And the cause of death?"

"The bodkin punctured the right ventricle of the heart.

Once the cells are deprived of oxygen, the blood fails to clot and the heart pumps harder to deliver blood to both it and the brain. That would explain the amount of blood."

"How long would it have taken her to die?" Gemma asked, her mouth drooping with sadness.

"Not too long, but long enough to realize there was no hope. She would have been terrified until she lost consciousness. I believe she tried to stem the flow of blood with her hands, but there was nothing she could have done."

"Was she sexually assaulted?" Sebastian asked. Colin still shied away from talking of such matters in front of Gemma and might have left that bit out.

"No, she was not, and I saw no evidence of sexual congress," he said, coloring slightly. "Whoever killed her had no interest in her in that way."

"I see. Thank you," Sebastian said.

"I hope you find the information helpful," Colin said as he pushed to his feet, "but there's little to go on in terms of identifying her killer. She could have been murdered by anyone, man or woman, left- or right-handed, tall or short. All they had to do was stab her hard enough and the deed was done."

"How very sad," Gemma said, and used her knuckle to wipe away the tears that had slid down her cheeks. "To die all alone in a strange town and get consigned to a pauper's grave, without so much as a single mourner to grieve your passing."

"I will be there," Colin said. "I will mourn her."

"I will go as well," Sebastian said. "I will let you know when the arrangements are made for the body to be collected."

"She won't be ready until at least three o'clock tomorrow. Mr. Danvers has a lecture in the morning, and then he will make his way here to finish up. I will bid you goodnight, then," Colin said.

"Goodnight, Colin. And feel better," Sebastian said.

Colin smiled tiredly and left the room.

THIRTY-FOUR

"What was that all about?" Sebastian asked once Colin had gone, and he was sure they wouldn't be overheard.

"What was what about?"

"Is Colin angry with you?"

A heavy sigh escaped Gemma, and her shoulders sloped in defeat. "I took it upon myself to examine the body after Mr. Robinson left. Colin became upset when I told him and reprimanded me in rather strong terms."

"So don't tell him next time."

Gemma's eyebrows lifted in surprise, then she smiled at Sebastian playfully. "Are you advising me to lie, Inspector?"

"Only by omission."

Appreciating how deceitful his advice must have sounded, Sebastian hurried to explain. "This is my case, and I have no objection to you examining the body. You don't need Colin's permission, therefore you're not obligated to inform him."

"You weren't happy for me to examine the body before," Gemma reminded him.

"I changed my mind," Sebastian admitted gruffly.

Gemma looked incredibly pleased, since he'd just given her carte blanche when it came to his cases, and Sebastian realized that he truly didn't mind. Gemma's input was invaluable, and Colin had no call to get territorial. The bodies were there to learn from, and, if Colin could use the victims as a teaching opportunity for his paying students, he hardly had any right to object to Gemma performing a non-invasive examination.

"Were you able to learn anything useful?" Sebastian asked.

"I jotted down my findings, but Colin covered all the salient points." Gemma pulled a folded sheet of paper from her pocket and handed it to him. "And I couldn't have known about the tumor," she added a bit defensively.

"Thank you," Sebastian said and unfolded the page. He skimmed the list, then refolded it, and put it in his pocket. "This is very helpful." Glancing at the clock, he said on a sigh, "I'm afraid I don't have much time."

More than anything, he wanted to stay, but he couldn't turn his back on Simian again, not if he hoped to rebuild the relationship with his brother.

"It's all right," Gemma absolved him. "You should spend some time with Simian. Another opportunity might not present itself for a while."

Or ever, Sebastian thought, but he couldn't bring himself to go just yet. "I don't have to leave for a half-hour," he said, although he wished he could stay for dinner.

They had much to discuss, and the postmortem results had put them both in a somber mood, but as Sebastian gazed at Gemma he felt momentarily transported. So many times he had imagined what it would be like to finally be alone with her. His imaginings didn't stop with dinner, but to finally enjoy a private meal where they could speak freely and not be overheard or observed by others would truly be a dream come true. Too many of their interactions revolved around murder, but, despite the macabre nature of the subject, there was a hidden benefit. Whenever they theorized about a case, Gemma's excitement and intellect overshadowed her somber gown and the less-than-ideal setting, and she sparkled like a precious gemstone caught in a ray of light.

Gemma was a woman who craved intellectual stimulation and purpose, and working a case provided her with both. She couldn't bring back the dead, but she could offer them justice, and, when a guilty verdict was read out in court, that verdict was in part due to her diligence and tireless pursuit of the truth. Sebastian had come to accept that he couldn't stop Gemma from sleuthing any more than he could apply for a position as a porter or become a shopkeeper. They each had their strengths and their shortcomings, and he was prepared to accept Gemma's, even though at times his stomach lurched as if he'd suddenly walked off a cliff and realized there was nothing beneath his feet but empty space, and he was dropping with no hope of breaking his fall.

She would thrill and terrify him for all the days of his life, and, even though he still feared what may come, he was ready. Their eyes met, and Sebastian thought that he would give anything for the simple pleasure of having dinner with her every evening and knowing that they would retire together and spend the night in each other's arms, only to rise in the morning and face another day as a couple, and then as a family.

And in that moment, he decided he was through waiting, and that, as soon as the current case was closed, he would use part of the money he had saved since moving into the boarding house to buy Gemma a ring and propose the instant she was out of mourning. He had no right to rush her and had not asked how long she planned to mourn or if she planned on a period of half-mourning, but he would be ready and waiting when the time came.

"You are very pensive. Were you thinking about the post-mortem results?" Gemma asked, looking at him with concern.

"I'm sorry," Sebastian said, realizing that the silence had stretched on for too long because he had been woolgathering. "Yes, but I don't think Colin's findings change anything. Do you?"

"No. We had already deduced the basics."

"The only other new piece of evidence is the hair trapped beneath the victim's fingernail, but we don't know that the hair belongs to the killer. She could have picked it up anywhere that didn't require she wear gloves."

"I was thinking the same thing," Gemma said. "I wonder if she knew about the tumor."

"She must have felt reasonably well if she had decided to travel to London."

"Women push through pain all the time," Gemma replied. "This may have been her last chance to say goodbye to someone she loved. And tell him about the child they had lost."

"Perhaps," Sebastian replied noncommittally. "We don't have enough evidence to say for certain that she came to London to see her husband."

That furtive look passed over Gemma's face once again, and Sebastian realized she was waiting for an opportunity to share something with him.

"Come on. Out with it," he cajoled.

Gemma didn't pretend not to know what he was talking about. That was one of the things Sebastian loved about her. She did not rely on coyness to avoid discussing a difficult topic or try to mislead him by changing the subject. Gemma was as straight as an arrow.

"I went to Paddington today," she confessed, and fixed Sebastian with a stubborn look that suggested she was ready for whatever he was going to say because she'd heard it all before.

She also had the air of a woman who had something vital to share, which was surprising since Sebastian had already interviewed nearly everyone at the terminus and had come away with precious little.

"Did you find anything out?"

Gemma seemed pleased when Sebastian failed to chastise her for the second time that evening, then nodded eagerly. "A porter who recognized Helen confirmed she arrived on the 1:47 from Oxford on Monday and had come from Birmingham. She had been traveling on her own, but she had expected to be met. She didn't say by whom, but she looked worried when they failed to show. She asked the porter to recommend a reputable place to stay and then asked for directions to St. Thomas's Hospital."

"Recognized her?" Sebastian asked, thinking he must have misunderstood.

Gemma grinned, and her face lit up with obvious pride. "I stopped by Mr. Robinson's studio before going to Paddington and purchased a copy of the victim's photograph."

"But he only made one."

"He had taken two photographs," Gemma explained. "He thought the first one was too dark to be used for reproduction, so he took another one. I purchased the darker image, but the features were clear enough for someone who'd seen the victim to recognize her."

"Clever girl," Sebastian said, and Gemma's smile grew wider at his compliment. "Did she tell this porter why she wanted to go to St. Thomas's?"

"No but, given what Colin discovered, it's possible that she had hoped to see a doctor. And I already knew she had given birth, and I suspected the child had died," Gemma said, referring to her notes.

"Why did you think she lost the baby?" Sebastian asked.

Colin had shared his reasons but, as a woman, Gemma might have a different perspective, based on the victim's behavior rather than physical evidence.

"She was in mourning, and a nursing mother is not likely to leave her baby behind. I thought the baby had died and she had bound her breasts to stop the milk."

"So, this woman traveled to London shortly after her baby died. She expected to be met by someone close to her, possibly her husband. The man failed to show as was previously arranged, and she took a room at the nearest hotel. She was so distressed, her hand shook when she signed the register, which made her crabbed handwriting even more difficult to decipher, and requested one of the cheapest rooms. Presumably, funds were short, and she didn't know how long she would need to remain at the hotel, so she decided on two nights. Perhaps she simply wished to be reunited with whoever she had come to see, or maybe she'd traveled to London because she knew she was ill and thought she might get more advanced treatment at one of the London hospitals."

"That sounds plausible," Gemma agreed. "Except that we don't know for certain if she had come from or through Birmingham. The porter also mentioned that the woman spoke with a Highland burr. He was quite certain she was Scottish. Which means that she might have come from Scotland by way of Birmingham."

"That would explain why she arrived in Paddington," Sebastian mused. "I believe there's a way to go through Carlisle with connections in Stafford and Birmingham. And if she was from Scotland, then that makes Gordon McTavish a person of interest, especially since his hair matches the color of the hair found on Helen."

"Who's Gordon McTavish?"

Sebastian suddenly realized he hadn't seen Gemma since before he had searched the victim's room, so he filled her in on what he'd found and the tenuous connections he had been able to establish.

"Gordon McTavish is a Highland Scot who lives at one of the two possible addresses," Sebastian explained.

"There are plenty of Scots living in England, especially in the north," Gemma argued. "Do you have any reason to suspect he was related to Helen or had a motive to murder her?"

"No, but he's unaccounted for on the night of the murder, and no one was able to confirm that he arrived at work on time on Thursday. McTavish claims that his wife left him for another man, but it is possible that he was involved with the victim and was the one to visit her in her hotel room."

"His name starts with G," Gemma said.

"It does. And he's a porter."

"But what would be his motive though?"

"McTavish had not left London in the past year, so if the victim had been pregnant and had recently given birth then that might mean the child wasn't his. He might have flown into a jealous rage."

"Unless she'd come to London before and had become pregnant then," Gemma pointed out. "But if she knew where he lived, why would she not go straight there?"

"If she knew that the man she had come to see was staying at a boarding house, she would also know that the landlady would not permit her to stay. So she took a room at the hotel and went to see him on Wednesday."

"She arrived on the 1:47," Gemma pointed out. "She could have easily taken a room, set down her things, then gone to the boarding house to speak to whoever she had come to meet. And she did inquire about St. Thomas's Hospital specifically. Both Mr. Danvers and Mr. Rushton have ties to St. Thomas's and reside in Albion Street."

"Yes, they do, but I found nothing to connect either of them to the victim," Sebastian said. "Helen was considerably older and not the sort of woman to catch the attention of a young man. Presumably, she was also married. However, Gerald Quince, who must be closer to her age, asked for a cab to St. Thomas's Hospital. Perhaps he had expected Helen to go there after she arrived."

"And he also wears a uniform."

"As does his brother," Sebastian said.

"Whose penny dreadful was in the victim's pocket at the time of her death."

Sebastian and Gemma shared a conspiratorial smile, silently acknowledging the pleasure of following each other's reasoning and working in tandem to unpick the knotty mystery.

"As far as we know, Helen did not leave the hotel on Monday," Sebastian recapped. "Perhaps she was tired or felt unwell. She went out on Tuesday and was murdered on Wednesday."

"Perhaps she never met with whoever she had intended to see and left a message instead. They came to find her at the hotel and murdered her," Gemma exclaimed.

"If Helen had arranged to meet her killer, then they must have been in contact," Sebastian pointed out.

"So why would this person kill her once she arrived? If she posed a threat, why not leave her where she was? She could hardly have hurt the killer from Birmingham, or Scotland."

"I didn't find any letters among her possessions. And there was no coin purse or reticule inside the room. She had stuffed the address into a glove, as if she was afraid someone would find it," Sebastian reminded Gemma.

"She might have put the address into the glove for easy access, in the same way women tuck a handkerchief into their sleeve," Gemma replied. "The porter did say that she carried a rather distinctive reticule. It was made of black velvet and had a metal frame embossed with flowers."

"The killer must have taken the reticule because it was the

only item of value and probably contained something that could identify them," Sebastian concluded.

"Have you been able to formulate a theory?"

"At the moment, my thoughts are all over the shop," Sebastian admitted. "I have a number of disjointed facts that don't add up to a cohesive narrative, and I have no proof that the facts even relate to the same story."

"Maybe I can help you separate the wheat from the chaff," Gemma offered.

Sebastian glanced at the clock again, acutely conscious of the time. "I very much hope so because just now I can't see a way to fit the facts together, even though there does appear to be a common thread connecting the clues."

"Go on," Gemma invited, and leaned forward in her eagerness to help.

"Jory Dixon, who works at Paddington, came upstairs after his shift for a tryst with a chambermaid who cleans the fourth floor. They met in a vacant room next door to Helen's. Jory heard raised voices coming from Helen's room and was certain that one of them was male. A guest whose room is on the other side went to use the lavatory at the end of the corridor and saw a man dressed as a porter walking toward the victim's room when he came out."

"That fits with what you know so far," Gemma said.

Sebastian shook his head. "Jory might have heard voices from the room on the other side, and the guest who saw a man in uniform most likely saw Jory and not the killer, since that was right around the time Jory arrived for his assignation, and the witness said the porter carried a red rose, which both Jory and the chambermaid mentioned." Sebastian sighed. "Jory also said that he'd noticed a porter wheeling a trolley toward Platform 4 the following morning. The porter's cap said GNR, which stands for the Great Northern Railway."

"Which comes into King's Cross," Gemma observed.

"Exactly. Gerald Quince's name starts with G, his wife's name is Hettie, which could look like Helen, he was in London on the day of the murder, his wife lives in Birmingham, and he asked for a cab to St. Thomas's Hospital. Evidence or mere coincidence?" Sebastian asked, not really expecting an answer. "According to the station manager, Gerald Quince had to have left on the returning train, since the driver did not report his absence or ask for a replacement conductor."

"Is that enough to eliminate Gerald Quince from your inquiries?" Gemma asked.

"No, because he could have been working with his brother, who was employed at King's Cross until last week. Bertram Quince was dismissed, but according to the station manager he's still in possession of his uniform. The page torn out of his penny dreadful could underline the victim's connection to Quince, or it might mean nothing at all," Sebastian said. "She might have bought the penny dreadful when exiting the station."

When Gemma failed to respond, Sebastian added, "Giles Rushton's name starts with G, he works at St. Thomas's Hospital and resides at one of the two possible addresses, and he called on Colin, who was charged with performing the postmortem on the victim. He had also spent time in Scotland during his student days and might have crossed paths with the victim. It's unlikely, but I'm not prepared to rule him out."

"That's four possible suspects," Gemma said. "If you could isolate a motive..."

"The motive for three of the four eludes me at present since I have no real evidence that implicates any of them," Sebastian said. "My theories are pure conjecture."

"So, who's at the top of your list?" Gemma asked, her curiosity instantly piqued.

"Bertram Quince is about to marry Mathilda Poole, who just happens to be the sole proprietress of a three-story boarding house and probably has a tidy sum squirreled away since she cuts as many corners as she dares when it comes to the running of the business. She even dismissed Hank, who used to help her around the house and ran errands, so that she could save on his wages."

Sebastian took a deep breath and continued. "As soon as they are married, Mrs. Poole's assets will become the property of her husband, which will make him financially secure. Quince used to live in Birmingham and claims that he never married, but what if he was married and his wife had become an impediment?"

"Do you have any evidence to suggest that Bertram Quince knew Helen?"

"No, but I don't trust the man, and will not rule him out until I'm absolutely certain he had nothing to do with the victim's death."

"So what evidence do you have?" Gemma asked.

"The only incontrovertible proof is the address in the victim's glove. One of those four men knew her. Possibly more than one. Bertram Quince mentioned that his brother stood to inherit a textile mill when his father-in-law died. Perhaps he had died, and Gerald had decided to rid himself of a wife he no longer had any use for and asked Bertram to help him cover his tracks. That would explain why the body was moved the following morning, after Gerald had left. And perhaps he had asked Hettie to meet him in London to make certain she was never identified."

"But how would he have known where to find her?" Gemma asked.

"Perhaps he made an educated guess and decided to check at the hotel that adjoins the station. He would have had enough time to get to Paddington, murder his wife, then return to King's Cross and leave on the outbound train. Saying he was ill and needed to go to the hospital could have been a clever misdirection. And Colin did say that he couldn't be sure about the time of death. Perhaps the victim was murdered earlier in the day."

"You think the Quince brothers are experienced fortune hunters?" Gemma asked.

"They could be, but until I can prove that they knew the victim all this is mere speculation. I don't even know her name, not for certain."

"So, what will you do?" Gemma asked.

"I'm going to have a word with Mr. Quince and Mr. Rushton."

"Will you go to St. Thomas's tomorrow?"

Sebastian shook his head. "It would take too long to locate someone who might have seen the victim or come across Gerald Quince. The place is enormous."

"Can you not send Constable Bryant or one of the other men to ask around?" Gemma asked.

"The Yard is short-staffed at the moment, so Ransome can't spare anyone for an errand that might take most of the day. He sent Constable Forrest to inquire at other stations, but unless there's a note waiting for me when I get back to the boarding house I'm right back where I started."

"I can go," Gemma said eagerly. "I can take my half-day tomorrow instead of on Sunday."

"Gemma, you need your rest," Sebastian replied. "I know looking after Mrs. Ramsey is not as draining as the work you did at the hospital at Scutari or even at the Foundling Hospital, but it's emotionally taxing, and you need those few hours a week for yourself."

Sebastian tried to carve out a few hours each week to spend with Gemma on her afternoon off, but, when he wasn't able to make the time, Gemma met up with Poppy or spent the afternoon on her own, running personal errands, browsing the bookshops in the Strand, or sometimes just going for solitary walks that helped her to clear her mind.

Gemma's expression was one of infinite sadness. "You're right. It is taxing. One can try to help someone who's in physical pain, but there's no way to help Anne, and it's my inability to do anything for her that I find exhausting. I try to remind her of things and correct her when the situation calls for it, but then I think, what's the point? I'm only making her feel worse when she's already so fragile and lost. Perhaps it's kinder to allow her to live in a world of her own making, in which she's still a little girl playing with her dog or a young wife and mother, just starting out on her life rather than finishing it in such a cruel, undignified way."

"Your kindness and sensitivity are all the help Anne needs," Sebastian said, acutely conscious of the fact that Gemma had just echoed his own thoughts. "We don't get to choose our end, but to know that there's someone who genuinely cares when we reach that point and who will see us out can make all the difference."

Sebastian glanced away so Gemma couldn't see his face, but she could probably guess what he was thinking anyway. He tried not to dwell on the past, but it was always there, at the back of his mind and at the forefront of his heart. Louisa had died alone as she crawled across the cold, hard floor towards the door that represented hope and, in her desperation, help. No one could have saved her, not even the most competent surgeon —her injuries had been too grave—but it might have eased her passing if there had been someone with her, someone like Gemma, who was gentle and kind and would have made her feel less alone at what had to be the most terrifying moment of her life.

He looked up to find Gemma watching him, and he was sure she had divined his thoughts because she smiled sadly and said, "You needn't hide your grief from me, Sebastian. I will never fault you for feeling. It's a lack of emotion that would frighten me off."

Sebastian nodded, suddenly unable to speak. He was feeling more every day, opening up after years of self-inflicted exile, and, although it felt truly miraculous to have found love again, it was just as terrifying, because now he had something to lose, and it was that emotional connection that made a man truly vulnerable since he would do anything to protect it.

"It's always about love in the end, isn't it?" Gemma mused. "That's the motive for every murder."

"In a way," Sebastian replied, hoping they were now on firmer ground since they were speaking about the case again.

"Love of a person, of money, of power, of freedom. Even when the motive is hatred, it's because that hate had grown out of some form of love. No one starts out with murder in their heart."

"No, they don't, but most people never cross that line, at least not right away. Something causes them to snap."

Gemma shook her head, as if trying to understand. "What was it about that poor woman that made someone snap? She looked so harmless, and she had to be very sad."

"I don't know, but she was clearly a threat to someone, a threat they hadn't seen coming."

"What makes you say that?"

"If the killer had intended to murder her all along, they would have come prepared, and they probably wouldn't have killed her in a hotel full of people. Instead, they grabbed a sewing tool that was in her box and plunged it into her chest in a moment of madness. Perhaps she had threatened them or had humiliated them or had unwittingly crushed a cherished dream," Sebastian mused. "The killing was spontaneous, but the disposal was not. The killer discarded the body in a way that was both elaborate and impersonal. That speaks to cunning, daring and, most of all, an ability to keep a cool head in a situation where most individuals would panic. It also points to someone who has a good imagination and certain tools at their disposal."

"Someone like Bertram Quince, who has the imagination and the means to go unnoticed at both the hotel and the station, where half the men are in uniform," Gemma replied.

"Quince was dismissed from his position at King's Cross, so he now has an even stronger motive to eliminate anyone who might stand in the way of his marriage to Mathilda Poole. But I can't discount the others, not until I can conclusively rule them out. Tomorrow, I mean to interview the porters who work the day shift at the Great Western Royal Hotel. They might have seen or heard something."

"Surely a woman with a Highland accent would stand out," Gemma said.

"Elsewhere maybe, but not at a busy hotel. I'm sure guests from Scotland are not a rarity."

"And neither are porters," Gemma said with a sigh.

Sebastian gave her a wry smile. "Quince asked me to be his best man."

"Bertram Quince wants you to be his best man?" Gemma exclaimed, her incredulity written all over her face. "What about his brother? Surely he would be the more appropriate choice."

"Gerald is rarely in London, and Bertram doesn't care to wait."

"Does he not have any friends he can ask?"

"It seems I'm the only friend he has."

"Might he have asked you to throw you off the scent?" Gemma smiled ruefully, clearly concerned with causing offense.

"I didn't think so at the time, but I can't dismiss the possibility now that he's a suspect."

"That puts you in a rather awkward position, doesn't it?"

"That's the understatement of the year."

Gemma shook her head. "This really is a corker of a case."

"Let's see what tomorrow brings," Sebastian said and reluctantly pushed to his feet. If he didn't leave now, he would be unforgivably late.

"I'll see you out," Gemma said. "Will you come by tomorrow?"

"I'll stop by in the afternoon," Sebastian promised.

THIRTY-FIVE

Sebastian got in just after eight o'clock and immediately made his way to Bertram Quince's room. He saw a sliver of light beneath the door. So the writer was in, which was fortunate since Quince sometimes went for a stroll after dinner. He said walking through nighttime London made him feel alive and fueled his creativity. Sebastian knocked and waited. After a few moments, he heard hurried footsteps, and then Quince opened the door, his expression of pleasurable anticipation immediately replaced by one of surprise. Quince wore a silk dressing gown and leather slippers and appeared to have been preparing for a romantic assignation with Mrs. Poole, since there was an open bottle of wine on the small table by the window, and two glasses.

"Is something wrong, Inspector?" Quince asked, doing his best to rearrange his features into an expression of concern. "If you were looking for your brother, Mathilda put him in the vacant room. Mr. Bell refused supper and decided to go for a drink instead. I'm sure he'll be back at any moment now, if you were worried."

"It's not that," Sebastian replied and inwardly thanked Simian for not sitting in his room and waiting for him with a look of reproach on his face because Sebastian had come home later than expected. He would hate for Simian to think that he'd forgotten or had stood him up again. "My apologies for disturbing you, but I wanted to speak to you for a moment."

"Of course. Of course," Quince said, and moved away from the door. "Is it about the wedding? I do apologize if I put you on the spot and will completely understand if you've changed your mind about being the best man. I suppose I can ask Mr. Danvers, or Mr. Rushton."

"It's not about the wedding," Sebastian said once Quince had shut the door behind him.

Quince gave Sebastian a quizzical look that said, *What then?*

"May I see your uniform?"

"My uniform?"

"Yes. Or have you already returned it to King's Cross?"

"Erm, no. I haven't."

Quince didn't budge, and Sebastian could tell that he realized precisely why Sebastian was asking.

"I didn't kill anyone, Inspector Bell," Quince said. "I believe in the adage, the pen is mightier than the sword."

"I'm sure the Earl of Shatsbury would agree with you, Mr. Quince, but I would still like to see the uniform."

Quince's eyebrows lifted in surprise, but then he nodded and walked toward the bedroom. Through the open door, Sebastian watched Quince pick up the folded garments and the cap that rested atop the pile that had been left on the chest of drawers. Quince returned to the sitting room and held out the uniform. He looked like a man who was surrendering his most prized possession.

"I was going to return the uniform on Monday," he said. "Once Mathilda had cleaned it."

"This looks clean to me," Sebastian said as he set aside the cap and unfolded the coat.

"Yes, she had time this afternoon."

Sebastian carefully examined the front and the sleeves but found no evidence of blood. Either it had never been there in the first place or Mrs. Poole had done an exceptional job cleaning the coat.

"When did you give Mrs. Poole the uniform?"

"On Tuesday. That was when I told her that I had left my position." A guilty look passed over Mr. Quince's face. "I expect you know I was dismissed."

"I do. Why did you do it, Mr. Quince? Surely you must have understood the risk."

Quince nodded. "I did, but the earl really is a shit and hadn't even bothered to thank me after I had helped his man with a dozen cases, much less given me a tip. And the Duchess of Devonshire had stepped on my foot and hadn't bothered to apologize because I'm not human to her. Just another flunky she can verbally abuse, and she *is* abusive," Quince added. "To be frank, I didn't think they would ever find out, but what's done is done. The end of every chapter is the beginning of another."

Sebastian handed the coat back to Quince. If he was telling the truth—and Sebastian would check with Mrs. Poole when she had cleaned the uniform—then Quince hadn't been in possession of it when the victim had been murdered and couldn't have been the porter who had been seen at Paddington.

"Do you have just the one uniform?" Sebastian asked. "Is there a spare coat or a second cap?"

"No. We're issued one uniform, and it's our responsibility to keep it tidy. Mrs. Poole did an excellent job of brushing down the coat and the trousers."

"Thank you, Mr. Quince," Sebastian said.

He could see the hurt look on Bertram Quince's face as he

shut the door behind himself, but he wouldn't apologize for doing his job. He would be remiss if he didn't check on the whereabouts of the uniform and its owner.

Sebastian was just about to head upstairs and check on Gustav when Mrs. Poole emerged from her own room, a strong floral scent filling the foyer and the fabric of her dressing gown swishing against her bare calves. She reared back when she saw Sebastian, then raised her chin defiantly. This was her house, after all, and she was about to be married. She had nothing to be ashamed of.

"What are you doing lurking in the shadows?" she demanded.

"I wasn't lurking. I was going upstairs," Sebastian said apologetically. "But I'm sorry if I frightened you."

"Well, get away with you, then," Mrs. Poole hissed.

"Can I ask you a question?"

"What, now?"

"Yes, now."

"What is it?" Mrs. Poole asked, her voice still low.

"When did Mr. Quince ask you to clean his uniform?"

Mrs. Poole answered immediately. "On Tuesday, but I didn't get to it until today. Why?"

"Where was the uniform in the interim?" Sebastian asked without bothering to answer Mrs. Poole's question.

"In the laundry room."

"Which you don't lock." It wasn't a question; he knew Mrs. Poole never bothered to lock the door.

"No. Why would I lock up soiled laundry? If someone wants to steal someone's drawers, they can just as easily take them once they're clean and hanging on the line."

"So anyone could have taken the uniform, and you wouldn't have noticed?"

"I suppose so."

"Do you recall if it was there the entire time?" Sebastian asked.

Mrs. Poole shook her head. "Monday is laundry day, so I've only been in there once since Tuesday." She fixed him with an imploring look. "Why are you asking? Is it to do with the case you're working on?"

Sebastian didn't respond, but his silence was answer enough.

"Do you really think Bertram is capable of murder?" Mrs. Poole asked.

Sebastian could sense her horror and see the questions in her eyes. He had warned her about Bertram Quince a few weeks ago, but she had decided to ignore his advice. Now she was wondering if she had done the right thing and if she was about to be duped or, worse yet, murdered once Quince got what he wanted.

"We're all capable of murder, Mathilda." Sebastian lifted his hand to forestall her when she opened her mouth to protest. "Most people would kill only in the most extreme circumstances, but there are those who would do anything to remove an obstacle or neutralize a threat. I don't have any solid evidence against Mr. Quince, but the woman was murdered by a man who was seen wearing a porter's uniform, and she had an address for someone who lives in this street."

"Who?" Mrs. Poole whispered.

"I don't know."

"Do you suspect anyone else?"

"I'd like to have a word with Mr. Rushton. Is he in?"

Mrs. Poole shook her head. "I didn't see him come in, and when I brought his supper tray he didn't answer the door."

"What about Mr. Danvers?"

"He's in his room. He told us over supper that he'd spent the day at his tutor's house, working on a cadaver," Mrs. Poole said, her expression one of utter disgust. "What sort of person would want to do that for a living, I ask you?"

Sebastian didn't bother to answer since he often wondered the same thing as he watched Colin go about his work. He did know that Mr. Danvers had been with Colin, so he turned his attention to Mr. Rushton.

"Do you have a spare key to Mr. Rushton's room?"

"Yes."

"I think we should check on him, don't you?"

Mrs. Poole looked dubious. "It's just gone eight. There's hardly any reason for concern. And if he finds out I allowed you to search his room, he'll be sure to move out and badmouth me to anyone who'll listen. I have a business to run, in case you forgot."

"Harboring a murderer won't do your reputation any favors. And as the landlady, it's your responsibility to check on your tenants' welfare."

Mrs. Poole quickly recognized the validity of Sebastian's argument, and returned to her room to fetch the crowded ring that held the keys to every door in the place. Together, they made their way to the top floor, Mrs. Poole hovering behind Sebastian as he unlocked the door. Sebastian didn't expect Mr. Rushton to lunge at him like a jungle cat, but he stepped to the side as soon as he pushed the door open, just in case.

Mr. Rushton had one room, unlike the lodgers on the lower floors, who had a small sitting room and a bedroom. In this instance it was a bonus, since Sebastian could take in the entire room with one glance to make certain that Mr. Rushton wasn't hiding in the other room, weapon at the ready. The room was empty and dark, the only sign of habitation two medical texts stacked on the writing desk next to an inkwell, pen, and blotter. The bed was neatly made, and the coatrack was bare, so Mr. Rushton had definitely not come back and fallen into a deep sleep.

Sebastian took a quick look inside the narrow wardrobe, then checked the drawers of Mr. Rushton's desk, while Mrs. Poole stood guard by the door. Sebastian didn't find anything aside from some clothes, a spare pair of shoes, and some writing paper inside the desk. There was nothing even remotely incriminating. Disappointed, he stepped out into the corridor and asked Mrs. Poole to lock the door. She did as he asked, then slid the key ring into her pocket and walked slowly down the stairs. Sebastian thought she might turn toward Mr. Quince's room, but she entered her own room, and he heard the key turn in the lock. It seemed she was no longer in the mood for romance.

Tired and disheartened, Sebastian unlocked his own door and went inside. Gustav jumped into his lap as soon as Sebastian had taken off his coat and hat and settled in the chair without bothering to light the lamp. He stroked the purring cat and stared into the depths of the empty hearth until he heard footsteps on the stairs and went to check if Giles Rushton had returned. Simian stood in the hallway.

"I'm sorry I kept you waiting. I needed a breath of air. Are you ready to go, Seb?"

"Mr. Quince said you went for a drink," Sebastian said, relieved that Simian wasn't angry with him and there was no need to grovel.

Simian looked sheepish. "He said he likes to walk in the evenings, and I thought he might volunteer to accompany me if I said I was going for a stroll. Never met a man who likes the sound of his own voice as much as B.E. Ware."

"Say no more," Sebastian said with an understanding grin.

He stepped inside to grab his things, shooed Gustav out of the way, and locked the door.

"We can go to that tavern you mentioned," Simian suggested.

"Yes, of course," Sebastian replied absentmindedly as he

peered up the stairs towards Giles Rushton's room. He couldn't see a light beneath the door, so Rushton had not come back.

It was too soon to worry, but, as he stepped into the crisp spring night, Sebastian knew without a shadow of a doubt that whatever happened tomorrow would irrevocably alter the course of the investigation.

THIRTY-SIX

Sebastian led the way to Mann's, which remained open until midnight on Fridays and Saturdays. The tavern was busy. Every table was occupied, and the din from the bar was loud enough to wake the dead. Sebastian looked around but didn't see anyone who looked like they were ready to leave. He nodded in acknowledgement when the proprietor, Thomas Mann, came forward to greet them.

"Inspector Bell," Mann said. "A pleasure to see you again."

He led them to a back room that was normally reserved for private engagements and showed them to a table by the wall. The two men sat down, both silent now that the moment was finally upon them and it was time to address their estrangement. After Mann's daughter, Dixie, had stopped by to take their drink order and list the dining options, Sebastian decided to plunge in. There was no point putting off the inevitable, and he wanted to get the reproofs over with and make the most of the time he had left with Simian.

"I'm sorry, Simian," he said. "I shouldn't have left the way I did."

"No, you shouldn't have. I was angry with you for a long

time. Too long, but there was a point when I stopped hating you and began to miss you instead." Simian sighed heavily. "I'm sorry too, Seb. I should have been there when Louisa died. I should have come to London and stood by your side at the funeral, then brought you home, where Hannah and I could have looked after you. I was proud and selfish, and I allowed my grudge to get in the way of our relationship."

"I never meant to hurt you, Sim," Sebastian said. "I just wanted a life of my own, so I left you the farm, because you had always loved that life. I never asked you for anything." He didn't want to sound like a whiny, accusing child, but the only way forward was to admit how hurt he'd been by Simian and make him see that they were now even.

"I only ever wanted your support, and your friendship," Simian said. "Without you, nothing was the same. I lay awake at night, listening to the creaking of the house and the nighttime noises coming from the outside, and I felt so alone, and so betrayed."

"Was that why you married so quickly, because of me?" Sebastian asked after Dixie had set their plates before them and unloaded two more jars of ale from her tray.

Simian took a long pull, then set the cup down with a sigh of pleasure. "I always wanted Hannah. With you out of the way, she had nothing left to hold out for, so I proposed, and she accepted. I know it was petty, but in some childish way I felt like I got back at you by marrying the girl who loved you."

"Hannah was never the sort to marry out of spite. She liked you well enough, and going from sharing an attic room with her sister to having her own farm would have been an added incentive. It sounds like you've made a wonderful life together."

Simian chuckled. "You make her sound grasping."

"Not grasping, no. Pragmatic. Hannah wanted a better life for herself, and she got it. Speaking of which, how are the children?"

"They're well. Luke just turned nine, and Kathy is seven." Simian took another gulp of ale and added, "Mark would have been thirteen, had he lived."

"I'm sorry," Sebastian said. "How old was he when he passed?"

"Nearly three."

Sebastian didn't ask how Mark had died, and Simian didn't volunteer the information. The loss of children was a painful topic, and it was for that reason that Sebastian didn't bring up his own unborn son. Sharing one's grief didn't lessen it, it only made the other person feel bad.

"The children would like to meet you," Simian said. "Luke has told all his friends that his uncle is an inspector with the police. In his mind, you're larger than life."

"I wouldn't want to disappoint him," Sebastian said, and wondered how he would seem to Simian's children, and to Hannah, who hadn't seen him since he was a brash youth.

"You couldn't disappoint him if you tried," Simian replied.

They both ate in silence for a few minutes, each lost in his own thoughts. Then Simian asked, "Do you remember Uncle Stanley?"

"The name sounds familiar, but I can't bring up a face."

"You would have been around six when he left. He was Mum's cousin. Uncle Norm's son."

"Right. Now I remember. He came to see us and brought boiled sweets."

"That's him, all right. Always a pocketful of sweeties."

"So, what about him?" Sebastian asked, wondering why Simian had brought up a man they hadn't seen in nearly thirty years.

"He passed last week. That's why I was in Maidenhead."

"I thought Stanley had gone to America," Sebastian said, now recalling why they had never seen their uncle again. Maybe that was when the dream of America had first taken root in Sebastian's soul. He had heard Stanley talk about it to their parents and had thought it sounded like the most exciting place on earth.

"He did. Braved the Oregon Trail and eventually settled in the Nebraska Territory with a woman he'd met on the way. But he sold up and came back to England after his wife and son died of typhoid fever a few years back."

"I'm sorry to hear it," Sebastian said. It seemed that death stalked even those who had survived one of the most treacherous journeys a person could undertake.

"Stanley came back for a reason. He wanted to spend his remaining years among family."

"Did he?"

"He lived with his sister, Janet, but she passed a few months before him."

"I would have come with you to his funeral had I known," Sebastian admonished Simian.

"To be honest, I wanted to get it over with and didn't care to make the situation more complicated than it needed to be."

"So, why did you write to me?" Sebastian asked, hurt by Simian's brutal honesty.

Simian sighed. "In the end, there's nothing left but those few people who care for us, and despite my anger towards you, I do care, and I hope you still care about me. I want us to turn over a new leaf, Seb, and I want you to have this."

Simian reached into his breast pocket and took out an envelope. "Stanley left this to us. It's the proceeds from the sale of his homestead. He always loved Ma, and he wanted to do something nice for us, even though there are other cousins he could have left his life savings to."

Simian laid the envelope on the table and pushed it toward Sebastian. "I never bought out your share of the farm or shared any of the profits with you. You deserve this."

Sebastian set down his cutlery and reached for the envelope, opening it just enough to see a stack of notes. He closed the flap and set the packet back on the table.

"I can't take this. Set it aside for your children or buy something nice for Hannah."

"I have a sum put by for the children's future, and Hannah doesn't lack for clothes and trinkets. I want you to have a home, Sebastian. Seeing that mean boarding house and those two chiselers only magnified my guilt and reminded me of my responsibility towards you."

"I earn a fair wage, Simian. I live at Mrs. Poole's because it suits my needs. Or used to."

Simian's face relaxed when he smiled. "You've met someone."

"Yes."

"Does she love you?"

Sebastian felt a pleasant warmth in his chest. "I think so," he replied modestly.

"When is the wedding?"

"Gemma is still in mourning for her brother, who died in November."

"I'd like to meet her sometime."

"Perhaps the next time you're in town."

"I don't expect I'll be back soon. I can't leave the farm for too long, so tonight is my last night of freedom." Simian sighed deeply. "I hate to lose you again, Seb, but at least now I will be at peace knowing you're all right. Sometimes when I think of you, I still think of you as a little boy." Simian smiled wistfully and his gaze clouded with memory. "You probably don't remember this but, when you were about two, you got into a pot of raspberry preserves that Ma left cooling on the table. You were halfway through the pot by the time she realized you were no longer playing in the yard while she was hanging out the washing. Father was going to punish you, but you got so sick, he decided that was punishment enough." Simian looked like he was about to cry. "Mark looked so much like you when you were that age. All big eyes and golden curls."

"I'm really sorry, Sim," Sebastian said as he reached out and laid a hand on Simian's arm.

Simian nodded. "Life hasn't been very kind to us, has it, Seb?"

"I don't think life is kind to too many people. We're not the only ones to experience loss."

Sebastian couldn't help but think back to all those photographs in Zeke Robinson's studio, especially the ones of the children. There were too many deaths, and too many young lives cut short.

Simian gave him a watery smile. "Take the money. Please. I want you to have it."

"The only way I will accept it is if we share this inheritance," Sebastian said. "It's only fair, and I think that's what Uncle Stanley would have wanted."

Simian nodded. "All right. Half for you and half for me, but dinner is my treat. Think of it as an early birthday present."

"My birthday is more than a month away," Sebastian reminded him.

"I know when your birthday is. I remember the day you were born, even though I was hardly more than a baby myself. I was so happy, and so proud to have a brother. I still am," Simian said softly. He lifted his nearly empty cup and raised it. "Do you remember the toast Dad used to make?"

Sebastian nodded, a lump in his throat. "May the Bells keep ringing."

Sebastian raised his own drink, and they touched cups, like they used to do when they had been little boys and only allowed milk.

"To the Bells," Simian said, but, instead of joy, all Sebastian felt was sorrow.

THIRTY-SEVEN
SATURDAY, MAY 7

The morning was cool. The sun tried to peek out from behind a thick layer of clouds, appearing for a few seconds then disappearing again for long stretches and leaving the city shrouded in shades of gray. Sebastian walked Simian to the cab stand and wished him a safe journey home, then set off for the Great Western Royal Hotel. He was glad he and Simian had finally cleared the air and had parted on good terms, but they would likely not see each other again for a long while and he'd miss his brother more now that he'd found him again. Strange that, in a city that boasted half a dozen train stations, Simian and his family seemed as far away from Sebastian as if they were on the other side of the ocean, but perhaps the ocean was a representation of Sebastian's own reservations rather than actual miles.

Melancholy as he felt, Sebastian couldn't afford to dwell on his personal problems. He had until the end of the day, but he was no closer to solving the case. Giles Rushton had still not made an appearance, which was extremely worrying, and the morning edition of the *Telegraph* screamed:

Paddington Killer Still At Large

Sebastian could almost believe that Marshall Lawrence was taunting him, but then reminded himself that everything the man did was based on profitability, people's feelings be damned. Sebastian's wounded pride had nothing to do with sales and everything to do with his own failure to solve the case. When Sebastian had been new to the job, he'd sometimes given in to despair, but he'd learned long ago that, when the pieces didn't fit, the worst thing one could do was to allow one's personal feelings to get in the way. The only option was to rely on dogged policework, which eventually yielded new clues that allowed one to view the case from a different angle.

This morning, his first order of business was to return to the hotel and speak to the clerks and porters who'd been on the day shift when the victim had checked in and while she had still been alive. It was a long shot, and it wasn't likely that they had seen or heard anything significant, but it was still worth it to check. And if he were truly honest, he didn't have any other leads except for the hospital connection, which was even more tenuous since merely going to the hospital or working there didn't make one guilty.

When he got to the hotel, the reception area was busy. Several guests had just arrived, and a number of people were checking out, harried porters helping them with their luggage so they wouldn't miss their trains. Sebastian had no choice but to wait his turn to speak to the clerks, who worked their way down the line with practiced efficiency. When Sebastian finally got to the front, the first clerk shook his head when he looked at the photograph, but the second, who introduced himself as Mr. Winchell, remembered the woman. He was friendly and polite, and seemed eager to help.

"I was the one to check her in," Mr. Winchell said. "I cannot believe the poor woman was murdered right here in the hotel. I've worked here nearly two years, and there's never been a major incident."

"Never?" Sebastian knew that to be untrue and wondered if Mr. Winchell thought he would be rewarded for his loyalty if he didn't mention any past occurrences that might tarnish the reputation of the hotel.

"Well, of course there was some unpleasantness, but never murder," Mr. Winchell amended when he realized that Sebastian didn't believe him.

"What sort of unpleasantness?" Sebastian asked.

"There was a guest who helped himself to the silverware, and Countess Steffen once accused a chambermaid of stealing a diamond bracelet and demanded that we call the police and have the girl arrested. it turned out that the lady's maid, Fraulein Dinker, had taken the bracelet to a jeweler because it had a broken clasp. The countess apologized to the chambermaid she'd so nearly sent to prison and even made her a gift of a fur-trimmed cape. The maid was quite pleased with the outcome."

"How long ago was this?"

"Last November."

Sebastian had little interest in some German countess, since the incident clearly had no bearing on his case, but found it odd that there had never been a suspicious death or more incidents of thieving. In a hotel this size, surely unexpected occurrences were bound to happen every week.

"Tell me what you recall of the victim, Mr. Winchell," he invited.

The man cast his gaze toward the ceiling as he tried to remember the details. "I think she was upset," he said at last. "She kept looking toward the door, as if she expected someone to turn up any minute. I suppose I should have asked her what was wrong, but we were terribly busy that afternoon. I rushed her through the check-in process. Now I wish I had taken more time."

"Did you ask for her name?" Sebastian asked.

"I did, but her accent was rather impenetrable, and I didn't want to keep asking her to repeat herself. It seemed rude. And when she signed the register, her hand shook quite badly," Mr. Winchell said. "It was only after she had gone upstairs that I realized I couldn't make out her name."

"Could you tell what sort of accent she had?" Sebastian asked, wondering if Mr. Winchell would confirm what the helpful porter had told Gemma.

"I hear a lot of different dialects in my capacity as reception clerk, and I would have to say it was Scots, Inspector. From the Highlands."

Sebastian's thoughts leapt to Gordon McTavish once again, but just because the man was a Scot didn't automatically mean he had known the woman. And just because the victim had a Highland accent did not prove that she'd come directly from Scotland. There were plenty of Scots living in England, especially closer to the border, where the accents blurred into a dialect all its own. But Sebastian did not believe in coincidences, and the fact that McTavish was Scottish, worked as a porter at King's Cross, and lived in Albion Street made him a suspect, especially since there was a period of time during which no one had seen him.

What Sebastian lacked was a motive and the reason for the cover-up. Gordon McTavish was strong enough to murder the woman with his bare hands, and he could have just as easily killed her elsewhere or left her body in the room. If he had been the one to murder Helen, why go to the trouble of coming back to move the body? Unless her surname was McTavish, which it clearly wasn't, no one in their right mind would make the connection between the Scot and the victim.

Same went for Bertram Quince. He had a uniform and a possible motive, and lived in Albion Street, but why hide the woman in the trunk and take her to the station unless she could somehow be connected to him?

"What does the name look like to you?" Sebastian asked the clerk.

"It's difficult to tell, but if I had to guess I'd say it looks like Owens or maybe Quinns. The handwriting really is atrocious." Mr. Winchell seemed to regret the criticism and added, "I really shouldn't speak ill of the dead."

The couple next in line were growing restive, and Sebastian heard heavy sighs and muffled comments about people who carried on as if they were the only ones there with no regard for others, but he wasn't about to leave until he'd asked all his questions. The guests would just have to wait until the other clerk was free to help them.

"Do you remember anything else about the victim, Mr. Winchell? Did she take breakfast in the dining room? Did she come down to dinner?"

"I don't know about dinner, since my shift ends at four, but I think she had breakfast. I saw her going into the dining room."

"Did she need directions anywhere or ask for a cab?"

"Yes," Mr. Winchell replied proudly, evidently glad to have recalled something of significance. "She asked one of the porters to find her a cab."

"Which porter?"

"Billy Lark. That's him over there." Mr. Winchell pointed to a lad of about eighteen, who preened with self-importance when Sebastian approached him.

"I 'ave 'eard what 'appened, sir," Billy said, lowering his voice so that only Sebastian could hear him. "They're trying to keep it quiet"—Billy jutted his pointy chin in the direction of the manager's office—"on account of not wantin' to frighten the guests, but word gets 'round, ye know? Cor, to think the poor gulpy got snuffed right in 'er room. Tragic is what it is. And 'er so far from 'ome."

"What makes you think she was gullible?" Sebastian asked.

"Well, she let the killer in, didn't she?" Billy leaned in even closer. "I sneaked up there during me dinner break to case the room, and there's no sign of a break-in, is there, Inspectah?"

"No, there isn't," Sebastian agreed, but that didn't mean the victim had been duped. What it told Sebastian was that she had not been afraid.

"Just like I said. The poor pigeon ushered in 'er own death," Billy concluded.

"Mr. Winchell said the woman asked you to get her a cab."

Billy nodded. "There's a cab stand inside the terminus, but she asked me to fetch one for 'er, so I 'ad to go to the stand at the corner."

"Did she tell you where she was going?"

"Not me, but I 'eard 'er tell the cabbie to take 'er to the Royal College of Surgeons."

"Did she say anything else?" Sebastian asked, hoping against hope that the victim might have revealed something more.

"No. She didn't. But I saw 'er come back later."

"How did she seem?"

"Lost," Billy said. "She 'urried across the foyer with 'er 'ead down, 'er reticule clutched to 'er breast, and then she were gone."

"Thank you, Billy."

The lad clearly expected a tip, but Sebastian didn't see any reason to part with the funds he needed to travel across town multiple times a day. He asked to see the victim's room one more time, but was advised by Mr. Sykes that the room had been cleaned and all possessions had been packed into her valise and taken to the storage area. Sebastian riffled through the items belonging to the victim but didn't find a reticule. The woman might have been mugged, or the more likely explanation was that the killer had taken it with him and had either held on to it or disposed of it somewhere far from the hotel.

There was nothing more Sebastian could learn at the hotel, so he set off for the Royal College of Surgeons. Perhaps someone would remember the victim and furnish him with the name of the person she had come to see.

THIRTY-EIGHT

"Would you like to go for a walk, Mrs. Ramsey?" Gemma asked once Anne had finished her breakfast and they had adjourned to the parlor, where Anne immediately gravitated toward the window and looked out anxiously.

Anne shook her head. "George and I have been invited to a garden party, so as soon as he gets home you can help me dress. Oh, I do love garden parties," she gushed. "Do you think it's going to rain?"

"I think not, it looks like the sun is trying to come out."

"Good. I hope it will be a nice day. Where is George?" Anne asked, staring out the window and wringing her hands in agitation.

George Ramsey had passed away three years ago, but Gemma chose not to remind Anne that her husband was gone. There were days when Anne remembered and grieved for him, and days when she didn't and the news came as a terrible shock and left her tearful and confused.

"Mr. Ramsey won't be back for a while yet," Gemma said. "Perhaps I can read to you, or maybe we can play a game of cards."

Anne's expression was mulish. "I don't have time for that. Has the new maid laid out my frock for the party?"

"New maid?"

"Yes, the one who was here the other day. She looked a bit dour, but I expect she'll do. So difficult to find competent help," Anne moaned. "Make sure to tell her to check the bonnet and steam the silk flowers if they are creased. And I'll wear the lavender kid gloves and the matching slippers."

"I'll see to everything," Gemma promised.

"It's not your job to look after my clothes, Gemma dear. That's what servants are for. Where's the new maid? Oh, I can't recall her name," Anne said irritably.

"Did you interview her yourself?" Gemma asked.

"No, of course not. Hiring new maids is the providence of the housekeeper, but I saw her in the street. She waved to me."

Gemma smiled in understanding. Mrs. Ramsey was referring to their neighbor's new maid. She was a sweet girl of about seventeen who often waved to Anne when she walked past the house, mainly because Anne waved to her and the girl had no option but to respond, since it would be rude to ignore the lady of the house.

"Oh, where is George?" Anne wailed, and slumped into a chair in a fit of despondence. "I don't want to be late."

"I'll check if he has arrived," Gemma replied.

"Thank you, dear. You were always such a dutiful daughter."

There was no sense in reminding Anne that the time for parties had long since passed and that Gemma was her nurse, and at times her keeper. If Anne wanted to believe that Gemma was her daughter, it seemed cruel to tell her otherwise. She would forget the conversation soon enough anyway.

Gemma went upstairs and fetched her book from her bedroom, exchanged a few words with Colin, who was on his way to the cellar, then rejoined Anne in the parlor. Anne's gaze was blank, both George and the garden party forgotten, and her attention on the street beyond, where a carriage drawn by a fine pair of grays was gliding past the window. Anne loved horses, and watched their progress with mute admiration.

Once Gemma settled across from Anne, she found that she was unable to concentrate on the story. She shut her book and stared out the window, longing to be outside. It galled her to realize how many hours of her life were spent waiting. Waiting for permission, for approval, for a sense of purpose, for a life. She had survived nearly four years in Scutari, praying every day that the war would soon be over and she could finally return home, and just as many years in mourning for those she'd loved. It was as if her real life had been delayed, all the joyful things suspended until further notice. It wasn't that she didn't miss or love the people she'd lost, but the constraints of the mourning period made it that much harder to come to terms with her grief. Gemma needed to keep busy to still her mind and soothe her heart.

Her chest felt tight, and although Mabel routinely aired out the room there didn't seem to be enough air, and perspiration moistened her forehead and upper lip. She couldn't bear to spend another minute waiting for anything. Leaving the book on the chair, Gemma asked Mabel if she would mind keeping an eye on Anne for about an hour, and went to fetch her reticule and put on her cape and bonnet. She still had the photograph of the victim, so she would go to St. Thomas's and see what she could learn. At best she would discover why the woman had wanted to go there, and at worst she would get out of the house for a little while, a small treat she felt she had earned after nursing both Ramseys for nearly a week.

Although she hated to waste time on travel, Gemma found that she was enjoying the ride to Southwark. It was a nice day, and a pleasant breeze caressed her face as the hansom rolled onto Blackfriars Bridge. From her vantage point, the Thames resembled a sparkling ribbon that wound through the city and flowed toward the sea, an ever-changing giver of life and a facilitator of commerce. The sad truth was that the river was really a highway of death, especially during the summer months, when the water was contaminated by waste, the remains of decomposing animals, floaters who hadn't yet washed up on the slimy banks, and rotting fish. The previous summer, the reek had been so foul that the awful months had been named the Great Stink. Those who could afford to leave had fled London, while those who couldn't had tried to keep the awful smell from getting into their homes by washing the walls with chloride of lime. Several hundred tons of lime had been dumped into the river to break down the sewage, but another summer was on its way, and there was nothing to suggest that this year would be any better.

Gemma spotted activity in the distance and, peering over, saw several people and a constable bending over what looked like the body of a man that had washed up near Billingsgate. Another poor soul who'd either had enough and had thrown himself off a bridge, or had been killed and then dumped in the river. Life was so cruel and so unpredictable, and the end was all too often too gruesome to contemplate, those final hours filled with pain, terror, and hopelessness. Her grim thoughts seemed to summon Victor's presence once again, and she experienced a moment of intense longing for her brother when she realized that, as time went on, these visitations would become less frequent and she would be forced to let him go a second time, this time forever. Victor would not age with her, and there would come a time when she would no longer be able to anticipate his reaction or channel his thoughts. But for now, he still felt close, and she could hear his voice in her mind.

"It's time, Gem," Victor said quietly. "Go forth and live your life before something else happens and you find yourself unable to move forward."

"But I'm not ready to let you go," Gemma whispered into the wind.

"You don't need to let me go. I will always be with you, but you need to fight for your happiness, or it will pass you by. Life is so precious, and so short. You know that better than anyone."

"Coming out of mourning feels like a betrayal," Gemma replied inwardly.

"The only way you can betray me is by hiding behind your mourning weeds and allowing what's left of your youth to pass you by." Victor was silent for a moment, but Gemma could feel his presence and knew he was still there, hovering near. "You have my blessing, sis," he said at last.

"Blessing to come out of mourning?"

"No, silly. Blessing to marry your policeman."

"He hasn't actually asked."

"Well, if he doesn't, I'll haunt him for the rest of his days," Victor quipped.

"Please don't. He's haunted enough already."

Gemma could sense Victor's amused chuckle. "I'll haunt the pair of you if you don't finally make it legal."

Thank you, Gemma thought. *I needed to know you approve.*

"No, you didn't. You always did what you wanted anyway. Just look at you, off on another mad errand. You never could stay where it's safe. One of these days, the risk will prove too great."

"Are you saying my time is short?" Gemma asked the spirit at her shoulder.

"Everyone's time is short, Gemma, and the only thing that matters when your life is done is whether you were loved."

"You were."

"I know," Victor replied dreamily. "I was lucky."

Dying at twenty-seven didn't seem lucky to her, but she was glad Victor was at peace. Or maybe she wanted to believe he was at peace and had conjured up the entire conversation in order to reason away her doubts. But she could feel Victor near and knew that he really did want her to be happy, and then the feeling passed.

Gemma felt a momentary emptiness, but then the hansom pulled up before the hospital gates, and her mind instantly turned to the task at hand.

THIRTY-NINE

The Royal College of Surgeons of England, located in Lincoln Inn's Fields, was a grandiose multistory building, its massive portico supported by six Ionic columns. It resembled some of the more exclusive men's clubs and was probably a club in its own right, and just as exclusive by the very nature of its membership. Sebastian couldn't help but wonder how Helen must have felt as she gazed at the intimidating façade and what she had hoped to find within its walls.

He walked up the steps and entered the foyer. The marble floors and tall ceiling magnified the sound of his footsteps, and at first he thought he might have to find the office of the director or the president of the college himself, but then he spotted the reception desk near the far wall. Perhaps the directors wanted to make certain the visitor was sufficiently intimidated before they asked for permission to enter.

An older man with white hair and bushy whiskers hailed him politely. "May I be of assistance, sir? I don't believe I've seen you here before."

In other words, *You're clearly not one of us and you'd better have a damn good reason for being here.* He would have been even less welcoming to a woman, especially one with a thick accent and serviceable attire.

"Inspector Bell of Scotland Yard," Sebastian said, and showed his warrant card.

The man looked momentarily surprised, then drew himself up and fixed Sebastian with a disdainful stare. "We do not pay for stolen corpses, Inspector, so if you're looking to make an accusation against one of our members you had better have irrefutable evidence of wrongdoing."

"I'm not here to accuse anyone, Mr....?"

"Hewitt."

Sebastian took the photograph of the victim out of his pocket and placed it on the desk. "Do you remember this woman?"

Mr. Hewitt's reaction was instantaneous. As someone who was employed by the College of Surgeons, he would be able to tell right away that the portrait had been taken after death. He stared at the image in horror. "She was just here. Two days ago. What happened to her?"

"She was murdered, her body stuffed into a trunk and left at Paddington."

"I read about that. Terrible business," Mr. Hewitt said.

"Why did she come here?" Sebastian asked.

Mr. Hewitt seemed surprised that Sebastian knew the victim had called at the college, but he seemed willing to help, unlike so many gatekeepers whose only objective was to protect the members of whatever exalted institution paid their wages.

"She was looking for someone."

"Who?"

The man sighed heavily. He looked conflicted about revealing confidential information but eventually relented, either because the woman was dead or because he realized Sebastian wouldn't be easily fobbed off.

"She seemed very anxious and wouldn't give her name, but

explained that she had come to London to find her husband. She said they married in Scotland while he was studying at the University of Edinburgh, but that he had returned to England because his mother wasn't well and needed looking after. He had promised to send for her but never did." Mr. Hewitt puffed out his chest with self-importance. "I told her I couldn't possibly let her in. No women are permitted on the premises, and I would be remiss in my duties if I allowed the meeting to take place here at the college."

"Did she explain why she hadn't tried to find her husband at his home?" Sebastian asked.

"No, but I got the impression that she was nervous about the upcoming reunion and would have preferred to meet in a public place."

"Did she give the man's name?" Sebastian exclaimed. For the first time since coming face to face with Helen's remains, he felt like he was on the verge of a breakthrough.

"I'm afraid I'm not at liberty to share that information with you, Inspector."

Sebastian was tempted to reach across the desk, grab the man by the lapels of his coat, and shake him until he saw sense, but managed to keep his head.

"Why not?" he asked as calmly as he could.

"Because you don't know that it was her husband who murdered her, and if I give you the name you will besmirch the reputation of a well-respected member of our community."

Sebastian sucked in a calming breath, then tried again. "Mr. Hewitt, a woman was brutally murdered. Surely you can see why I would need to know the name of the man she had sought to find. If he wasn't the one who killed her, then at the very least he should be informed of her passing and see to her burial. And she might have had family. Parents, siblings, and possibly children. They deserve to know what happened to her."

Mr. Hewitt nodded sorrowfully. "Yes, they do. There's nothing worse than not knowing what happened to a loved one."

Sebastian could think of a few things that were considerably worse, given that he had experienced them for himself, and the terrifying images still tormented him in his nightmares, but this was neither the time nor the place to dwell on the past.

"Any information you share with me will be held in the strictest confidence."

"Unless the man is the killer," Mr. Hewitt pointed out. "Then his name will be splashed across the papers, and this institution will be maligned by the press. The papers are always looking for an excuse to make lurid accusations."

"This institution will be maligned only if it tries to shield a killer," Sebastian replied. "Surely the Royal College of Surgeons does not condone murder."

That statement was debatable since every surgeon who held a membership in the College had killed his share of people either due to an error of judgment, sheer incompetence, or, worst of all, hubris. Many surgeons treated their patients like sides of beef and refused to heed advice or consider what was best for the patient rather than the surgeon's prospects. Sebastian had heard enough stories from Colin to comprehend just how dangerous it was to permit oneself to be operated on.

"How dare you even suggest such a thing!" Mr. Hewitt cried. "Every one of our number is a respected member of the surgical community and can prove his credentials should his conduct come into question."

"The name, please," Sebastian said again.

He would have preferred not to threaten the man, but he would if it came to it, and charge the receptionist with obstruction. The silence dragged on, then Mr. Hewitt nodded resignedly.

"All right. But you never heard it from me."

"You have my word of honor that you will not be implicated."

"The woman asked after Colin Ramsey."

Sebastian went hot, then very cold, and then a wave of infernal heat seared his innards as he tried to formulate a response.

"I see the name is familiar to you," Mr. Hewitt said, his brows knitting with consternation at Sebastian's visceral reaction.

"Erm, yes. We've met."

The clerk looked as though he was about to inquire about the circumstances of their acquaintance, but Sebastian had no intention of explaining himself. He was reeling with shock and needed a moment to make sense of what he'd heard. Hell, he needed a few hours, but time wasn't on his side. If Colin was somehow involved—and that was the extent of his culpability that Sebastian was willing to entertain—he had no time to waste. The victim was in Colin's cellar, and Gemma, who had been asking questions and making observations, was in his home. The soles of Sebastian's boots slapped against the marble floor as he took off at a run.

FORTY

St. Thomas's Hospital was a palatial compound that was built around three courtyards and had to be one of the largest holdings in all of London. Without knowing who Helen had come to see, there was no way to isolate the correct department or wing. Since St. Thomas's was a teaching hospital, doctors, patients, nurses, and students came and went all day long. To find someone who'd seen Helen and remembered her was nigh on impossible, but Gemma was willing to give it a try. After entering via the main entrance, she walked into the reception area and approached the desk.

There were several ledgers, some thicker than others, an inkwell, a blotter, and a wooden cup filled with pens. A man sat behind the desk, his shoulders hunched, his kinky hair unruly, and his bespectacled gaze radiating impatience. He gave Gemma a brief once-over, his irritation on full display, and snapped, "It's not open yet."

"What's not open?"

"The nursing school. Isn't that why you are here?"

"No—"

"You clearly don't work here, you don't look ill, and visiting hours don't start until noon. So what, pray tell, do you want, madam?"

"I'm looking for someone," Gemma said.

"Who?"

She took out Helen's photograph and showed it to the man. "This woman came here on Tuesday. Do you recognize her?"

"You must be joking," the man scoffed, his exasperation mounting. "First of all, I can barely make her out, and second, do you have any idea how many people walk through that door? Do you think I'll remember your face once you've gone?"

"She was murdered after she came here," Gemma retorted angrily. She hadn't wanted to lose her temper, but this man was insufferable. "Surely the least you can do is take a closer look."

"Was she murdered *because* she came here?" the man demanded.

"Possibly."

"Possibly, she says," he scoffed again.

"Can you just look at the photograph?" Gemma asked. "Please."

"And what's your interest in this?" the receptionist asked belligerently. "Is she a relative of yours?"

"I'm working with the police."

"Are you now? I didn't realize the police service had become desperate enough to rely on meddlesome women."

"Your insolence is quite uncalled for, sir," Gemma said haughtily as she pulled back her shoulders and glared at the man. "This woman deserves justice, and, if you are too hard-hearted to even try to help, then perhaps you should not be employed by an institution whose sole purpose it is to heal."

The man's mouth fell open at Gemma's impertinence, but she held her ground. There was no excuse for such rudeness, and the receptionist was only treating her with such disdain because she was a woman and he had clearly come to the conclusion—not erroneously—that she was unmarried, since no man would permit his wife to gallivant around London on her own, assist the police with their inquiries, or attempt to assert her rights over her betters.

"I think you should leave now, madam, or I will have you forcibly removed," the receptionist said, his tone bordering on threatening.

"You will do no such thing, Perkins," said a deep voice from behind Gemma, and she spun about to find herself face to face with a tall, dark-haired man who had obviously just walked in from the outside. He smiled, and his dark eyes twinkled with amusement. "Good morning, Miss Tate. It has been entirely too long."

Gemma smiled at him. "It's a pleasure to see you again, Mr. Price."

And it was. Gemma had known Godfrey Price at Scutari and had assisted him on countless occasions, both in the course of patient rounds and during surgery, which he'd had to perform in a drafty, ill-equipped room that had boasted nothing but a table, a box of straw to soak up the dripping blood, and a long cabinet used for surgical tools and bandages. His efforts had been nothing short of heroic, and it was only due to his tireless dedication that some of the men had come home instead of moldering in mass graves that had been dug into inhospitable Turkish soil and filled in without so much as a marker to commemorate them.

The surgeon had no way of knowing that Gemma had been part of the investigation into the murder of Jacob Harrow, of which he had been accused. Price had been arrested and charged but subsequently released, an outcome that had been largely due to Gemma's involvement. He would be mortified to discover that she knew all about his recent difficulties and personal failings that had almost cost him his freedom and his family.

"I didn't know you worked at St. Thomas's," Gemma said.

Last she'd heard, Price had been on the surgical staff at Guy's Hospital.

"I worked at Guy's after returning from Crimea, but I have recently accepted a position as chief of surgery here at St. Thomas's."

He smiled proudly, and Gemma thought the position must have come with a sizable pay increase and professional accolades, both of which he more than deserved. He was not only a dedicated surgeon but also a kind man who deserved a bit of good luck for a change.

"Then allow me to offer my congratulations, Mr. Price," Gemma said. "That's quite an accomplishment."

"Thank you, Miss Tate. You are too kind," the surgeon demurred. The praise seemed to embarrass him, and he quickly changed the subject. "Are you here regarding possible employment? I can put in a good word," he offered. "Or were you looking for Miss Nightingale? I'm afraid she's not here, if you were hoping to speak to her about a place at her school."

"No, I'm not here about that," Gemma replied. "I was actually trying to find someone."

"Perhaps I can help."

Turning her back on the nasty clerk, whose gaze was boring holes in her skull, Gemma held out the photograph and explained the purpose of her visit. Godfrey Price studied the photograph carefully, then handed it back to her.

"I didn't see her myself, and I think your chances of finding someone who did are rather slim, but I will do what I can to help. I was just going up to the surgical wing. Perhaps we can ask there."

"Thank you, Mr. Price."

There was no evidence to suggest that Helen had come to see a surgeon, but Mr. Rushton worked at St. Thomas's and had called on Colin while he had been working on the victim. There had to be a connection, so this was as good a place to start as any. Gemma shot the now-silent Mr. Perkins a triumphant look and allowed Godfrey Price to lead her toward the stairs. Once they reached the surgical floor, he directed her towards the doctors' lounge and promised that he'd meet her once she was finished.

After more than an hour, Gemma was ready to admit defeat. No one recalled seeing the woman in the photograph, and there was scant possibility that she would have found her way to the surgical floor. Likewise, no one had seen Mr. Rushton, even though he had been expected at work and was meant to be assisting one of the senior surgeons during an operation that was already in progress. Gemma had to admit that she was relieved not to have run into the man. She wasn't sure what she would have said to him and suspected that Sebastian would disapprove of her questioning him on her own. It was one thing to inquire about the victim, and quite another to interrogate one of his top suspects without Sebastian's knowledge or blessing.

Gemma had a decision to make. She could try the other two wings of the hospital, which would take hours, or give up on this wild goose chase and go home. She settled on home. She had a job to do, and it was unfair to ask Mabel to look after Anne while also seeing to her many chores. Just as it was callous to take advantage of Colin's goodwill. She had got away with going out yesterday, but leaving two days in a row was sure to get noticed.

"Thank you, Mr. Price," she said when she met the surgeon in the corridor, and they fell into step. "I'll be going now."

"I was happy to help, Miss Tate," Godfrey said. "It was the least I could do after all the help you have given me."

Gemma wondered if Godfrey was aware after all of her role in the Harrow investigation, then decided he was probably alluding to their work in Crimea.

"Please don't hesitate to call on me if you ever need a character reference or would like a place with the nursing school, although I don't think you would need any help from me. Miss Nightingale would be lucky to have you, and I am certain she would welcome you on board."

"You're too kind."

Godfrey Price looked like he was about to say something, then thought better of it and bowed stiffly from the neck as they approached the stairs. "Good day to you, Miss Tate. I hope we meet again soon."

"Good day, Mr. Price, and give my best to your family."

Gemma stopped to put the photograph away before heading down the stairs, then smiled at a young woman who had approached the stairs. She was no older than eighteen and wore a short blue cape and a spoon bonnet decorated with silk flowers. The woman smiled back and lifted her arm to lay a hand on the banister. The motion shifted the folds of her cape to reveal the black velvet reticule in her other hand. Gemma stared at the frame, charmed by the roses etched into the metal.

FORTY-ONE

"Pardon me," Gemma said as the two women sedately descended the stairs, "but your reticule is really lovely. May I ask where you purchased it?"

The young woman's cheeks turned pink. "It is lovely, innit? I didn't buy it, though," she confessed, lowering her voice when a young man overtook them and hurried down the stairs. "Found it while I were cleaning, didn't I? Someone stuffed it into a rubbish bin. I couldn't bear to throw it away, so I brushed the velvet and polished the frame, and it's as good as new."

"It certainly is. What luck to find something so useful. Was it in the nurses' lounge that you found it?" Gemma asked.

Most hospitals didn't see fit to provide the female staff with a place to rest or safely store their belongings, but it was a way to inquire about what she really wanted to know, and the young woman immediately took the bait.

She chuckled. "There's no nurses' lounge, miss. Thank the Lord there's a ladies' cloakroom on the ground floor, or we'd have to hold our water till we burst. It's only the men that 'ave lounges on every floor. The reticule were in the surgeons' lounge, buried beneath old newspapers and pipe tobacco. It smelled a bit, but the smoke's all aired out now."

"Why would a surgeon throw away a lady's reticule?" Gemma asked.

She had to ask her questions quickly, since the woman would leave as soon as they reached the ground floor, and Gemma's chance to discover the details would go with her.

The cleaner shrugged and laughed merrily. "Lord knows, but their loss is me own gain, innit?"

"Was there anything inside when you found it?"

"Just an old letter. It was stuffed behind the lining."

"Gosh, how intriguing, did you read it?" Gemma asked, lowering her voice conspiratorially.

The young woman blushed and nodded. "It were addressed to someone named Helen."

"What did it say?"

"Nothing important. Just that the writer had moved to new lodgings and were working here at the hospital and that a mutual acquaintance were courting some woman. There was also something about dissection, but it made little sense to me. I think the first page of the letter were missing."

"Was the page signed?"

"Just initialed. G.R. I threw it on the fire. Nothin' to do with me."

They had reached the ground floor, and the young woman looked fearfully at Gemma, probably wondering if she should have been so frank. "Ye're not going to tell I took something from the lounge, are ye?"

"Of course not," Gemma promised. "Enjoy the reticule."

"Oh, I will. I still can't believe me good fortune."

Neither can I, Gemma thought as she hurriedly crossed the courtyard and practically trotted toward the cab stand. She had to get home, then send a message to Sebastian to tell him she knew who the killer was.

FORTY-TWO

Sebastian decided it would be faster to get to Blackfriars on foot than look for a cab and take the chance of getting stuck in heavy afternoon traffic that could come to a standstill if the road became blocked. He had to get to Colin's house, and fast. Colin and Gemma were safe as long as they remained in ignorance, but either of them could unwittingly say something that would immediately place their lives in danger. The man had already killed once. He wouldn't hesitate to do so again, and, given that Colin's mortuary was filled with scalpels, saws, and the bodkin the killer had used, he wouldn't have to search too hard for a weapon.

Sebastian's visit to the Royal College of Surgeons had helped him to narrow down the list of suspects to two men. Three, if he included Colin Ramsey. He refused to believe Colin was involved, but the fact that the victim had asked for him by name had provided a valuable clue. Sebastian thought he knew who the killer was and had deciphered the motive on the way to Colin's house, but he had to tread carefully. He had no backup, and he could hardly ask Colin to jump into the fray when he'd been ill. And if Gemma got in the way... It didn't bear thinking about. Sebastian sprinted up the stairs, took a moment to catch his breath, then knocked on the door, making sure not to bang the knocker in a way that would reveal his anxiety. He had to remain calm if he hoped to keep everyone safe.

Mabel opened the door and smiled in welcome. "If you're here to see Miss Tate, she's just returned."

"Returned from where?" Sebastian asked, suddenly filled with dread.

"I don't know," Mabel said as she took his things, "but she was gone for ages, and Mrs. Ramsey was beginning to fret, the poor dear. She's so attached to Miss Tate. Sometimes she thinks she's her daughter."

"Where's Gemma now?" Sebastian had expected to find Gemma and Anne Ramsey in the parlor, but Anne was standing at the top of the stairs, her brows furrowed with confusion as she tried to place him. Gemma was nowhere to be seen.

"Good afternoon, Mrs. Ramsey," Sebastian said, keeping his voice low so as not to announce his presence in case the killer was already there.

"Good afternoon, erm, Mr. Melville?"

Anne seemed proud to have remembered the name, and Sebastian didn't try to correct her. Just now, it was better if she called him by the wrong name.

"Miss Tate went down to the cellar a few moments ago. She said she had something to tell Mr. Ramsey," Mabel said, replying to his earlier question.

"Thank you, Mabel."

Sebastian carefully opened the door to the cellar and stood still, listening. And then he heard Gemma's voice.

"Get away from her this instant, you despicable man," Gemma cried.

"I beg your pardon?" a male voice replied, the speaker clearly stunned to be spoken to in such a rude manner.

"I know it was you. Giles Rushton had written to Helen, to tell her what you were up to."

"And how would you know that?" The man sounded outraged, but a note of fear had crept into his tone.

"It doesn't matter how I know," Gemma retorted, equally angry. "But you've been discovered, sir. And you won't get away with your crime."

"I think you'll find you're quite deluded, Miss Tate. And I would thank you not to throw around accusations you are unable to prove."

"Gemma, what on earth?" Colin exclaimed, but Sebastian didn't wait to hear Gemma's response.

He hurried down the steps and found Colin, Gemma, and Eugene Danvers frozen in a gruesome tableau as they stood over the corpse, whose chest cavity was still partially open. Eugene turned toward the sound, his gaze darting around in panic when he saw Sebastian. Sebastian thanked everything that was holy that Danvers held a needle and not a scalpel. That would have given him an advantage, and Sebastian couldn't afford to tackle the man in such a small, densely furnished space.

Danvers' gaze went to the oil lamp on the counter, but it was on the other side of the dissecting table, behind Colin, next to Colin's instruments and the kidney dish that still held the bodkin. Sebastian's breath caught in his throat as he weighed the possibilities, but Danvers' gaze shot to the door that led to the alley. It was bolted, and he would have to get past Colin to get away. Colin, who'd finally caught on, had moved to stand in front of the instruments, but he'd noted the direction of Danvers' gaze and would lunge for him if he tried to flee.

Eugene Danvers was trapped, but he wasn't going to give himself up, not after he'd gone to such lengths to distance himself from the murder. Sebastian sensed the desperation that was building inside him and tried to anticipate which way he would go, but there weren't many options, and Danvers knew that.

"You bitch," Danvers ground out when his gaze met Gemma's triumphant stare. "You summoned him, didn't you?"

"Speak of the devil, and he shall appear," Sebastian said, his voice low and menacing as he inched toward Danvers. "Step away from the table."

"Or what?"

"Or I'll make you."

Sebastian mentally willed Gemma to move away, but she remained where she was, her gaze fixed on Eugene Danvers, her breath coming in jerky gasps and her cheeks an angry red. She was furious, and, for one mad moment, Sebastian thought she might hit the man. If she did, Danvers would no doubt hit back, and he would hit hard. He was a desperate man, and he had nothing left to lose.

"Gemma," Sebastian said, keeping his voice even but urging her to listen. "Step away."

He wasn't even sure Gemma had heard him, but Danvers had, and he realized it was now or never. He shoved Gemma with all his might toward the cabinet that held Colin's specimens. She cried out as she lost her balance, and tried to right herself, but the impact had been too great and she crashed into the cabinet, her breath coming out in a whoosh as her head collided with one of the shelves. The jars shook precariously, rocking back and forth, until the biggest one, the one that held the fetus, tipped forward and crashed to the floor.

The sound of breaking glass reverberated off the walls, and sharp, pointed shards flew in all directions. The formaldehyde splattered, instantly soaking the hem of Gemma's skirts, but she wouldn't have noticed. Her eyes were closed, and her hands gripped her head as she moaned with pain. The fetus that had been inside the jar slithered across the floor and came to a stop when the head smashed into the stone wall with a dull crack.

Taking advantage of the momentary distraction, Eugene Danvers sprinted toward the stairs. Bending low, he hurled himself at Sebastian and headbutted him in the chest, knocking him off balance long enough to get past. Danvers pounded up the stairs, Sebastian, once he regained his equilibrium, close on his heels. Danvers was within reach of the door when it suddenly opened, and Mrs. Ramsey's feeble voice called down the stairs.

"Colin. Gemma. Are you down there? Children, I told you not to play in the cellar."

Everything happened rapidly after that. Eugene Danvers reached the top of the stairs and grabbed Anne by the shoulders. She screamed in terror as Danvers spun her around and pushed her down the stairs, using the velocity of her falling body to knock Sebastian down like a bowling pin. Sebastian felt his legs go out from under him as he and Anne tumbled in a tangle of limbs down the steps. Stone walls bracketed the staircase, and there was nothing to grab onto to break the fall. Anne shrieked with fear and pain as her limbs smashed against the walls and the steep steps. Sebastian landed heavily, the sharp edge of a step just beneath his lower back, Anne atop him.

The pain was excruciating, and Sebastian thought he might have broken his back, but he could still feel his legs, which he supposed was a good sign. His head was pressed against the wall, his knee throbbed, and the shoulder he'd broken in November ached dully. Anne continued to scream, her screeching slicing into Sebastian's pain-addled brain, but suddenly she stopped. She lay motionless, her face bone white even in the dim light of the stairwell, her features weirdly hazy. Then Sebastian realized that his vision was blurred, probably due to the blow he had taken to the head. He was dizzy, disoriented, and severely nauseated. His back pulsated with agony, and he was grateful when Colin sprang into action and lifted Anne off him, cradling her in his arms.

"Mother. Mother, can you hear me?" Colin pleaded.

When Anne didn't answer, Colin's face, which already looked distorted due to Sebastian's impaired vision, twisted, and he looked demonic, his eyes dark with fury, his mouth a gaping hole.

"He's getting away," Colin hollered. "Danvers is getting away."

Colin's cry brought Sebastian to his senses, and he scrambled to his feet and held on to the wall. He was still winded, his legs were wobbly, and his back was stiff and throbbing, but he couldn't allow Danvers to get away. He would melt into the crowd, and Sebastian would never find him again. He could go anywhere, do anything, and no one he met would ever know that he'd killed his wife, and possibly Anne Ramsey. Sebastian glanced toward Gemma, who, although ashen and clearly in shock, seemed to be all right. Their eyes met, and he saw Gemma's anguish. Danvers was escaping. Helen and Anne would never get justice.

Pushing through the pain, Sebastian summoned what was left of his strength and hobbled up the stairs. Once he got moving his limbs loosened, and he experienced a surge of energy that was fueled by fury, desperation, and the need for retribution. Danvers had not only killed Helen, but he had intentionally hurt the people Sebastian loved. Mabel looked horrified as Sebastian pushed past her.

"He went left," she called after him.

Sebastian looked to the left and saw Danvers running toward St. Paul's Cathedral. He had a healthy head start, but Sebastian wasn't about to let him get away. The pain displaced by the thrill of the pursuit, Sebastian sprinted after Danvers, his mind on nothing but the chase. He couldn't allow himself to think about Anne or Gemma or wonder what had happened to Giles Rushton. If he hoped to catch Danvers, he needed razor-sharp focus.

Sebastian directed every ounce of energy into his legs, but the distance between the two men widened. Sebastian was older and heavier, and had already run all the way from the college to Blackfriars. The muscles in his legs burned and his back was so tight he thought his spine might crack. But luck or God or maybe both were on his side. A loaded dray wagon turned the corner and trundled into the road just as Danvers tried to cross the street. Unable to stop in time or maneuver around the wagon, Danvers ran straight into its side. Stunned by the impact, he tipped backward and fell hard. That was all the help Sebastian needed. He closed the distance between them and charged Danvers, bringing him down just as the other man managed to clamber to his feet. Danvers thrashed, and kicked, and tried to scratch Sebastian's face, but even though he was a decade younger he lacked experience when it came to bare-knuckle fighting, and couldn't hold his own against a man who'd broken up countless brawls.

Traffic had come to a stop and a crowd had gathered to watch, the onlookers egging the two men on. There was no substitute for free entertainment on a slow afternoon. Sebastian got in a few good punches, but also took a few kicks before he gained the advantage. He worked to maintain it by rolling Danvers onto his front and grinding his face into the grit and muck of the road below. Sebastian wrenched Danvers' arm behind him until the man screamed in agony.

"Please," he panted. "You're going to dislocate my shoulder."

"That's the least you deserve for what you've done."

"I never meant to do it," Danvers insisted through sobs. "It was an accident."

"How does a bodkin accidentally wind up in someone's heart?"

"She fell on it," Danvers cried.

Sebastian yanked his arm harder, and the man let out a sound worthy of a renowned soprano.

"You can tell me all about it at Scotland Yard. Flag down a cab," Sebastian called out to the swelling crowd.

"Sure thing, guv," a rough voice called back.

"'E's tough for an old cove," a small boy who'd pushed to the front of the crowd announced, clearly in awe of Sebastian's fighting skills. He held a bunch of birch twigs, which marked him as a crossing sweep.

"I thought 'e were going to kill 'im for sure," his friend replied.

"Nah. Rozzers don't do the killing theirselves," the first boy said. He clearly thought himself an expert on the subject. "They get the magistrate and the 'angman to do it for them."

Sebastian straddled Danvers, planting his knees on either side. He kept hold of his arm, ready to twist it if Danvers attempted to throw him off. Sebastian's leg muscles quivered with fatigue, and the pain in his back was so intense he wanted to howl. He breathed a sigh of relief when he heard a shrill whistle and spotted the tall hat and blue uniform of a constable, who was pushing his way through the crowd, his truncheon at the ready.

"What's going on here, then?" the man asked as he approached, glowering in a way that suggested he thought Sebastian was the perpetrator.

"Inspector Bell of Scotland Yard," Sebastian said, and noted the change in the constable's expression. He'd clearly heard of him, and it wasn't all bad.

"Constable Burrows. B Division. How can I help, Inspector?"

Constable Burrows was some way from his own patch, which was Chelsea. Sebastian was relieved he wasn't employed by the City of London Police, which was a separate organization and not always eager to help its counterparts at the Met.

"This man is a suspect in a murder investigation, and he just attacked two innocent women. I need to get him to Scotland Yard."

Constable Burrows nodded. "Get up nice and easy, and I'll take hold of him."

He must have realized that Sebastian was in no shape to get up without help because he held out his hand. Sebastian grasped it, and Constable Burrows pulled him to his feet. Danvers didn't even bother to try to get up. He lay on the ground, whimpering. Constable Burrows hoisted him to his feet and pushed him toward the hansom that had just pulled up.

"Get in slowly. You try anything, I'll knock you out," Constable Burrows said to Danvers, and watched him climb into the cab.

Sebastian was desperately tired and wanted more than anything to return to Colin's house and check on Anne and Gemma, but he didn't know Constable Burrows, not even by reputation, and couldn't trust the man with his suspect. He got in next to Danvers and closed the folding doors just as Danvers moved as far away as possible and pressed himself to the opposite side of the cab. Sebastian thought he might try to get out, and wrapped his fingers around the man's wrist, his grip as tight as a vice.

"You're hurting me," Danvers whined.

"Good. I'm going to hurt you much worse if I find out that Mrs. Ramsey has died of her injuries or that Miss Tate has suffered a concussion."

Danvers stared at Sebastian fearfully, no doubt realizing it wasn't an empty threat.

There wasn't enough room for three people inside the cab, so Constable Burrows stepped up onto the narrow platform behind the horses and grabbed hold of the fender.

"I'm coming with you," he told Sebastian, who felt nothing

but gratitude towards the man. He didn't have the strength he'd need to tackle Danvers if he tried to escape.

"Thank you, Constable."

"Don't mention it, Inspector."

Sebastian gazed out as the cab began to move and the onlookers dispersed, disappointed the show was over. He said a quick prayer for Anne and thanked God that Gemma had seemed all right. Had he come a few minutes later or not at all, Gemma might have provoked Danvers enough to do her serious injury. Sebastian shook his head in disbelief. She was so brave, and sometimes unbelievably naive. What had she thought was going to happen? Had she imagined Danvers would feel remorse and turn himself in? But Gemma, who could never do anything truly underhanded even if she wanted to, had been simply unable to contain her outrage once she'd realized that Danvers was the murderer. Seeing him handle Helen's remains must have infuriated her and she had snapped.

And she had figured it all out, possibly even before Sebastian had. "Clever girl," he said under his breath.

"What was that?" Danvers asked sullenly.

"Nothing. Just thinking how you were outfoxed by a woman."

Danvers looked confused, the whites of his eyes too bright in a face that was covered in muck. *Serves him right*, Sebastian thought viciously. And he would give Gemma credit for the solve, at least to Ransome if not the other men, who resented a woman's involvement in an occupation reserved strictly for men and which they believed to be fit only for their superior intellectual ability.

Sebastian glanced at Danvers, who sat quietly now, his gaze fixed on the river that sparkled in the distance and on a small craft that was gliding toward the open sea.

Constable Burrows took hold of Danvers as soon as they arrived at Scotland Yard and hauled him through the doors, while Sebastian walked slowly behind them. Every bone in his body ached, and his head tolled like a bell. His mouth twisted into a sardonic smile as he recalled what Quince had named him. Inspector Knell. At this moment, the name seemed particularly apt.

FORTY-THREE

Constable Bryant sprang into action as soon as Constable Burrows pushed Danvers, who was twisting like an eel, through the door of the duty room. The constable seemed a little resentful that a policeman unknown to him had assisted Sebastian in making an arrest, but he put a brave face on it.

"Thank you, Constable. I'll take it from here," he said.

Constable Burrows relinquished his hold and smiled in a non-threatening way. "Just lending a hand," he explained. "Inspector Bell was a tad winded."

Constable Bryant and Sergeant Meadows both turned to look at Sebastian, then nodded in unison.

"Good man," Sergeant Meadows said to Burrows. "Would you care for a mug of tea?"

"Thank you, no. I must be about my duties, and I'm too far from my beat, so I had best be getting back. But I might take you up on that offer one day. Always hoped for a place at Scotland Yard."

He gave Sebastian a meaningful look, and Sebastian nodded. "You're welcome to use me as a character reference."

"I appreciate that, Inspector," Constable Burrows said. "Good day."

"Constable Bryant, please put Mr. Danvers in an interview room and let Superintendent Ransome know that I've made an arrest in the Paddington murder case." Sebastian turned to Sergeant Meadows. "I need you to send someone to pick up Giles Rushton. You will most likely find him at St. Thomas's Hospital."

"I doubt it," Sergeant Meadows said, and shook his head.

"Based on what?" Sebastian asked, hoping that an explanation was forthcoming.

"Mr. Rushton is already here," the sergeant said.

"He came in on his own?"

"Not exactly. He was fished out of the Thames this morning, near Westminster Bridge, so the Yard was called in."

"Drowned?" Sebastian asked, wondering if Giles Rushton had topped himself.

"Slit throat."

"How did you know it was him?"

"He had a calling card case in his pocket. And his watch and cufflinks were still on him, so not a robbery."

Sebastian nodded sadly. Had he been able to crack the case sooner, Giles Rushton would most likely still be alive, but Sebastian wasn't about to accept the blame. Rushton must have known what was going on. That had to be the reason he had called on Colin; he had realized that Eugene Danvers was autopsying his own wife. Rushton could have said something to Sebastian at any time, but he had chosen to remain silent. And now he'd been silenced forever. Sighing, Sebastian headed down the corridor to apprise Ransome of the new developments.

Ransome smiled happily, then his expression changed when he noticed how awkwardly Sebastian was moving and the state of his clothes.

"Are you all right, Bell? Do you need a doctor?"

Sebastian shook his head, and even that minuscule motion hurt like hell. "No, but I would like to get the suspect booked so I can go."

"Tell me what happened."

Sebastian relayed everything he had discovered, and what he had overheard Gemma saying to Danvers, and Ransome nodded approvingly. "Good work. And bravo, Miss Tate. Please pass on my compliments. And tomorrow, I will be sure to alert the newspapers that the culprit has been apprehended, and the Metropolitan Police Service has prevailed."

Sebastian chose not to point out that the service had done nothing to help him solve this case, but there was no point splitting hairs.

"If you have no objection, I would like to sit in on the interview," Ransome said. He was already getting to his feet and moving toward the door.

Sebastian didn't object. He had to admire Ransome's management technique. Unlike Lovell, who rarely left his office, Ransome was everywhere and knew everything, and would do whatever it took to raise the profile of Scotland Yard with the public, who were skeptical at best, hostile at worst. The two men walked together in silence until they reached the interview room, where a filthy Eugene Danvers waited for them, his earlier defiant expression replaced by one of childlike innocence.

He looked at Ransome and cried, "I didn't murder anyone. I swear."

"So, why did you run?" Ransome asked once he was seated.

Sebastian remained silent, waiting to hear what Danvers would say.

"I knew no one would believe me and I would be falsely accused."

"You don't have any reason to worry on that score," Sebastian said. "There will be nothing false in the accusation."

"You have no proof of wrongdoing," Danvers insisted.

"But I do," Sebastian replied. "And if I can't get you on the murder of your wife, I will have you sent down for the murder of Giles Rushton and for the attempted murder of Anne Ramsey."

"I never laid a finger on Giles, and I never meant to hurt Mrs. Ramsey. She got in the way."

"You hurled an elderly woman down the stairs," Sebastian bellowed. "And assaulted Miss Tate."

That shut Danvers up for the moment, but he continued to glare at Sebastian from beneath his furrowed brow.

"Would you care to tell us what happened, Mr. Danvers, or should I leave it to Inspector Bell to fill in the blanks?" Ransome asked conversationally.

"I'm not telling you anything that might incriminate me."

"That's all right," Sebastian replied. "You can remain in the cells while I send someone to Edinburgh to find a record of your marriage to Helen Danvers. Shouldn't take more than a fortnight."

Eugene Danvers looked horrified, then exclaimed, "It was Giles. He made me do it."

"Do what?"

"He made me marry her."

"If it was a case of, say, self-defense, the judge might go easy on you and show mercy. You might get off with a prison sentence," Ransome said, looking at Danvers as if he was on his side and only wanted to help.

Sebastian didn't think a life lived out in one of London's many prisons was necessarily more merciful than a quick death, but he wasn't about to say so, not when Danvers seemed to be teetering on the brink of confession.

"I never meant to kill her," Danvers cried desperately. "But she wouldn't leave me alone. And then she started to make threats."

"From the beginning, son," Ransome asked pleasantly, and Sebastian settled more comfortably, certain he was about to finally hear the truth.

FORTY-FOUR

Eugene Danvers looked like he was going to cry, then fixed his attention on Ransome, his gaze pleading for understanding. He suddenly appeared very young and frightened, and his shoulders slumped in defeat, all the fight going out of him. When he spoke, his voice was soft, and he looked down at his hands as if he couldn't bear to see the judgment in the eyes of the policemen—or maybe because he realized that his life was over and he would never again be free, no matter how vehemently he proclaimed his innocence.

"I arrived in Edinburgh two years ago. I was alone and a little frightened, but I wanted to become a surgeon, and that was the best place to learn. I got a room in a cheap hotel and planned to stay until I found permanent lodgings. During my first week, I met a few other students, Giles Rushton among them. We got to talking, and he recommended his boarding house. He said it was affordable, not too far from the school, and there was a vacancy since one of the lodgers had up and left. And that was how I met Helen McDougal. She was nice and kind and made me feel at home."

"So, what happened, Mr. Danvers?" Ransome asked. "Sounds like the beginning of a love story for the ages."

"I realized Helen liked me as more than just a lodger, but I never meant to encourage her. I was only being polite," Eugene replied miserably. "But then..." His voice trailed off.

"But then she slipped between the sheets, did she?" Ransome asked with a knowing smirk.

Danvers nodded. "She started coming into my room at night."

"And you did nothing to discourage her," Sebastian said, recalling Mrs. Poole's attempts to seduce him and his own evasive maneuvers because he knew exactly where such an association could lead.

"I was lonely. I had never been away from home before, and she reminded me of my mother," Danvers replied. He sounded like a child who had been sent away to boarding school. "She called me Gene, just like Mum. And she looked after me. Helen was always knitting. She made me a muffler and woolen socks when she saw I was cold. I know I should have moved, but I was busy with my studies, and Helen made it so easy to stay."

Sebastian and Ransome both waited for Danvers to continue, but it wasn't difficult to imagine what had happened next.

"After a few months, Helen announced that she was with child and said I had to marry her."

"You must have realized that could happen," Ransome said.

The young man's eyes grew misty. "The only women I had ever touched before Helen were the cadavers at the school. I knew it could happen in theory, but I didn't expect..." He took a moment to compose himself. "I thought Helen had done that kind of thing with previous lodgers and knew how to avoid falling pregnant, since she didn't have any children. But I think she'd singled me out because I was young and trusting. She wanted a family, and a husband, and didn't care how she came by it."

Danvers swiped at his eyes with the back of his hand and continued. "I felt trapped. Backed against the wall. So I confided in Giles. He was furious with me. I think he had feelings for Helen, but she didn't like him in that way."

"So what did Mr. Rushton advise you to do?" Ransome asked.

"Giles said I had to do the honorable thing. What could I do? I had to take responsibility for my actions, so Helen and I were married. After the wedding, Helen took her ring to a jeweler and had it engraved with our initials. She was so worried about scratching the gold that she wore the ring on a string around her neck and only put it on when she left the house, so that the neighbors could see it. Helen carried on like we were this great love story, when all I wanted to do was shrivel up and die. I had never been so unhappy."

"So you ran away," Sebastian said.

Danvers nodded. "I told Helen my mother was unwell, which wasn't true since she had passed a few years before, but Helen didn't know that. We never really talked about my family or my life in England. She had no interest in any of that. I promised to come back as soon as I was able, but all I wanted was to stay away. I didn't love her, and I didn't want the child. I found a place to live, and then I heard from one of the chaps at the RCS that Mr. Ramsey offered private lessons and thought I could finish my education without returning to Scotland."

Sucking in a quivering breath, Danvers continued. "At first I wrote to Helen and continued to reiterate my promises, but the longer I kept away the angrier I became, and the more I wanted to permanently cut ties with her. She had manipulated me and forced me into a marriage I couldn't get out of. And then I met Miss Chandler."

Eugene hung his head and went silent, so Sebastian decided

to fill in the blanks. He hurt more with every passing minute and had no desire to draw out the interview. There was no question of Danvers' guilt, so all he had to do was sign a confession, and then Sebastian could finally head to Colin's. He couldn't stop thinking about Gemma and Anne.

"Was Giles Rushton blackmailing you?" Sebastian asked.

"Giles sought me out when he arrived in London, so I couldn't really avoid him. To his credit, he never asked me for anything. He only wanted my friendship, but he disapproved of my conduct towards Helen. I told him I would return to Helen and the child once I had completed my studies, and he believed me, at least until I started to spend time with Miss Chandler. We had quite the row about that, and I was forced to swear that I had no designs on Miss Chandler."

"Did you know that Mr. Rushton and your wife were in contact?" Ransome asked.

Eugene Danvers shook his head. "I had no idea, but I had underestimated just how much Giles cared for Helen. He couldn't bear to see her hurt."

"So Giles Rushton wrote to your wife and told her that she had better come to London and remind you of your responsibilities," Ransome concluded. "Was the child stillborn?"

Danvers shook his head. "Helen left the child with a cousin who'd recently had a child of her own. She promised to look after the boy until Helen came back."

"How old is your son?" Sebastian asked.

"Four months."

"So why was your wife dressed for mourning?"

"Her grandfather died. The old coot was ninety-two and still sharp as a tack," Danvers said with admiration.

"Did Helen know she was ill?" Sebastian asked.

"I don't think so. She was always a very private person, so she probably didn't speak to anyone about her symptoms. She would have thought it was natural for her body to take so long to get back to normal."

"Presumably, Mr. Rushton promised to meet her at Paddington on a prearranged date, but she either arrived on the wrong day or he failed to show up. Why did she not find lodging closer to Albion Street?" Sebastian asked.

"I moved not long ago, and Giles never told her where I lived. She only had his address. I expect he didn't want her to show up, make a scene, and reveal that he'd gone behind my back," Eugene Danvers explained. "But she probably would have turned up at the boarding house in due course. The woman was relentless."

"So, Helen asked a porter for help, and he directed her to the Great Western Royal Hotel," Sebastian concluded. "She took a room and went in search of you. She knew from her correspondence with Giles Rushton that you attended lectures at St. Thomas's Hospital and also that you took private instruction with Colin Ramsey."

"Why didn't she confront you at either of those places?" Ransome asked.

"She was embarrassed," Danvers replied. "Helen was a big one for appearances, and wanted to speak to me privately. The best way to do that would be to accost me in the street and demand that I come to her hotel."

"Did she *accost* you?" Ransome asked, a tad sarcastically.

Danvers nodded. "She tried to find me at St. Thomas's and, when she couldn't, she went to the RCS and asked for Mr. Ramsey's address. She was waiting for me when I left Mr. Ramsey's house on Wednesday. I told her I couldn't speak to her just then because I had to get to a lecture, but I promised I would come to the hotel that evening. When I got there, she was waiting for me. She'd curled her hair and she carried on as if we were these star-crossed lovers who'd been reunited."

"What happened then?" Ransome asked.

"I tried to explain how I felt, but she wouldn't listen. She said we were man and wife, we had a son, and I had to come home. I lost my temper. I told her I hated her, accused her of trapping me into marriage, and said I suspected I wasn't the first lodger she'd tried to seduce, but I was the only one stupid enough to fall for her antics."

"I don't expect she liked that very much," Ransome scoffed.

"She went for me, so I grabbed her by the wrist and wrapped my fingers around her neck when she tried to scratch me. That only made her angrier, and she threatened to tell Miss Chandler that I was already married and to destroy my reputation with the RCS. She said she would make me unemployable in England, so I would have no choice but to return to Scotland."

"So you grabbed a bodkin that was inside the sewing box she'd left on the nightstand and stabbed her," Sebastian said.

"Yes," Danvers admitted. "I knew I'd killed Helen, even though she wasn't yet dead, so I washed my hands, tossed the towel and the bloodied water out of the window, and fled. I didn't want to walk out the front door—I had blood on my cuffs and coat—so I went in search of a back exit. I passed a room with lost luggage and another that held spare uniforms. And then I saw one of the porters pushing a loaded trolley into the ascending room. That was when I got the idea to move the body to the storage area. By the time the body was found, no one would be able to recall anything pertinent."

Danvers inhaled sharply and continued. "I hid in the storage room and waited until it was safe to come out, then I emptied a trunk someone had left behind, put on a porter's jacket and cap, found a trolley, and made my way upstairs. There were several Do Not Disturb signs hanging from a hook, so I grabbed one, to put on the door."

He sucked in a quivering breath and continued. "I didn't encounter anyone, since the dinner service had finished and everyone had gone up to their rooms. The foyer was empty, and all the porters had gone off shift. I stuffed the body in the trunk and brought it down to the storage room. Then I left by a back door."

"Did you take Helen's reticule?" Sebastian asked.

"Yes. I had to make certain there was nothing in it that would incriminate me. I disposed of the reticule when I was next at the hospital, where no one would have any reason to connect it to me."

"Except there was a letter, apparently," Ransome said.

"And your wife had hidden the address of the boarding house in her glove," Sebastian added.

"She was always hiding things," Danvers replied angrily. "She didn't want anyone to know her business."

"Why did you go back and move the body?" Ransome asked, but Sebastian thought he already knew.

"I couldn't sleep at all that night. I kept thinking about what I had done, going over every detail and worrying that I had left some obvious clue to my identity. It was then that I realized that the clerks or the manager might be able to provide the police with Helen's name and address, and the police might connect me to her murder, especially if Giles felt duty-bound to reveal that we were married. I'd noticed Mr. Quince's uniform when I went into the laundry room to wash my shirt and try to clean the blood off my coat, so I took it upstairs and then headed out directly after breakfast. I had to make certain everyone saw me, including you," Danvers said, looking pointedly at Sebastian. "I went to the lavatory at the terminus, put the uniform on over my own clothes, and used one of the hotel trolleys to bring the trunk to Platform 4."

"But you missed the 7:42 to Oxford," Sebastian reminded him.

Danvers nodded. "The trunk was heavy, and it took longer than I expected to load it onto the trolley."

"Why Oxford? Did you hope the trunk would be transferred to a Birmingham-bound train because of the address on the tag?" Ransome asked.

"I didn't care where the trunk went. I heard one of the porters say that the next train would be departing from Platform 4, so that was where I went."

"Why didn't you wait for the next train, to ensure the trunk was well away from London?" Sebastian asked.

Eugene Danvers sighed, clearly regretting his decision not to do just that. "I couldn't afford to tarry," he explained. "I was spotted by a passing porter, and would no doubt draw more attention to myself if I didn't leave right away. And I was due at St. George's Hospital. It would not go unnoticed if I was late. I assumed the trunk would be loaded onto the next train to leave from Platform 4. Once it was gone, no one would be able to connect me to Helen's murder, and I would be free to live my life."

"Except that I happened to be at Paddington and got the case," Sebastian pointed out, "and when Giles Rushton heard about the murder he began to suspect that you were responsible. Did he confront you?"

Eugene Danvers nodded. "He'd seen Helen at the hospital and knew she had arrived. He wanted to know what had happened to her when I didn't mention that I had seen her. I told him Helen had left, but he didn't believe me. Then he put two and two together when he saw the story in the *Telegraph*."

"Is that why he went to see Mr. Ramsey, to warn him that his star pupil was working on a woman he'd murdered, his own wife?" Sebastian asked with disgust. Danvers nodded miserably. "So you killed him too."

"Giles threatened to expose me. I had no choice," Eugene Danvers wailed. "Helen and Giles were out to ruin my life. I never wanted to hurt anyone."

"But you did," Sebastian replied pitilessly. "How did you murder Mr. Rushton?"

"He liked to walk across the bridge, so I followed him. I came up behind him when he stopped to look out at the river, slit his throat with my scalpel, and threw him in. Then I walked across, found a hansom, and was back at Mrs. Poole's in time for dinner."

Ransome glanced at Sebastian, who nodded, giving Ransome the floor. Ransome stood and faced the young man, his expression solemn.

"Eugene Danvers, you are hereby charged with two counts of murder, as contrary to Common Law. You will be taken to prison to await trial, and, if found guilty, transported to a place of execution."

"But you said the judge would be merciful," Eugene whimpered.

"Given what we've heard here today, I very much doubt any judge would feel sympathy for you."

"What about my son?" Eugene wailed. "I've never even seen Donald. He's all that will be left of me when I'm gone."

"It's too late to worry about your son," Sebastian said. "I expect your wife's family will look after him."

Ransome walked to the door and called out to Constable Bryant, who appeared immediately.

"Take Mr. Danvers down to the cells, Constable, and tell Sergeant Meadows to arrange for transport to Newgate."

Ransome turned to Sebastian once they were alone. "Take my brougham and get yourself home. You look like you're about to keel over."

"Thank you, sir."

"It's the least I can do. I'm sorry you didn't have more support on this case, Bell. Three new constables are due to start on Monday. They'll need training, but I expect it won't take them long to learn the ropes."

Sebastian nodded. He couldn't help but admire Ransome's tenacity. He had clearly managed to convince Sir David to increase the budget and had used the funds to hire more men rather than find a way to benefit in some more personal way and explain the expenditure away as a necessity.

"I couldn't have brought Danvers in without the help of Constable Burrows. He's with B Division. He's interested in transferring to Scotland Yard."

"I'll see what I can do," Ransome said.

"Thank you."

Ransome nodded and patted Sebastian on the shoulder. "Get some rest."

Sebastian hobbled toward the front door and stepped outside, where he signaled Ransome's driver. When the brougham pulled up, Sebastian gave the man Colin's address, then climbed into the carriage and leaned heavily against the seat.

FORTY-FIVE

The sky was just turning a delicate shade of lavender when the carriage merged into the early-evening traffic and crawled toward Blackfriars. Although he had solved the case and had made an arrest, Sebastian didn't feel a sense of satisfaction. A woman was dead, and a promising young surgeon would go to the gallows because he'd made a terrible mistake and had compounded it by giving vent to his frustration and fear. No animal was more feral than a man who found himself trapped and believed he was fighting for his life. And once a sentence was passed and carried out, a little boy would be orphaned. Sebastian hoped Helen's family would care for the child and love him, and maybe they would, but it was also possible that they would resent him and never miss an opportunity to remind him that he was a drain on their resources. Sebastian hoped it was the former.

He felt more than a little apprehensive when he finally walked up to Colin's door and lifted the knocker. He had no idea what he was about to face, but there was no black bow on the door and the parlor curtains were open, the light of the gas lamps reflecting in the mirror that hung above the fireplace.

Either Anne was still alive, or no one had yet got around to preparing the house for mourning. When Mabel finally opened the door, she looked grim, but smiled sympathetically when she saw Sebastian. He was sure he was a sight to behold with his bruised face and soiled clothes.

"Come in, Inspector," Mabel said as she ushered him in, and held out her hands for his things. "Can I get you anything?"

Sebastian shook his head tiredly. There were many things he wanted, not the least of which were hot water to wash his face and hands with and something to dull the pain, but first he needed to speak to Colin. And see Gemma.

Colin was in the parlor, slumped before the hearth, his gaze fixed on the leaping flames. He instantly sat up when he heard Sebastian's footsteps on the hardwood floor and turned to face him. He must have seen the question in Sebastian's eyes because he replied right away.

"Mother is alive, thank God, but she's badly hurt. She suffered a severe concussion, her left arm is broken in two places, and she has dislocated a hip. It was quite a job to get her upstairs without doing her further harm and causing indescribable pain." Colin's eyes filled with tears. "She is so broken, Sebastian."

Sebastian knew Colin was referring to both Anne's physical and mental states, and patted his friend on the shoulder before sinking into the chair opposite.

"She will recover, in body if not in spirit," he said.

"And how are you feeling?"

"I'll be all right," Sebastian replied, even though he felt anything but.

"Did you get him?" Colin asked, his gaze growing flintier and his hands gripping the armrests as if he was preparing for bad news.

"I got him. Eugene Danvers murdered Helen. She was his wife."

"Why?"

Sebastian offered a brief explanation. He was tired of talking about the case, but Colin had additional questions.

"And Giles Rushton?" he asked.

"Giles knew the truth and would have come forward eventually. He came here to warn you that Eugene was working on his own wife."

"He never flinched, not until he discovered the tumor," Colin said.

"He probably realized that if he had waited she would have died on her own."

"He would have made a fine surgeon. What a sad waste of potential."

"What a sad waste of life," Sebastian replied.

Colin nodded, then fixed Sebastian with a pleading stare. "There's a favor I must ask of you."

"Whatever you need."

"I know how you feel about Gemma, but I can't manage without her, Sebastian. Not now. Mother trusts her, and I know that she is safe in Gemma's gentle hands, so I have asked her to stay. Gemma will be more likely to agree if you support her decision. Please, all I ask is that you wait a few months. Will you do that for me?"

Every fiber of Sebastian's being wanted to say no. He had waited so long already and wanted only to start his life with Gemma; but how could he refuse? Colin was his friend, and Anne was hurt because of Sebastian. And he had no right to put Gemma in a difficult position.

He nodded. "Of course. I quite understand."

"I knew you would," Colin said, his relief evident. "I just felt so awful to ask."

"Can I speak to Gemma?"

"I'll tell her you're here. She hasn't left Mother's side all afternoon."

"Is she all right?" Sebastian asked.

"A little shaken, a little bruised, and very sad, but otherwise she's fine."

Colin left the room, and Sebastian rested his head against the back of the chair and shut his eyes. He was so tired, and quite sad himself. His plans to propose and look for a house for himself and Gemma would have to wait. He knew it wasn't the end of the world. As long as Gemma still cared for him, he had a wonderful future to look forward to, but he wanted that future to start now, today.

Sebastian's eyes flew open when he heard the swish of Gemma's skirts. She looked worn out, her skin pale against the black fabric of her gown, and there was a large bruise on her left temple, but her gaze was clear and her smile warm.

Gemma sat down, then reached out and took Sebastian's hand. "Are you all right?"

"I'm fine."

"You look exhausted."

"I could use a drink."

"When was the last time you ate?"

Sebastian shrugged. "I can't recall."

"You must stay for dinner," Gemma said as she walked over to the sideboard, poured about four fingers of whisky, and handed him the glass.

Sebastian took a gulp, then shook his head. "Thank you, but I'm not fit for company tonight."

"None of us are," Gemma said, but didn't press him. Instead she asked Mabel, who'd popped her head in to see if they needed anything, to bring him a sandwich and a cup of tea.

"You figured it out," Sebastian said, a smile tugging at his lips.

He finished the whisky, and a pleasant warmth spread inside him, the pain dulled by alcohol and his sadness not nearly as bitter. He told Gemma about the arrest and hoped he wouldn't have to think of Eugene Danvers any more that night. He had other things he'd rather focus on.

"What an unexpected outcome," Gemma said with a sigh.

"Not as unexpected as you might imagine. Marriage often leads to murder."

"Why do you think that is?"

"Because matrimony can feel like a prison when it's not happy," Sebastian said.

"Still, most people don't resort to murder."

"No, but some people are predisposed to violence, and deceit. Danvers would have committed the perfect crime if the trunk had been loaded onto the train and had Simian not taken that particular train to Paddington."

"I'm sorry you didn't get to spend more time with your brother."

"But I will, and I would like you to come with me."

"I don't think that would be appropriate," Gemma said, and blushed delicately.

"Then we will go once it is," Sebastian said.

"I can't leave Mrs. Ramsey, Sebastian. Not in the state she is in."

"I know. And I will wait until the time is right."

"You won't go anywhere?" Gemma asked anxiously.

"Not without you."

She smiled at that, and Sebastian could see the relief in her eyes.

He wanted to tell her that he loved her and that he would propose as soon as she was free to marry, but he didn't want his declaration of love to be forever tainted by the memory of this awful day. So instead he asked, "Will you come to Mrs. Poole and Mr. Quince's wedding with me? I guess I'm not off the hook for the role of best man."

"All right," Gemma replied. "I will come to the church."

"Thank you. Perhaps we can sneak away after the ceremony."

"Perhaps." Gemma grinned. "And if we're really lucky, we won't trip over a dead body."

"We'll make our own luck," Sebastian promised.

"We will."

EPILOGUE

Gemma lifted the lid of the trunk and reached inside. She shifted a few items aside and pulled out an emerald and maroon striped silk gown. She hadn't worn the gown in years, and it was hopelessly outdated, but it was the nicest dress she owned, and she hoped it still fit. The fabric smelled a bit musty, and the skirt was creased, but she would iron it and air the dress so by Saturday she would look presentable.

She laid the gown on the bed and took out the other items. There was a shirred silk bonnet, dark green and decorated with deep-red stiffened silk flowers, and a burgundy velvet cape. There was also a yellow morning gown, a walking dress of dark blue wool, and a sprigged muslin gown in a pattern of beige and mauve. Those were all the clothes Gemma had in the world besides her mourning weeds, and she ran her hand over the fabrics lovingly, glad to finally shed the black she'd worn for so long.

Gemma held the striped gown before her and gazed in the mirror. She looked like a different person and thought the colors made her appear more vibrant and perhaps a little younger than her twenty-eight years. Come Saturday, she would accompany

Sebastian to the wedding, their first public outing as a couple. And then, once Anne was back on her feet, Gemma and Sebastian would finally talk about the future. She was terribly disappointed that they had been forced to wait, but, even if Colin had never asked, she would have offered to stay regardless. She loved Anne and wouldn't leave her at a time when both she and Colin needed help so desperately. But she meant to put the time to good use.

She had also asked Colin for a favor of her own, and Colin had promised to give her more time off and to permit her to spend time with Sebastian without himself there acting as chaperone. Gemma smiled at herself in the mirror as she recalled the lingering kiss she and Sebastian had shared last night. They both craved so much more, but patience was a virtue, wasn't it? So perhaps soon theirs would finally be rewarded.

A LETTER FROM THE AUTHOR

Huge thanks for reading *Murder on Platform Four*. I hope you were hooked on Sebastian and Gemma's latest case. Their adventures will continue. If you want to join other readers in hearing all about my new releases and bonus content, you can sign up for my newsletter.

www.stormpublishing.co/irina-shapiro

If you enjoyed this book and could spare a few moments to leave a review, that would be hugely appreciated. Even a short review can make all the difference in encouraging a reader to discover my books for the first time. Thank you so much.

Thanks again for being part of this amazing journey with me and I hope you'll stay in touch—I have so many more stories and ideas to entertain you with.

Irina

irinashapiroauthor.com

facebook.com/IrinaShapiro2
x.com/IrinaShapiro2
instagram.com/irina_shapiro_author

ACKNOWLEDGEMENTS

A big thank you to my editor Emily Gowers and the entire team at Storm for their hard work and dedication in bringing this book to life.

Printed in Dunstable, United Kingdom